ELODIE

EMMA NICHOLS

First published in 2021 by:

J'Adore Les Books

www.emmanicholsauthor.com

ISBN: 979-8-710966174 (pbk)

Also available in digital format.

Books by Emma Nichols

Other books by Emma Nichols...

The Vincenti Series:
Finding You
Remember Us
The Hangover

Duckton-by-Dale Series:
Summer Fate
Blind Faith
Christmas Bizarre

Forbidden
This Is Me (Novella)
Ariana
Madeleine
Cosa Nostra
Cosa Nostra II

To keep in touch with the latest news from Emma Nichols and her writing please visit:

www.emmanicholsauthor.com
www.facebook.com/EmmaNicholsAuthor
https://twitter.com/ENichols_Author

Thanks

Without the assistance, advice, support and love of the following people, this book would not have been possible.

Bev. Thank you for your candid feedback and dedicated time reading and re-reading the chapters as the book progressed.

Kim, Gill, Valden, and Doreen. Thank you for your instructive feedback. I am delighted you enjoyed this story.

Mu. Thank you for your exceptionally talented creative input and yet another awesome cover.

Thank you to my editor at Global Wordsmiths, Nicci Robinson. Your technical advice, patience, and skilled editing has had a significant impact on my crafting skills. I will be forever grateful. Thank you.

To my wonderful readers and avid followers. Thank you for continuing to read the stories I write. I have really enjoyed writing this wonderfully sensual love story.
I hope you enjoy it too.

If you enjoy my stories, please do me the honour of leaving a review on Amazon or Goodreads as this helps with visibility so that other readers may discover my stories too. You can also subscribe to my website at **www.emmanicholsauthor.com** for updates on my book releases.

With love, Emma x

Dedication

To those women who struggle to feel loved.
May you have the courage to open your heart,
and the faith to trust that you really are worthy of love.
It's your birth rite and don't let anyone lead
you to think differently.

Emma x

PROLOGUE.

Convent of the Sacred Heart, Paris, France, July 2000

BY THE FIRST SUMMER of the new millennium Elodie is in love. She knows it's love because her heart pounds in her chest at the sight of Mylene's red hair, her expressive blue-grey eyes, and her laugh that has become lighter and louder in the months they have spent together. This awakening dawns on her now, as they walk hand in hand, even though they have known each other for seven years. The grass has a strong earthy fragrance, lush from the last shower, and the sun is as hot as freshly cooked French toast. She tells Mylene the unpredictable weather is the result of the global warming issue, which the politicians should be taking more seriously or the world will definitely come to an end. Her feet slip and squeak in her open-toed sandals, and the sun tickles at the roots of her hair. She squeezes Mylene's warm hand and starts to run across the field with her and down to the lake. It's the place they claimed as their own when they became good friends at Christmas. The other girls won't stray this far, preferring instead to occupy themselves in the extensive gardens that enclose the convent. The other girls are too constrained by the convent's draconian rules, and their spirit is cast in pastel hues that blend to form one indistinct and uniform character as they wait for their Prince Charming to rescue them.

The grand lake is the place they both like to sit and talk of their dreams of the future and where Mylene shares her discoveries of what goes on behind the convent's closed doors. It's exciting that she likes to sneak around at night. Elodie listens to tales of the antics she has spied and feels fuzzy inside. Today, something is different, electric between them. It's the last day before Elodie goes home for the summer holidays. She hopes her mother won't come to collect her, but she's sure she will. Her mother has work that Elodie needs to do. She needs to learn how the vineyard works for when she takes over. It's mind-boggling to think of the future, almost too distant to be real, and the work isn't going to be fun, like this is.

They sit on the bank with the large rock behind them, take off their sandals, and dip their feet in the shallower water. Clear becomes quickly murky with the flicking of their feet but is no less enticing.

"Sister Mary touched Sister Clarence on the breasts last night," Mylene says, nodding.

Elodie turns and faces her. "Really?"

"They were both dressed, but it was a real touch."

It's disappointing that they were clothed. Elodie thinks Sister Mary has fine breasts and in her imagination, she has seen them naked. They are like ripe peaches with chocolate buttons where the stalks on the fruit should be. The image makes the fuzzy feeling stronger below her stomach, and she fidgets her bottom on the grass. The sensation becomes a pulse, and she's not sure if it feels worse or better. "How do you mean, a real touch?"

Mylene giggles. "You know." She lifts her hands palms facing away from her and makes an odd circling and squeezing motion in the air.

Elodie frowns. That isn't what she's imagined a sensitive touch to look like. Mylene's hands would fit around Elodie's breasts perfectly. Elodie automatically clasps her pounding chest. Her nipples are hard against her palms. She fidgets again then sits on her hands. "That's not a real touch."

Mylene turns and looks at Elodie, then her eyes track down to her breasts, and Elodie can barely breathe. "Want me to show you?"

Elodie's heart races faster than she imagines is good for her, like when she's running cross-country up the big hill at the back of the house. There's more chance of it bursting through her chest than there ever was of the millennial bug happening. Her hands are clammy beneath her and it feels as though her legs are heating up the water quicker than a kettle boils water. Her mouth is as dry as the cardboard they used to make the Christmas and Easter decorations. Mylene inches her hand toward her. She can't bring herself to speak, let alone to say no. She is undoubtedly going to go to hell for what is about to happen. It's a risk. Mylene's hand is getting closer, and she knows unequivocally she wants to feel her touch more than she wants to go to heaven. Heat is everywhere: inside her, outside her, and in every place in between. And then the contact comes, and she quakes inside. She gasps as a tremble tingles across her skin. This isn't really touching though, because her dress is a barrier between them.

Mylene's movement isn't as it was when she demonstrated in the air a moment ago. The squeezing motion is slower and tender, and the way Mylene stares at her is beguiling. Tiny shocks pulse into her stomach with every beat of her heart and the feeling moves lower, running faster than the waterfall that spills into the far side of the lake. Her toes are probably heating up the water with that amount of fire in them, and she still can't take a breath.

"Like that," Mylene says and then swiftly removes her hand.

Elodie tries to swallow. Mylene's eyes are darker, and her cheeks are flushed, and Elodie knows what that feels like. Her body is on fire, and there's only one way to cool down. She stands, removes her dress and bra, and steps into the lake, keeping her back to Mylene. She walks out into the deeper water where she can drop her body below the surface before turning back toward the bank. "Come on in."

Mylene makes a move to remove her dress, then stops.

"I won't look." Elodie turns away and swims into the lake. The water is soft and tastes of nothing in particular. Maybe a little like rain. At least it's wetted her mouth so her tongue can move more feely around her mouth, though her heart still thunders as she swims, and there is a giggle bubbling up inside her that she's losing control of. She dives under the surface to feel the cool envelop her whole body and feels something she has never felt before: liberated. As she breaks back through the water, Mylene is swimming toward her. She turns and swims away from her. Elodie knows they will kiss soon, but she wants this heady feeling to last forever. After their lips meet, nothing will be the same between them. She swims toward the small island in the middle of the lake wondering who will lead. It's going to happen sooner rather than later.

She stops swimming as the water becomes shallow again and enjoys the silt at the bottom of the lake spilling between her toes. She avoids the larger pebbles as she pushes her body slowly through the water. She's feeling brave and magnificent, and her tummy flutters like butterflies' wings. Excited and scared, it's a sensation like nothing she's ever experienced before. She has warm sensations when she imagines Sister Mary but nothing as intense as this. This is like an unstoppable force, compelling her to touch and kiss Mylene, and she couldn't do that with Sister Mary, not without getting into a heap of trouble, though she has considered whether it would be worth the risk. She stands with her breasts just above the surface of the water. Her nipples are elastic-band tight and small, and Mylene is staring at them with wide eyes. Slowly, Mylene stands and reveals herself. Her breasts are wonderfully large, her skin is far paler than Elodie's dark skin, and she delights in the contrast. Women are beautiful. The restraint is killing her and multiplying the force driving her to touch Mylene's breasts. She takes a step closer. Mylene is a little taller, broader, and has shape to her body where Elodie is like a stick, and Elodie has already explored every millimetre of her in her imagination. The pulsing between her legs is deep and fiery, and the more Mylene stares at her with eyes that are now as blue as the sky, the more Elodie wants her.

"You can touch me," Mylene says.

There's a quiver in Mylene's voice. Elodie takes another step closer. Heat itches her palm. She's so close she can feel the finest, almost invisible hairs in the prickling of Mylene's skin. Mylene leans forward. The delicate texture of Mylene's hard nipple at her fingertips and the soft skin of her breast takes her breath away. Elodie can't recall ever feeling more powerful. She makes gentle strokes and holds Mylene's breast delicately in her palm and without thinking, she leans down and kisses her nipple.

Mylene gasps. Elodie lets go quickly and stumbles, splashing in the water. "I'm sorry. I..." Her stomach turns as the wrongness of what she is doing strikes like lightning sent from the gods. It takes a moment for the darkness in Mylene's eyes and the quivering of her lips to register as desire. Elodie's heart pounds harder and heavier.

"It feels nice," Mylene says.

The words slowly sink in and Elodie smiles. The taste of salt and caramel lingering on her tongue are her new favourite flavours. She holds out her hand and Mylene takes it. Together they walk out of the water and onto the island. There's a small area of grass and a single palm tree surrounded by bushes that make walking anywhere impossible without a scythe. Elodie kneels on the warm grass and draws Mylene down to kneel facing her. The sliver of space between them fills with their heat and longing. Elodie looks up and stares into Mylene's eyes. If she were the black hole in the universe, Elodie would jump in without question.

She reaches up and cups Mylene's breast in her hand. The puckered nipple grows at her touch and soft moans fall from

Mylene's lips...lips that Elodie is desperate to kiss. She wraps her arm around Mylene's waist. Their stomachs are touching, breasts too, and the urge is too strong to resist. Mylene's eyes close and her lips part. Then there is just the softness of Mylene's mouth against hers. There is tenderness and warmth in the silky wetness as their tongues touch for the first time, and Elodie is immersed in the sensations on her lips. The softness of Mylene's mouth and face feels sensual, there's a lightness of pressure and then a heaviness, a depth and then the barest of contact. Shivers slip down her neck and shoulders. She's trembling inside and out. They achieve an easy rhythm that Elodie wants to never end. The sense of Mylene's lips on hers is more exquisite than she imagined possible. She has no words, nor does she need them. Their bodies are conversing without spoken language. She kisses Mylene, marvels in the warmth of her breath and the wetness they give to each other. Nothing between them will be the same again...

1.

Loire Region, France, September 2018

ELODIE WAS GREETED BY the distinctive, delicate scent of eucalyptus oil as she opened the door and stepped inside the Lalla Spa. It was as if the aroma and melodic notes effused from the azure blue and white tightly stencilled patterned tiles that formed the walls from floor to ceiling. The scent drifted with the movement of the people who worked here. The temperature in the reception seemed cooler than normal despite the thermometer reading the usual twenty-two degrees on the wall behind the white marble reception desk. The clock's long thin hand glided over the Roman numerals on its face, even though time stood still for Elodie when inside the spa. There was nothing more satisfying than the sexual attention of other women, giving pleasure and gratification without regard for the otherwise empty reality of her personal life.

The reception was spotlessly clean and brightly lit. Moroccan authenticity featured in the marbled surfaces and natural pine doors that welcomed guests. The pictures on the walls, of women enjoying the company of other women, were original works of art. Radiant smiles reached out from the canvas and revealed the promises to come to those who could read the signs. And Lalla Spa never failed to deliver when a woman knew what she was looking for. And Elodie knew exactly what she was here for and where she would find it.

Her skin prickled in the cooler air. She walked toward the desk, scrutinizing the two guests ahead of her. Aside from the reassuring familiarity of the spa, admiring beautiful women was another of the aspects she enjoyed. The darker skinned of the two women turned and her gaze tracked the length of

Elodie's body slowly, lingering for a moment at Elodie's breasts before settling on her face. The woman's expression radiated pure joy, and her smile signalled an offer for Elodie to join them inside. Elodie gave an indecisive smile, though she wouldn't refuse her. There was a fine line to tread in keeping a woman wanting, and she enjoyed creating the hint of anticipation.

Her core twitched. Maybe that was why other women came to the spa, to feel powerful, to feel alive. To immerse in the thrill and exquisite pleasures on offer in the hope that the sensations would linger long after the brief moment had roused them back to life.

Elodie watched the two guests make their way from the desk toward the door that led to the inside of the spa. The sensation in her core deepened. No, she wouldn't resist if the offer was there.

"Bonjour, Madame Elodie."

Preeda looked up at Elodie from behind the desk and smiled as she always did. Dressed in a traditional silk gown, she looked like a porcelain sculpture. The coffee cream material that moulded perfectly to her petite frame, accentuated her narrow waist and small breasts, and she glided gracefully when she moved.

Elodie swept her fringe from her face. "Bonjour Preeda. How are you today?"

"I am well, thank you. How is the grape harvest?"

Even if Preeda wasn't well, she wouldn't say. It would be unprofessional to discuss personal matters with a client. A level of formality was afforded to those with wealth and title, and affluence was an important distinction between the women who frequented the spa for the purpose of doing business within the club and those who didn't. The typical client would come to soak up the relaxing atmosphere, the saunas and steam rooms, the swimming baths, ice baths, and aroma massages. They would sample the fresh mint, thyme, and fennel teas, and the spa's own blend of detoxifying herbs in a chilled fruit juice. One thing was guaranteed...everyone who left the spa did so with a smile on their face. "It's an exceptional year. Picking starts in a couple of weeks."

"So, you will not be in for a while?"

Preeda's skin was flawlessly smooth, seemingly unaffected by life or conditions outside the spa. Even in her tight-fitting traditional dress, she looked cool, and fresh, and younger than her years. She was a perfect exemplar for the rejuvenating effects of the spa, should a visitor need any evidence. Elodie didn't need convincing. A visit to the spa enriched her mental and physical health ten-fold. "I'll pop in when I can. It'll be a crazy few weeks though."

Preeda took a key from the rack and slid it across the marble top. "Enjoy your time here, today."

"Merci."

Elodie's thoughts wandered to the upcoming harvest. It was going to be a tough month, and she was still a few hands short, especially since some of the students who had signed up wouldn't bother to show up. Fortunately, they had a strong core of seasonal pickers and locals who saw it as their duty to help. As the owner of one of the most prestigious vineyards in the region, Chateau Marchand, she had elected to maintain traditional methods of harvesting, as her mother had before her. It was important that the grapes were handled gently rather than being ripped from the vine by a machine for the sake of speed. Grapes picked with care held their shape and always looked happier, her grandmother had said to her as they had picked grapes together. She had been a young child then, no more than six or seven, but the fond memory had stayed with her. Whether it was true mattered not. The fact was that hand-picked grapes produced a better quality of wine and their reputation was based on producing the best wines in the region.

She went through the door from the reception. It was several degrees warmer and the soft orange hue, mellow and inviting, made for a nonchalant mood inside the chill-out bar. It was the perfect place to enjoy a glass of chilled champagne or Sancerre. Unpretentious, the social strata were suspended among clients here. Madame Yvette Bourbon reclined on a softly furnished chaise-longue. Wife of Louis-Jean Bourbon, of the House of Bourbon, a French dynasty and the only remaining branch of legitimate descent to the French throne, Yvette was the club's owner. The towel draped across her stomach did little to cover the flesh of her inner thighs and beyond. She could have been an artist's muse. Elodie contemplated her, giving an audience to the three captivated women courting her and smiled. Lively gestures, uninhibited laughter, and radiant cheeks were clear measures of client satisfaction. The three women sipped their tea. Fennel and mint infused the warm air. Their attention remained fixed on their queen as Elodie headed for the changing rooms.

In the absence of women's voices, the sound of waves lapping against a shore echoed inside the room. She sat on a bench and closed her eyes. Inhaling warm air deeply, she coaxed the tension from her muscles. She replaced her clothes with a thin white towel tucked around her waist and exited the changing room through a door with a polished brass sign that read, *Blue Room. Private members' club.*

The comforting rich blue tones that reflected from the tiled floor and walls, accentuated by soft blue lighting, soothed her eyes. She stood beneath the shower, turned up the heat, and rubbed the lavender soap into her skin, then tilted her head back and allowed the water to cleanse her. Naked, she walked along the side of the hammam bath, fully aware that the other women were watching her, as they always did. Whether it was her slightly above average height or her androgynous appearance that appealed to them, or her naturally muscular form, or even her charm and intellect for those who were inclined to talk to her outside the baths, it didn't matter. These women could lose themselves inside their imaginations and that was a part of the appeal of the club. They could wish for more or think they'd touched a part of Elodie that no other woman had managed to reach. But that would be misguided and delusional. *Reaching* Elodie could never happen. There was something deeply erotic in knowing they secretly wanted more than they could have. It was like an aphrodisiac. The fuel that stoked the fire that would flame between them. Want fuelled desire, whereas the act of *having* always dissipated want. There were always rules to the games they played at the club, and the first rule was, no hearts involved.

She hooked her towel on the wall and put her locker key on the shelf directly above it. The cooler water in the bath caused a shiver to fly across her skin, increasing the thrill that sped through her veins. She made her way to the side of the bath and leaned her head back against the tiled edge of the pool. Her body rose on a deep breath, her taut nipples broke the surface of the water, and she closed her eyes. The floating sensation merged with the gentle moans of delight coming from the women she'd seen earlier in the reception. The sweet sound of them pleasuring each other seemed to blend with the music of waves crashing the shore. The throb between her legs intensified. She opened her eyes and watched. Being observed was one of the acceptable rules for those who frequented the Blue Room.

The darker skinned woman turned to face Elodie. She could read the invitation as if it were written in neon lights on the blue walls. The signals were always clear. A smile that conveyed secrets, a narrowing of the eyes, a slight nod, or tilt of the head. The woman turned away and brought the other woman's breast to her lips. She slid her hand down the other woman's body, and Elodie's pleasure ignited. The other woman moaned, and waves rippled across the bath when the darker skinned woman made slow rhythmical movements between her legs. A flash of fire sparked through Elodie, and she stifled a moan. The darker skinned woman glanced across at Elodie again, her smile broad.

Elodie made her way slowly, slipping her fingers across the water. She pressed her breasts into the darker skinned woman's back, trailed her fingertips down her side and tugged the woman's firm buttocks into her crotch. The woman pushed back into Elodie and rocked against her as she continued to pleasure the other woman at her side. The woman's dark skin pimpled when Elodie kissed down her back, and she turned to face Elodie. Elodie leaned forward and kissed her full lips. The darker skinned woman stopped kissing her and went back to kissing the other woman's breast as she took her to orgasm. Elodie rubbed her nipples against the woman's back and moaned as the sensations became more intense. She reached around the front of the woman and massaged the tender flesh of her breast, and her nipple became taut between Elodie's fingers. Elodie kissed her long neck, then she moved her hand below the water and stroked the tight curls between the woman's legs. The other woman cried out and shuddered at the actions of the darker skinned woman, who spread her legs wider for Elodie to enter.

Sexual gratification needed no conversation inside the Blue Room.

2.

London, England, September 2018

KAYE PRESSED THE BUTTON on the wall firmly and watched her world slowly disappearing behind the black metal shutters, grinding as they unrolled then clunking as they locked into the rail that ran the length of the door's opening. Twelve years of married life and just like that, everything she owned was locked away inside a two-metre square container with room to spare. Some might say it was pathetic and sad. That's what Sylvie had called her when she'd left their house, never to return. Her ex's look had been colder than the arctic, her posture deathly rigid, and her jaw clenched so tightly that Kaye though she might fracture her teeth. Sylvie hadn't spoken, and she'd kept her arms firmly crossed in a clearly defiant gesture.

Ice had crawled down Kaye's spine at the thought that Sylvie might lash out at her again. Sylvie had lost it with Kaye more times than she cared to recall, especially in the later years. She'd always apologised, of course, and Kaye had forgiven her. Sylvie had fiery passion. It was part of her creative character and in the beginning, her energy had been exciting, and driven, and directed at Kaye in a positive way, wooing her with thrills. The incident that finally led to Kaye filing for divorce was when she'd shown her true colours and landed Kaye in hospital. Kaye could have pressed charges, but she'd chosen not to.

If Kaye were honest, she'd been on edge around Sylvie for a very long time, and she'd just been happy to see the back of her ex, swiftly and without a fuss. Even though her best friend, Courtney, had been there with her as she packed up her things and walked out of the house for the last time, Kaye hadn't been able to breathe properly until the front door had been shut behind them and she was sat in the white van with Courtney at her side. The experience had left her exhausted, drained, and nauseous. But she'd done it. The past was now in the past, and she'd work hard to forget it.

Kaye thought about the balance in her new special saver account but couldn't bring herself to smile, though with six zeros on the back end she had no real reason not to. One million pounds would have stung her ex's pocket, though that didn't bring any satisfaction either. She was just relieved to have the whole ordeal out of the way and be able to move on with her life. Kaye's solicitor had virtually begged her to go for three million, but she hadn't wanted to unnecessarily hurt the woman she had loved enough to marry, and she certainly hadn't wanted to face Sylvie in a courtroom to fight over their dirty laundry. Though she'd had to go to court in the end, the battle had been marginally less painful for the lesser settlement figure she'd pursued. She should feel happier, justice had been served, but she didn't. She wanted something else, but she wasn't sure what. She *was* sure that, in time, she'd figure it out.

She felt grateful in one moment and then pain oozed through her pores and her thoughts oscillated between self-loathing and incoherence. She wanted to run but to where? Her sense of relief at her new freedom was tinged with remorse and guilt. So many times she'd considered walking away with nothing in the past two years and would have been happier for doing so. It would have been much easier than negotiating, and she would have been done with the process sooner. She had rights, her solicitor had reminded her, and he had exercised them for her within the narrow bounds of her tolerance.

She studied Winston in her hand, stroked his orange and white furry head and the knotted cotton thread where his left eye should have been, and smiled wearily. She poked the loose stuffing back into the gap in his right paw. He was the mirror of her. Damaged and run-down. She wiped an imaginary tear from his fluffy cheek as a cool streak ran down her own.

She'd been given Winston for her fifth birthday and loved him as if he were real. She'd wanted a tiger cub and wasn't happy that having a real tiger as a pet wasn't possible. She'd taken Winston to university with her and then to London. He'd been her good luck charm. While married, he'd lived in her suitcase in the loft. If only she'd realised that was a sign of things to come. Sylvie didn't like furry animals, living or otherwise. Sylvie didn't like much that Kaye valued.

She stared at the black-shuttered storage unit, one in a row of ten. Other people's lives entombed for safe keeping next to hers. Did their owners ever return to claim their things? She didn't know when she would be back to retrieve hers, if at all. Maybe, she'd find somewhere else in the world she wanted to live and have everything shipped to her. It wouldn't take much. Half a dozen boxes filled with a few bits and bobs, a bedside cabinet, an antique wooden bed frame, a tall lamp, and the two small pieces of art she had bought that had also resided in the loft during her marriage. She'd forgotten she had them. The thought of living somewhere other than London seemed inconceivable and yet entirely plausible. A soft sigh fell from her lips and she turned away from the unit.

Courtney frowned at her then smiled. She looked concerned. "You okay, kiddo?"

The term of endearment that she'd adopted for Kaye, a small indication of Courtney's northern English roots, always made her smile. It made her feel as though she had an older sister looking out for her, even though they were about the same age and mature women. "Yeah, I'm sound." She heard the fatigued lilt of her words and knew Courtney would see straight through her pitiful attempt at bravado. She tucked Winston under her arm and released a long sigh. The past was over. The future was yet to begin. In the middle, now, she felt a state of confusion tinged with regret.

"You need a drink." Courtney linked her arm through Kaye's and tugged her closer. They walked toward her rented van. "Well, you might not want one, but I sure do. You did it, kiddo. You slammed the Satan from hell."

Kaye shook her head. The truth weighed heavily in her aching heart, despite the efforts of her mind to generate a feeling of elation. Good feelings seemed to fade all too quickly. The reality couldn't be denied. She was alone when she should be enjoying married life. She'd always wanted to create a home with her wife, a life lived to the end together. It was probably the most compelling reason she'd not wanted to acknowledge their problems earlier and why she'd tried to convince herself they could work at their relationship. Single and alone. "Sylvie wasn't that bad."

"What?"

Kaye cowered. It was an instinctive response, still fresh, and one she planned to unlearn. She lifted her head as she matched Courtney's stride. "We both struggled at times."

Courtney stopped walking abruptly and turned Kaye to face her. Kaye squished Winston to her chest.

"The bitch bloody broke you, Kaye. Remember that. She got what was coming. In fact, a million isn't anywhere near enough for what she put you through. There's a reason her colleagues call her Psycho Sylvie."

A shudder made its way down to Kaye's knees. Courtney had told her for years there was something weird about Sylvie, something dangerously odd. She'd heard the words but hadn't registered them. She'd questioned Sylvie's behaviour occasionally, but they'd slipped into a new norm. She had hoped that things would go back to how they'd been at the start of their relationship before they'd gotten married. But time passed, and she'd forgotten to hope. Now it was finished, and she wanted to leave the past behind. All twelve years of it.

Sylvie wasn't the only one to blame for the deterioration in our relationship. "That's what many victims of abuse say," her doctor had said.

She never hurt me, not badly. Not until the end, and that last time, I don't think she meant it. She never reacted well to me challenging her, and I guess I'd asked for too much. "That's the difficulty with psycho-emotional abuse. It goes undetected for a long time. It gets lost in the argument that both parties embroil themselves in. The abused feels guilt and shame for their actions and they think they're to blame, when they're the victim," her therapist had said.

Sylvie was a master manipulator and yes, Kaye had thought herself at fault for everything that had gone wrong. Until she'd found the strength to go to her doctor, and then a therapist, and then a solicitor. The future was unchartered territory, and though she was without a compass or map, she was ready for the exploration. She stared into Courtney's light blue eyes, cupped her cheek, and smiled. "I need to move on, sweetheart. It's time to let go and start again."

Courtney inhaled sharply, as if she was about to raise an objection, but Kaye pressed her finger to Courtney's lips. "I know you care deeply about me, and I love you for that. But what's done is done, and I can't change the past. So, please, no more talk of Sylvie," *or the million pounds that I really don't deserve,* "and let's go and get that drink."

Courtney cleared her throat. "We need to get this back first."

"Then dinner is on me. Where shall we go?"

Courtney climbed into the driver's seat. "Bill's?"

Kaye took Courtney's hand and squeezed it. "Thank you for being here for me." The sudden urge to celebrate blossomed inside her and who better to do that with than her best friend since uni? She smiled. "Bill's, it is."

Her thoughts drifted as Courtney drove. The urge to leave London was compelling and emotional fatigue had caught up with her over the past months. Courtney's offer of the long-term flat share was kind, and she'd be happy staying there for a few more nights while she finalised her plans but no longer than that. Her mum wanted her to go home, but that didn't feel right either. She loved her mum and three brothers and younger sister dearly, but they would all want to make a fuss of her. She didn't want to be surrounded by people who saw her as the victim, all of them trying to make up for the fact that they should have seen it coming and been there for her. They were supportive, mostly at a distance because of their own busy lives, and in fairness she hadn't asked for their help because she didn't want to inconvenience them. She didn't want to rush into any decisions that would affect her future either, especially not one that involved what to invest her money in. And she definitely did not want another relationship. A complete break from everything was the only way.

Bill's was packed and shrill voices ricocheted irritatingly around the room like a ball pinging around the inside of a pinball machine.

"So, let me get this right? You've got a million quid in the bank, and you're gonna take a narrowboat through France?"

Kaye looked up from her phone showing the waterways map from Paris to Nice and smiled. "Partly."

"You're kidding me, right?"

She squeezed Courtney's arm. "Nope. It'll be an adventure. You can come too, if you want. I'll pay."

Courtney eased back from Kaye's grip and looked around the room. Kaye's heart sank. She hadn't intended for her offer to feel like charity.

"I can't take an infinite amount of time off work, kiddo."

Kaye's chest constricted. It might take time to adjust to her newly found freedom and in that sense, she was on this journey on her own. She didn't feel lonely as such, though maybe a little. She was more worried that they might drift apart while she was away. Courtney had always been there for her and she'd depended on her. She couldn't lose her best friend as well or she really would have no one to turn to. "I'm sorry."

Courtney smiled. "Hey, don't be. You can have the time of your life, and I'm jealous as hell, but you deserve this break, kiddo. Maybe I can meet you somewhere...en route, as they say in that neck of the world." She raised her eyebrows. "Ideally, at a five-star chateau with a heated pool and a vineyard. Then we can drink wine all day in the sun, lounge in the pool, and stuff our faces on fancy French food."

"You mean, like snails and frogs legs?"

"Yuk. I was thinking...what's that steak they eat? The one they set fire to."

"Steak Diane."

"That's it."

"That's not actually served in France. They eat pepper steak. It's making me hungry talking about it. I can taste the creamy sauce." Kaye laughed as the waiter arrived with their burgers and sides.

"Right. So, find me that place, and I'll meet you there. I'm due a week off before Christmas."

Kaye studied the map on her phone again as she plucked a chip and dipped it in mayonnaise. She'd been planning this trip for weeks but today it had become tangible. "You know how you love white wine?"

"I'm not gonna forget that, kiddo."

"What about picking grapes for a week?"

"You just burst my bubble." Courtney chuckled, and Kaye held out her phone so she could read the screen. Courtney squinted at the tiny map. "Is that Sancerre? Now that's a fine wine." She looked closer and pointed to the location on the map as she chewed. "Is that the real Sancerre, where they grow the actual grapes?"

"Yeah. Though it used to be a predominantly red wine region until the phylloxera epidemic in the mid-nineteenth century. The white wines were produced on the other side of the Loire, the Pouilly Fumé. It was only after the epidemic they decided to plant Sauvignon Blanc grapes there."

"I salute you, wine historian." Courtney bowed her head.

Kaye laughed. "I did my research. They produce red and rosé wines there now. Marchand is one of the few vineyards that still handpick grapes." She took a large bite of her burger. The sauce dripped onto the plate, and she wiped it up with her finger and licked it freely, with only a small prickle of guilt. Sylvie would have hated her doing that and would have instructed her to use a napkin and take smaller bites. She took another bigger bite and repeated the process of licking the sauce from her finger. *Damn you, Sylvie.*

"Kiddo, I don't care what they produce. If it's wet and it's wine, I'm not fussy." Courtney patted her chest in some kind of tribal commitment ritual. "You just need to find the chateau with a heated pool, then we have a deal."

"What's wrong with a narrowboat?"

Courtney winced. "Where shall I start?"

"It'll be relaxing. You'd get to play with the locks and steer the boat. And we could stop off and visit restaurants and bars. And there'll be French women."

"It's on water, it's damp, and it'll be stinky. And it doesn't sound like a five-star stay with a four-poster bed the size of my bedroom and a downy mattress that I can sink into with a soft silky quilt that caresses my body. Need I go on? There'll be French women in a five-star too. Posh ones."

"You're so arty-farty."

"I'm just saying. A girl knows what a girl likes. And this girl likes her comforts. You, on the other hand, are the lost romantic. Or is it the last romantic?" Courtney shrugged. "How're you getting there?"

"I'll take the Eurostar to Paris then work my way south. I'm picking up the narrowboat south of Paris, heading to Sancerre for grape picking, then following the canal to Nice. I'm not in a hurry."

"So, you'll be in Sancerre when?"

"For the grape picking season." Kaye laughed. "I know it sounds daft, but I really fancied it. I booked a taster day already, and I've volunteered to pick."

Courtney spluttered on her beer. "Kiddo, seriously? I hate to tell you, but grape picking's for youngsters. Kids on a gap year with young strong bodies and bored brains, not someone nearing forty. What were you thinking?"

"Forty is the new thirty. Anyway, I'm not that close to forty, and I missed out on a gap year, so I'm making up for it now."

"Oh yeah. What else are you gonna be making up for?" Courtney winked as she dunked her last calamari ring in the remaining sauce and hovered it above the plate.

"Nothing that you have in that dirty mind of yours."

"You don't know what's on my mind."

"Sex is always on your mind."

Courtney chuckled. "Sometimes it's at my fingertips," she said as she licked the sauce from her hand, "and I'll have you know, the saucier the better."

"Like every other Friday night. Speaking of which, am I holding you back from your usual Friday night of cruising?" Kaye's laugh died as her concerns formed. She wouldn't be joining her. She wasn't ready for a relationship for one night or a lifetime...well, certainly not for a lifetime. She needed to get over the first failed attempt before diving into the next. Maybe she was a hopeless romantic. She wouldn't fall so easily the next time around though. No, next time, she'd have her eyes wide open.

"Girl's gotta have a bit of fun."

Kaye bit her tongue. She'd never liked the fact that Courtney flitted from one casual fling to another. And for all that Courtney joked about having fun, Kaye had been the one who had noticed the change in her over the years. The fun was always so short-lived. Courtney had become a workaholic and suffered long bouts of depression. Alcohol, like sex, always put a smile on her face and lit a fire in her belly, but they soon became dying embers and she returned to her dark place. Kaye had often thought that Courtney would do well in a long-term relationship with someone to look out for her. The last time she'd suggested as much though, Courtney had become defensive. "Well, while I'm away, you need to take care of yourself."

"And you, my friend, need to book that chateau, 'cause little old Courtney here's gonna join you...when you get to wherever that wine place is. But I'm not picking grapes."

"I'll book your flights, and—"

"You won't. I'll pay my own way."

"I didn't mean..." Kaye looked down. She wouldn't previously have offered to pay for Courtney to go on holiday with her so why was she offering now? Maybe she anticipated missing Courtney. If she knew her friend was definitely booked to visit, the journey would feel less intimidating.

"It's okay, kiddo. Just make sure you don't go bailing out every waif and stray on your trip or you'll be penniless before you get back."

Kaye might prefer that. Having nothing to lose seemed easier and a more relaxing way to live. If people liked you, it wasn't because they were after something from you. Courtney was staring at her through unfocused eyes, her broad smile an indication of the quantity of beer she'd already downed.

"Your problem is your heart's too big, kiddo. There's a sad and bad world out there, you know. You need to stay safe." She leaned across the table and kissed the top of Kaye's head. "I love you." She sat back down, her cheeks flushed and her eyes glassy. "When are you leaving?"

Kaye sighed. Though leaving Courtney in London was nothing to feel guilty about, she felt as if she were betraying her. "Soon, I guess." Her heart sank just a little further at the expression in Courtney's eyes. And then Courtney smiled, and a lump formed in Kaye's throat.

"What're you looking so glum about?"

"It's just...different, I guess. It's all so new, and I haven't had time to process the fact that it's actually happening. The divorce, being single, this trip, and travelling alone. What I'm going to do with my life. None of it has really sunk in yet."

"Well, you'll have plenty of time to ponder your navel on that canal boat. Actually, the idea of it is growing on me." She chuckled. "Fancy a liqueur?"

Kaye shook her head. "Fill your boots. It *is* the weekend tomorrow. But I'll have a coffee." She turned her attention back to her phone and clicked the link through to the narrowboat trips website as Courtney gestured to the waiter.

On the Eurostar website, she navigated to the booking screen. She hesitated. Even though she'd booked and paid for a taster at the winery, she'd always thought she might not make it for one reason and another. This was it. There was nothing to stop her, and it felt so...final, so terminal, which was ridiculous. She could return to the UK at any time. There was nothing holding her anywhere. Her heart thundered in her chest as she clicked through the screen that had retained her personal details and, without further thought, pressed the *book now* button. Her thumb print failed to register twice as she tried to validate her stored card details. The third time, the icon on the screen whirred and then the message confirmed her worst fears and her biggest dreams in a single line. *Thank you for your Eurostar booking.* She was heading to Paris in three days for the start of a new adventure. Her heart thumped against her chest, and her hands trembled.

Everyone she loved was in the UK, but they didn't need her. They were happily living their lives, and she needed to discover how best to live hers. There was always Facetime and Skype. Her stomach turned somersaults then butterflies took flight, and she had the urge to squeal like a child. She might only be away for a few weeks but the other voice that came from deep inside her head, the one that had coaxed her to explore her adolescent dreams in the first instance, corrected her.

She didn't plan to come back anytime soon.

3.

Loire region, September 2018

"SO, DO YOU THINK Baroness Carolina will accept the offer?" Elodie stepped out of the steam bath and pulled a white cotton robe around her body. "Honestly, it's the best deal we can get her."

Yvette shook her head as she patted a towel to her reddened face. She sat on the bench, leaned her head back against the wall, and took in a deep breath. "I'll take it to her. You've done well with a sensitive situation. The baroness needs to take control of her habits before they destroy her family. Thank you, my darling." She turned and looked toward the steam room door. "Is it me or was it hotter than hell in there today?"

Elodie laughed. "It was pretty hot."

"Will you take lunch with me, darling?"

Yvette's cheeks and jaw sagged more than her senior years justified, and her lips were thin and cast in a downward arc as she relaxed. Her eyes were uncharacteristically lacklustre, and she'd barely said a word in the past hour. It was as if a stranger had showed up to the party and discovered there wasn't a party after all. This was Yvette, the woman who had been a mother figure to Elodie for the past eight years, the woman who only last week was entertaining her flock with a regal air and the vitality of youth.

"What's up?" Elodie asked.

Yvette half-smiled, though her focus appeared distant. "I'm just feeling old and bored today."

It was hard to gauge Yvette's age. She'd been around for what seemed like forever, but if Elodie was to surmise, she'd put her in her late sixties, give or take five years. Today, she'd add another five years to that. "You need a glass of the best wine in the house to perk you up."

Yvette pinched her lips together and huffed through her nose. "You are right about one thing. Yours is the best wine in the house."

"Is this about Jean?"

Yvette lowered her eyes. "My husband's health has been deteriorating for fifteen years in his mind, but he's still kicking like a mule and as stroppy and demanding as ever."

Elodie smiled. Yvette and her husband, like many in the upper echelons of French society, had shared the same property and lived separate lives for almost as long as they'd been married. It was an established cultural norm, and one that kept the divorce rates down and the religious institutions happy. Elodie didn't care for established norms or religion. Why anyone would want to spend a lifetime with someone they didn't love was almost as mysterious to her as why someone would want to be in a relationship, full stop. Maybe it was a different type of love they shared, one that made life easier to bear, not one driven by passion. Elodie's father clearly hadn't cared much for social norms either, having upped and left her mother at the point he'd had enough. Elodie had been two, so she didn't really remember him, and her mother had swiftly burned all photos of him. He was a shadow in her life that she didn't feel any particular need to shine a light on. That's what she'd told herself. As a teenager she'd been a little bit curious to know something about him, but her mother had dismissed the notion. The father's name on her birth certificate was William Dupuis, but his date of birth hadn't been a match for any man of that name that she could trace, living or dead. She'd soon stopped caring about him and then stopped wondering, though the hurt that came with being abandoned by him had been buried and not yet fully decayed.

She hadn't had anything to do with Jean either, so as much as Yvette had been a mother figure to her, so Jean had been a second absent father figure.

"Ignore me. I'm feeling very dull today...and a little melancholy."

Elodie nodded. "Come on, let's get lunch." She held out her hand. Yvette hauled herself slowly to her feet and pulled on her robe and slippers. They made their way to the chill-out bar, and Yvette huffed with every laboured step. As she entered the bar, she assumed the vitality expected of her position and title, walking taller with her chin raised, and with a measured stride.

Yvette sat opposite Elodie. "This is nice, sharing lunch with you. I think champagne is in order. I feel much better already."

The place was filled with a bounty of aromas: bruschetta topped with Asian spiced calamari and tomato and olives; cold cuts of a variety of hams and salamis; and wild rice pancakes with smoked trout, cut sweet fruit, mint, and eucalyptus. The clink of glass on glass and the clunk of glass on wood was somehow comforting. Women's whispered voices merged in a chanting rhythm with the low background music, and then a burst of laughter broke the spell.

Madame Castelle approached their table. "Madame Bourbon, what a pleasure to see you."

"Madame Castelle, please do join us. Elodie, you don't mind, do you?"

Elodie shook her head. Madame Castelle was a good friend of Yvette's and would bring a smile to her face. Elodie had her eyes on someone else, an unfamiliar face, and she was enjoying the distraction. "Madame Castelle. I hope you are well," she said.

"Comme ci, comme ça, Elodie. You know how things are."

Elodie smiled at the standard response in those of a certain age. Neither good nor bad, which translated to there wasn't a problem that needed their attention, which technically meant that life was as good as it was going to get. The combination of champagne and familiar company always lifted Yvette's mood, and within a couple of minutes she was engaged in cheery gossip.

Elodie drew her attention back to the unfamiliar woman across the room she'd seen glancing at her from occasionally since she and Yvette had entered the bar. Her light brown hair, parted in a perfect line at the middle of her head, hung in bangs that shaped her face and fell beyond her shoulders.

"Don't you think?" Madame Castelle said.

Elodie nodded and hoped it was the right response. She smiled as the two older women continued to converse, their voices drifting and fusing with the other sounds in the room. She glanced around the bar, drawn to the new face again. The woman looked directly at her and smiled. Warmth flowed from Elodie's chest to her limbs. A chuckle bubbled lightly inside her chest, and she swallowed it down.

The woman looked away, and Elodie would swear that she was blushing. The porcelain white skin tone that had attracted Elodie's eye returned slowly and Elodie wondered if she'd never seen the light of day. The local women all had skin shades a lot darker from the Mediterranean sun and outdoor living, and some women's skin tones were on another colour spectrum altogether. They were all a beautiful manifestation of their unique history, an original work of art, to be admired.

Elodie smiled inwardly at being observed by the woman peripherally. She watched her as she tugged her robe tighter fully enclosing her ample bosom and smiled at the hostess who approached the table with a glass of fruit juice on a silver tray. Her teeth weren't perfectly straight or artificially whitened as was the folly of some clients. She had genuine attraction, modest and chaste, and the freckles that dusted her cheeks were very cute. Elodie noted her foreign accent as English, and her voice was quiet and unassuming. Maybe she was a little reserved about speaking in a foreign language, though she had conversed confidently with the hostess, or maybe she was bashful in the company of so many half-naked women. The fact that she had stolen fleeting glances at the women, shifted her attention as if to avoid detection, and returned her gaze with what appeared as more than a casual interest, intrigued Elodie and caused her to wonder at the stranger's intentions. She was more attentive to the hostess than was usual of their regular clients, asking after her welfare and whether she enjoyed her job and she had tried to help by taking the drink from the tray. She clearly wasn't used to being waited on. It was refreshing to see. Elodie couldn't look away, though she'd been staring for too long. The shadows beneath the woman's eyes shaded her skin and gave her a tired and drawn appearance, and Elodie wanted to know what had brought her here.

The woman spotted her watching and gave a warm smile before she looked away. Elodie smiled back as the heat rose into her cheeks. She tried to give her attention to the conversation at the table but drifted back to the stranger with the delightful English accent. Her pulse increased as she watched.

She was accustomed to welcoming and even entertaining new guests. Any woman visiting the spa could be a potential client, an investor, or a woman in need of financial assistance, but for some reason this woman didn't fit any of those things, and yet Elodie had the urge to talk to her. Maybe it was the fatigued appearance, or her polite and reserved manner, or the fact that their eyes had met several times and she had an adorable smile.

Tentatively, Elodie rose from her seat and crossed the room. She didn't want the stranger to think of her as overly familiar or hitting on her. She wasn't, and she didn't want that to be her first impression. She stood at the woman's table, her mouth dry, and words failed her. "Hello," she said and noted the uncharacteristically strained resonance in her voice and the fact that she was rubbing the back of her neck.

The woman looked up. "Hi."

A pause hung in the air for longer than was comfortable. Elodie tucked her hands into the large pockets of her robe, though she continued to fidget with the cotton material as she stared into the woman's blue eyes.

The stranger smiled faintly. "Can I help you?"

Elodie smiled. "No. Sorry. I saw you were alone. I work here." *Kind of.* "How did you enjoy the spa?"

She tilted her head and smiled, then took a slow deep breath. "It was incredibly relaxing, thank you."

"That's good. My name's Elodie."

"I'm Kaye."

"That's a pretty name." Elodie closed her eyes for what she knew was a second but felt as though it lasted a lot longer. Kaye's faint smile widened.

"Thank you. Elodie's a lovely name too."

How inane. "Can I offer you something to eat? The sea bass is excellent, as are the house hors d'oeuvres. Champagne maybe?" Elodie was itching to take the seat opposite Kaye. Wrestling with the notion, she shook her head. Her stomach fluttered as Kaye looked down her robed body to her bare legs and her feet.

"You work here, you said?"

Elodie glanced down at the cloth slippers that matched exactly those on Kaye's feet. "I should explain." She indicated the seat at the table and Kaye nodded. "I don't work for the spa as such, though I do business here. I'm an investment networker. But really, I'm a vigneron by trade. I own the winery close by."

"That's nice."

Elodie couldn't take her eyes off the light dusting of freckles across Kaye's chest where the robe had fallen loose. Kaye was staring at her with a gently inquisitive gaze that stopped her brain from communicating with her now-dry mouth and made her feel like the most incompetent networker that ever existed. "I…I was enjoying some down time today."

Kaye smiled. "Me too. I've never been to a spa like this before. In England they're in hotels and very different." The light danced in her eyes as she glanced around the room.

"This is a women's only hammam, a Turkish bath, I suppose you might call it. Did you swim?"

"No. I had a wonderful massage though." Kaye yawned. "I hadn't realised how tired I am."

"Are you on holiday?"

"I'm travelling. Which vineyard do you own?"

"Marchand. You probably won't have heard of it."

Kaye's smile grew and her cheeks coloured. "I'm booked on a taster event there tomorrow."

Elodie leaned back in the seat and raised her eyebrows. Knowing she would see Kaye again had the effect of cool silk sliding across her skin. She smiled. "You're planning to join us for the grape harvest?" She couldn't pull her attention from Kaye's mouth, as Kaye brought the glass of juice to her lips and sipped delicately. Elodie's lips tingled at the idea of kissing her.

"Yes, as a volunteer, if I can cope with it. I've never picked before. I think it's going to be hard work."

She'd make sure Kaye would succeed. "It's backbreaking but another pair of hands is very welcome." She studied Kaye's hand around the glass: petite fingers, well-manicured nails, and smooth skin. An electric current flashed across her shoulders and down her arms. She glanced across at Yvette for a break from the image. She was chatting animatedly with her new lunch guest and looked in good form, but Elodie had no desire to go and join them. Kaye staring at her caused her breath to falter. "If you don't have any other plans, would you join me for lunch?"

Kaye looked down for a brief moment. Elodie's stomach clenched.

"Thank you, but I think the massage killed my appetite."

"That happens to me sometimes." Elodie placed her hand on the table and stood. "I should leave you to relax in peace."

Kaye looked up, her hands clasped together in her lap. "I'd be happy to join you for a drink."

Elodie held her gaze. *You have the most stunning blue eyes.* "If I'm not disturbing you." She caught the attention of the hostess and sat back down.

"Not at all."

"What should we celebrate?"

Kaye laughed. "Celebrate?"

Elodie noted Kaye squeeze her hands tighter together. She looked as nervous as Elodie had felt a moment ago. She took a deep breath and warmth spread across her chest. "We French always like a reason to drink."

Kaye unclenched her hands and settled back in the seat.

Elodie smiled. "And of all the vineyards in all the regions in France, you just walked into mine." It was corny, but Kaye's laughter was delightful, so it didn't matter. She held her arms up in a mocking plea for forgiveness.

Kaye tilted her head and stared at Elodie. "True," Kaye said softly.

Elodie liked being looked at by Kaye that way, though she didn't know why exactly. She made herself comfortable and leaned forward, catching the familiar scent of eucalyptus and the less obvious fragrance of oranges. "Shall I tell you a little bit about grape picking so you have a head start for tomorrow's class?"

4.

A STRONG WHIFF OF diesel wafted across Kaye's path as she cycled past the moored narrowboat, the Kanab. The eucalyptus aroma radiated from her skin, and she couldn't remember the last time she felt this healthy. She'd kept her arms covered to avoid getting sunburnt, though her cheeks were tight and hot to the touch. Soaking up the sun's rays, she felt more alive than she had done in as many years as she could remember.

She'd decided less than a week ago, after the incident in Paris, she didn't like cities much, and she didn't like being around a lot of people either. Being the victim of a scam didn't make her unique, but it did highlight her gullibility. She could hear Sylvie's acerbic tone, telling her how stupid and irresponsible she'd been giving money to a complete stranger, no matter what their plight. Courtney would tell her she was too trusting and an easy target to be taken for a ride. She could feel Courtney's rage toward the perpetrator and then she would be protective, which unravelled into being controlling. Maybe they were right. But she couldn't conceive of living her life without trusting people, even if that did result in the occasional person taking advantage of her. No physical harm had come of it and she hadn't been inclined to alert the police, preferring instead to put the event behind her and continue on her journey. She had vowed to be a little more cautious and travelling the waterways had proved to be safe. Incidents like that were common in cities where strangers were of no consequence.

No matter where she ventured on this expedition, she wouldn't be going back to live in London. By comparison with the rural town of Sancerre, London, and equally Paris, felt oppressive. Here, hundreds of acres of vines were delineated only by the narrow track roads that led to either a small hamlet, or a farmhouse, or another narrow track. She'd breathed clear, clean air, stared up at the millions of shining stars in the warmth of the darkest nights, and discovered the joys of being in and around nature. Chaotic cities were tarnished by the wheels of high commerce and congestion in all manner of shape and form. She didn't miss London.

Her days getting to Sancerre had been filled with navigating the picturesque waterways, the hypnotic rattling of chains as she opened the lock gates and the gushing of water as the boat levelled itself inside the lock, and the metrical low rumble of the engine as she guided the craft leisurely onward. She'd taken on one of the oldest canals in France and traversed the peculiarly narrow Briare aqueduct, which was lined by pretty lanterns and overlooked the Loire river. The physical demands of travelling alone had cleared her head and while she still felt a little weary if she thought for too long about the life she'd left behind, she was mentally and emotionally stronger.

Being on the narrowboat reminded her of her holidays as a child with her family, when she'd first learned how to work the locks, moor the boat, and live in a confined space. It was different here though. The French canals and towpaths were wider and better kept than she remembered of the English waterways and being alone on the boat, it didn't feel overly small. Also, she'd spent so many years with other people at her side, either guiding her or deciding for her, some looking out for her, she felt an absence that was neither pleasant nor unpleasant. But the nagging sensation would lift at the next wonderous sight. She'd enjoyed having time to herself and the freedom to choose what to do next. She'd seen a hedgehog, a badger, foxes, and so many different types of birds whose names she would never know. She'd appreciated being able to visit the historical sites along the route without Sylvie's whining voice in her ear, stirring guilt. She did miss having someone to share her experiences with though, someone to talk with. In time, that need would shift, but for now there was a small niggling space within her that whispered for the special attention of another human being.

The Kanab boat had been tied to the same spot against the bank since she'd moored the Papillion next to it two days earlier. The craft appeared empty inside and judging by the flaking red paint along its cabin and the windows that were opaque from grime, it was probably privately owned. It seemed out of place compared to the well-maintained touring boats she'd seen along the canal. She wheeled her bike across the narrow gangplank onto the front deck of the Papillion and leant it against the guardrail. She removed the paper bag of shopping from the woven basket on the front of the bike and stepped inside the boat. The scent of orange and cinnamon potpourri escaped through the open door. Her phone rang. She juggled the shopping onto the galley's surface and smiled at the icon on the screen before answering.

"Hi, Courtney."

"Hey kiddo, how's it going? I'm sorry I missed your calls. Work stuff got all kinds of cocked up. If I had balls, they'd be busted after this week. The assholes are killing me. Anyway, where are you?"

"Sancerre. You should come. It's stunning, and relaxing, and wonderfully hot. The village is on top of a hill and overlooks the plains. You can literally see thousands of rows of vines for miles around."

"That's a lot of grapes you gotta pick, kiddo."

Kaye wandered onto the deck and stretched before leaning against the railing overlooking the water. "I can't wait." She chuckled. "Anyway, I got talking to the vineyard owner at the spa earlier." Lightness filled her chest.

Elodie had scared the life out of her when she'd walked across and introduced herself. Yes, Kaye had noticed her, and yes, she craved female company. And yes, Elodie was the sort of woman Kaye would be attracted to, if she were looking. But she wasn't looking for *that*.

"Oh yeah? You've been talking to a strange woman at a spa. Gotcha. Was she naked?"

Kaye laughed. "Stop yourself. She was very sweet and welcoming. It was just nice to chat. I'm going to her vineyard tomorrow to learn about grape picking." *So sweet and welcoming*. She was interesting, intelligent, and humorous and very attractive. Kaye had misjudged her in the first instance. She'd tried to remain calm and relaxed and had declined the generous offer of lunch before she fully appreciated who Elodie was, that she wasn't chatting her up, and that she was just being affable and kind. She'd smiled inside, like the child that had just discovered Christmas, for the whole time that they talked together, and she'd come away feeling a strange sense of exhilaration. Elodie was so much more than sweet and welcoming, but she couldn't tell Courtney that. "They produce over a hundred and seventy thousand litres of wine in the Loire region each year. Her vineyard is around twenty-four hectares and yields five tonnes of grapes per hectare for their special wines. That's seventeen hundred and fifty bottles. And nine tonnes of grapes for the cheaper wine that we usually drink. It's immense." She was wittering and had spewed facts that she hoped would capture Courtney's interest. "I'm babbling, aren't I?" She heard Courtney yawn as she wandered back inside the boat and made coffee.

"It means you're excited, and that's fab. Sounds like hospital hangover territory to me. Have you tasted it yet? Might be shite."

"They sell their wine worldwide, so it'll be good shite."

"I was messing with you."

Kaye rolled her eyes. "Anyway, tell me you'll come. We can pick grapes together. They pair people up on the opposite side of the vines. We'll be picking at night under the moonlight. It sounds so romantic."

"You're kidding me. At night?"

"Yes. It's cooler then so it helps the crop stay stress free."

Courtney laughed loudly. "Stress free. Are you gonna counsel the grapes as you pick them?"

Kaye sighed. She couldn't expect Courtney to understand what she hadn't experienced. It wasn't just about grapes. Nurturing them to create a fine wine was a form of art requiring a great deal of knowledge, and skill, and a judgement that Elodie had that couldn't be taught. "Elodie said that grapes are very sensitive."

"Elodie, eh. Cute name."

Kaye rolled her eyes, though her stomach fluttered as she recalled chatting with Elodie. She'd enjoyed learning about harvesting and the different types of grapes. She hadn't realised that the skin on green grapes was a lot tougher than red grapes and that different grapes are produced for eating. She'd been enthralled by Elodie's knowledge and passion. "If the grapes get bruised or stressed the quality of the sugars changes and the quality of the wine is affected. It's why they still hand-pick rather than use mechanised methods."

"Naturally."

Kaye stopped herself from rising to Courtney's lightly mocking tone. She stopped talking. The silence that stretched out between them mirrored their physical distance. "Please come, even if it's just for a long weekend. I really miss you."

"I miss you too, kiddo. I'll have to give a rain check for now though. Work's bonkers. Anyway, tell me about Paris. Did you go clubbing?"

Kaye rubbed her neck. "It was interesting, and no, I didn't." She sounded as evasive as she'd intended to be. She'd planned to forget about Paris as quickly as possible. The main reason she'd been relieved when she'd called and Courtney hadn't answered was that Courtney would ask questions. Kaye expected she'd have a go at her for being so utterly stupid and naïve.

"Interesting." Courtney's tone had shifted from light-hearted to mild concern. "What do you mean, interesting?"

"Well, just uneventful." She was a hopeless liar. She flushed and felt as though the narrow walls were closing in around her. She took a sip of coffee and wandered back onto the deck. Courtney knew her too well and would soon pressure Kaye to explain the events of her fated evening in Paris.

"What happened?"

There it was. The damned question she didn't want to answer. Worse still, Courtney had that low tone in her voice that said with total certainty, *I know something's happened that you don't want to tell me about, so just tell me now and stop beating around the bush*.

"It was nothing, really. Just a misunderstanding."

"Kaye." She drew out Kaye's name to the length of three syllables.

Kaye cleared her throat. "Yes?"

"Does this misunderstanding involve your wonderfully trusting nature?"

Kaye cleared her throat again. She stared from the rippling water to the longboat that was heading in her direction. She held the phone to her ear with her shoulder and waved as it passed, smiling at the crew on the other boat who smiled and waved back. It was a perfect distraction. "Uh huh."

"Seriously, kiddo."

The boat having passed, she swallowed repeatedly as the dull grey image of her night in Paris forced its way to the forefront of her mind. "Look, I met a woman. She was really kind."

"What, and then she fleeced you?"

"No. She didn't steal anything from me." Kaye sighed and rubbed the back of her neck, turning her back to the canal and leaning against the railings. "She said she was in danger of losing her home because she couldn't pay the rent. I offered her some money, that's all, to get herself back on her feet." She spoke quickly and could envision Courtney's face contorting with frustration. Courtney puffed out a deep breath. Kaye lifted the phone away from her ear. She didn't need any grief—she'd had enough of that to last a lifetime—and she didn't want to spoil the relaxing effects of the massage.

"I'm not going to ask how much."

"It wasn't a lot. I saw her doing the same thing with another woman later that evening. I was conned, I know, and it won't happen again. I'm on the boat now and that was last week's bad news. I've moved on, and this week is all good news. I'm having a wonderful time." The weight of silence lifted slowly.

"I'm glad you're having a great time. I just worry about you, kiddo. After everything else that's happened. It hasn't been easy for you, and it pisses me off that people take you for a ride like that."

"I know. And I love you for caring. The woman seemed genuine and I thought she was struggling, and even though I was scammed, the benefits to her far outweigh the cost to me. It was my own fault."

"Kaye, not everything that goes wrong in your life is your bloody fault."

Kaye jolted at Courtney's raised voice, laced with anger. The silence resumed, and after a long moment Kaye checked her phone to see if they were still connected.

"I'm sorry. Look, I'm stoked you're doing great. I'm stressed as hell at work. I'm surrounded by assholes who dish out deadlines that they couldn't even hit. They're doing my nut in, and jobs are on the line because they've just decided the margins aren't big enough, and we have to deliver more value.

It's a crock. We've been round this gig before, but I have to play ball, or I'll end up on some asshole's exit list."

Kaye's heart thudded a heavy beat. Courtney's job meant everything to her. If she lost that, she'd lose her flat as well. She worked hard and didn't deserve that. "I wish you could come here for a break from it all."

"Me too. Maybe in a few weeks. Anyway, how stinky is the boat?"

A chuckle got lost in the sadness she felt for Courtney. She wanted to take her away from the grief she got at work. She could afford to help her friend out now, but Courtney was too proud to take a penny from Kaye. Aside from that, Courtney had been the one looking out for Kaye over the years and now the tide had changed. She valued their friendship, but the nagging was tiring and reminded her too much of the past she wanted to leave behind. She didn't want to depend on anyone, and she didn't want a hard time from those she cared about for her decisions. Kaye felt unsettled as a result of the shift that had taken place in her since she'd left the UK, though she hoped Courtney didn't sense it. "It's not. It's really comfy, and it has a television so you can watch the sport if you get bored."

"Where's the nearest five-star?"

Kaye hesitated. "I don't know. I could ask Elodie tomorrow if it means you'll come."

"If I could come, that would be awesome."

A warm sensation filled Kaye's chest. She craved company. "I'd like to see you."

"Look, the place sounds amazing, but I can't promise anything. Any hot women?"

Kaye smiled, and the memory of Elodie's smile warmed her. "I haven't been looking. I had a massage today and it was very relaxing. We can go to the spa together when you get here."

"Are there naked women there?"

"Give over." Yes, there were naked women, but Kaye hadn't given them attention...at least, not a great deal of attention. She'd enjoyed the liberating feeling that the place inspired, and it had been very pleasant chatting to Elodie. "It was a therapeutic experience."

"Listen, you take care. Hear me?"

"I am."

Sancerre was a cultural village surrounded by vineyards with low crime rates and a community spirit. People seemed supportive of each other. Tomorrow she was taking a lesson on grape picking and then she would start work as a picker. In a week, she'd be moving on and having new experiences in new places. With every day that passed, she discovered things about herself that made her stronger and her past weaker. Eventually, Sylvie and the pain that she'd endured over the years would be a distant memory, and then she'd be able to think clearly about what she wanted her life to look like. A relationship, a home, a family, a job. Maybe, but with a world to explore, she was in no hurry to find them.

5.

ELODIE LIFTED HER HAND to form a visor over her eyes and squinted into the near distance along the track road leading to the chateau. She smiled. Kaye was heading toward the vineyard on a bicycle. She was wearing a large straw hat and a canary yellow dress that moved on the breeze she created from pedalling, revealing her slender legs. Her hiking boots looked too big for the pedals. Elodie was captivated by the level of determination Kaye appeared to be putting into the task of moving the bike along the road.

As Kaye came to a halt in front of her, puffing hard, Elodie's smile broadened.

Kaye stood astride the bike, placed her hat in the basket at the front, and blew out a long breath. "Hi there."

Elodie admired the dress that accentuated her feminine curves and came to rest just below her knees. She was mildly amused and deeply fascinated with the English woman who dared to cycle in the heat of the midday sun, and a hint of tenderness called from her heart for Kaye's apparent innocence. "Hello, again."

Kaye looked at Elodie for a long moment and then broke eye contact. "Is there somewhere I can leave my bike?"

Elodie gripped the handlebars. "Let me help you."

Kaye swung her leg over the low central bar, tossing her dress upward before gravity settled it again. She looked like a flower in full bloom, luminous and new to the day. She appeared as a wonderful fusion of susceptibility and robustness and so very unlike the other women Elodie knew. There was an enchanting innocence that radiated through her sun-kissed cheeks. Her appearance touched Elodie like a fine red wine, smooth on the palate with a lingering warmth. "How was the ride?"

"As the crow flies, it would have been a lot closer. I think I might have got a bit lost as well." Kaye wiped her forearm across her brow. "It feels hotter now I've stopped." She cupped her palm to her cheek. "Do you think I've caught too much sun? I thought the hat would do the trick, but I'm not sure it's helped much."

Elodie smiled. "You look a little flushed. Would you like some water?"

Kaye pulled out a bottle of mineral water from the bike's basket. "Got some, thanks." She unscrewed the cap and took a long slug. "That's better." She replaced the bottle and searched inside the bag. "Ah, here it is." She pulled out a tube of suntan lotion, squeezed a little onto her fingers, and rubbed it into her cheeks.

Elodie reached out and smoothed in a dab of white cream that Kaye had left on her nose.

Kaye jerked her head back. Her eyes widened, and she looked like a doe caught in the headlights.

"Sorry. You had lotion on..." Elodie pointed at Kaye's face, wishing she hadn't touched her, hadn't created that defensive response in her. She hadn't meant to scare or offend her.

"Oh, thank you."

Kaye smiled, and Elodie released the tightness in her chest with a long breath. "Your bike will be safe here."

Kaye took the bike and leaned it against the low wall that bounded hedged gardens beyond which lay Chateau Marchand. "The castle is spectacular. Is it around twelfth century?"

"It is. You know architecture?"

Kaye smiled and pointed at the building. "History, mostly. It's the Gothic style and the height. Like the Notre Dames. Architecture is a passion of mine...at least, it used to be."

"Used to be?"

Kaye continued to look at the building. "At one point I thought about studying it. I guess life got in the way."

"Life has a habit of doing that."

Kaye looked back toward the chateau. "Yes, it does."

Elodie put her hands on her hips and looked up at the precisely cut stone, the pointed spires that topped medieval-styled turrets, and the leaded stained-glass windows. "It was here long before the vineyard. It's reputed that Louis VII stayed here with his wife, Eleanor. She was a wealthy and powerful woman. She was also rather smart by all accounts."

Kaye turned to Elodie. "You studied history?"

"No. I just know this place. It's been in the family for over three hundred years."

Kaye sighed. "Wow. I wonder what it would have been like to have lived here all those centuries ago."

Elodie frowned as she continued to stare at the chateau, seeing its history through that perspective. "Pretty horrific." As stunning as the place was architecturally, it had never felt like a home, and it would certainly have supported a different lifestyle for a woman in the twelfth century. The vaulted ceilings in the corridors echoed her footsteps too loudly, and the rooms were so large that she rattled around inside them. That's why she'd made the barn her home. She marvelled at Kaye's genuine admiration and knowledge, and a warm feeling spread across her chest.

Kaye chuckled. "I think you're right. Losing your head for being a woman who can't bear a son isn't very romantic."

Elodie laughed. "That was Henry VIII, I believe."

"True." Kaye blushed.

Elodie stared into Kaye's blue eyes, the same shade as the autumn sky. She had a darker blue around the outside of her irises and there were tiny flecks of hazel closer to her pupils. Kaye's eyes had been dark blue at the spa and the hazel hadn't come through. They were the kind of eyes that conveyed deep emotion and were easy to read. Dark eyes were tricky, especially browns and greens, because the dilation of the pupils was harder to detect. Some women wore their hearts on their sleeves. Kaye revealed her heart through her eyes. Elodie tried to keep her heart away from both her sleeves and her eyes.

"Shall we get started?" She indicated to her right where the road led away from the chateau to three buildings, each very different in structure and design: a large factory-sized construction using bronze-coloured rusted steel with generous black glass windows; a smaller barn conversion replicating the stone design of the chateau; and a raised bunker covered in grass with the word *Cave* carved into its wooden door.

"This is like a piece of art. Old meets new. I love it."

"The steel structure helps us keep the temperature consistent inside the factory. The cave is a perfect and authentic place for our visitors to taste the wine, and the barn is where the main offices and other tasting rooms are hosted." It was also where Elodie lived but she didn't need to explain that to Kaye. She didn't want to revisit why she didn't live in the chateau and didn't want to be thought of as ungracious given she had so much when so many people in the world had very little.

"It's impressive," Kaye said as she looked around.

"Most of the staff are out preparing the vines for picking, setting up the lighting, the picking bins, and doing final inspections. Inside the factory over there is where the real hard work takes place, the fermentation, refining, and bottling. Maybe you'd like to take a look at that another time. Come, I want to show you how we assess the grapes, so you know what's ready to pick and what isn't. When we're picking, we work the same vines over a period of a couple of weeks or more. So, sometimes you need to leave the grapes a little longer to make sure they're perfect."

Kaye frowned. "Am I going to get it wrong?"

"No. You can't ruin anything."

There was charm in Kaye's open display of apprehension. It meant she was likely to take the picking seriously and in doing so, she would take care to do a good job. Elodie's gut twinged as if she were watching a young animal navigate a dangerous world. She didn't like to see Kaye anxious. "Honestly, you can't get it wrong, so please don't worry. We have seasonal pickers and locals involved who'll help you if you're really unsure. There are also two levels of inspection of the grapes, one at the vines and again in the factory, so there's nothing to fear. I want you to enjoy your time with us. Picking is hard work, but it's also very rewarding. It's about teamwork, and everyone has a great time while they pick. Odd as it sounds, we're all passionate about grapes and wine. You're a volunteer, so you can do as little or as much as you like, and no one is going to judge you."

The mild look of trepidation on Kaye's face softened into a half-smile.

"I'll be around most of the time. If you have any questions, promise you'll find me."

Kaye nodded but still looked a little overwhelmed.

Instinctively, Elodie reached out and touched Kaye's arm then let go quickly, reminded of Kaye's startled response just a moment earlier. She clapped her hands together. "So, are you ready? Excited?"

Kaye rubbed her palms down her dress. "Yes."

Elodie led Kaye past the buildings. She opened the passenger door to a grey Land Rover Defender and indicated for Kaye to get in. "We have a short drive." She waited until Kaye was seated before closing the door and getting into the driver's seat. "Have you been to France before?" she asked as she shifted into gear and pulled away.

"A long time ago, as a child. I don't remember much except fields and fields of artichokes that smelled of rotten cabbages."

A laugh burst from Elodie. “Rotten cabbage isn’t how we prefer to be remembered. Most people think of fine wine, cheese, the fresh smell of baguettes, and cured meats. Rotten cabbages...not so much.” The chuckle rumbled in her chest as she drove along a track wide enough for one vehicle. Vines three-foot high spanned the flat plains far into the distance on either side of them and beyond which lay green hills.

“Have you been to England?”

“No. There were English students at École Polytechnique, the university I attended in Paris, but we had to study in English. I’d like to go to London someday. I imagine it’s majestic. I confess, I haven’t travelled much, just Paris and other parts of France, mostly in connection with the business. I would like to hear Big Ben chime, see your Houses of Parliament and the changing of the guards at Buckingham Palace, and take a boat ride along the Thames.”

“I’m staying on a narrowboat on the canal. Water is very calming.”

Elodie thought about the baths in the Blue Room and the occasions she’d swam in the lake with Mylene while at the convent. She hadn’t thought about Mylene in a long time. She’d stopped wondering about what had happened to her by the time she went to university. Now, her image was as vivid as if Mylene were stood in front of her and they were kids again. Mylene’s eyes were blue-grey, different to Kaye’s, and yet with the same openness. “I thought you might be staying at one of the hotels in the village. That’s where most tourists stay.”

Kaye laughed. “I’m travelling south to Nice and then on to Cannes. There’s so much more to see travelling by boat.”

Elodie turned her attention to the road. “You see all these vines on the flat land? They’re the Sauvignon grapes. Up there, on the slopes you see in the distance, those are the Pinot grapes. That’s where we’re heading.” Orange, cinnamon, and a faint hint of lavender drifted into her awareness. Inhaling Kaye’s fruity perfume, she was reminded of her grandmother's baking and Christmas as a small child. It was a fond memory, fleeting, and from what seemed like a different lifetime. She settled it in the back of her mind, in a different compartment to the one reserved for memories of her mother.

They drove in silence, with Kaye looking out the passenger window, until Elodie brought the vehicle to a stop. Elodie leaned over and opened the glove compartment and pulled out a pair of small scissors. She stepped out of the vehicle and went around to the passenger side as Kaye jumped down.

Kaye's cheeks were a shiny peach colour, with traces of red where the sun had definitely caught them. She brushed the front of her dress down and bent down to tie a loose lace. A ripping sound accompanied her as she stood. "Damn it." She lifted the back of her dress and inspected the small opening along the line of the seam. "I didn't bring a huge wardrobe with me. Just a rucksack. This was my best dress."

Elodie rolled her tongue around her dry mouth. Why would someone wear their best dress to pick grapes? It was daft and adorable, and she struggled not to laugh. Kaye was fiddling with the hem and tutting. Elodie could watch her all day and not get bored. She stopped herself from reaching out and comforting Kaye and shoved her hands deep into her pockets. "Maybe we can stitch it up later."

Kaye let go of the dress. "I'm useless at sewing."

Elodie smiled. "I can sew." She laughed at Kaye's wide-eyed stare. "You look surprised. I was educated in a convent. Needlecraft was a compulsory subject." She felt the air trap inside her chest as Kaye looked her up and down.

"I didn't expect...sorry. I didn't really think...thank you."

Elodie smiled. "It's okay. Come on." She walked toward the vines and gave her attention to the grapes. "So, you see these?" She raised a large bunch of dark red grapes as high as they would lift without snapping them from their source and cupped them in her hand. Kaye nodded. Elodie took out the scissors and snipped the bunch from the vine. She held them up against another bunch further along the row. "And you see these? They're slightly more rigid to the touch, their skins have less of a shine, and they're a fraction smaller. They're not far off, but they're not ready."

"I see."

"Touch them. What do you feel?"

Kaye moved closer to Elodie and pinched a grape from the bunch attached to the vine between her forefinger and thumb. "They're firm-ish."

As Kaye bent closer to the vines, Elodie caught the distracting citrus scent again, and Kaye's dress brushed Elodie's leg. The contact was barely noticeable and over too quickly as Kaye moved, but Elodie felt the warmth of it and wondered if Kaye had noticed. Elodie turned the cropped bunch of grapes in her hand. She took hold of a single fruit and twisted gently, releasing it from its family. Their fingertips touched briefly as she handed it to Kaye, and Elodie's breath faltered. She tried to stop the heat inside her from reaching her cheeks and failed. "Can you feel it?"

Looking at the grape, Kaye frowned.

"The difference between them."

Kaye focused on Elodie as she gently rolled the fruit between her fingers and thumb. "Yes."

Elodie held Kaye's gaze. "It has a thin skin."

Kaye continued to look at Elodie as she rubbed her thumb over the surface of the grape. She smiled. "Yes."

"Would you like to taste? Try it."

Kaye popped the fruit into her mouth and chewed. "Wow, that's very sweet." She pursed her lips and narrowed her eyes. "So sweet."

Elodie plucked a grape from the bunch and ate it. "It's very good. Excellent." She offered the bunch to Kaye, who twisted off another grape. "Take the bunch."

Kaye cradled the grapes as if they were a tiny bird in her hand. Elodie imagined Kaye's fingers applying the same quality of touch to her skin, and a tingle made its way down her spine.

"If you see any mildew, or white colouration, or anything that doesn't look like those grapes in your hand, then don't pick them. Now, you choose a ripe bunch and snip them from the vine." She held out the small, bladed scissors.

Kaye put the grapes on the ground. She bit her lip as she glanced toward the vines. She stared at the scissors in Elodie's hand for a moment before taking them. She bent closer to a vine, stopped, moved down the row, and then snipped a small bunch of grapes.

Elodie smiled. "Now check them against the others we picked. Are they a similar size, colour, texture?"

Kaye squeezed a grape from the bunch she'd just cut. "They're a bit harder, I think. I went with the smallest bunch, because I didn't want to waste a big bunch on practicing."

Elodie shrugged. "A small bunch doesn't mean they're ready for picking." She gestured to the rows of vines that surrounded them. "We have plenty of grapes to be able to give a few over to trial and error. Have another go."

Kaye cupped another bunch of grapes delicately and turned them in her hand. She stroked her fingertip lightly across their surface and then, almost hesitantly, snipped them from the vine. "These are definitely ripe."

Elodie stood perfectly still, moved by Kaye's concern and tenderness. She didn't have an explanation for the effect that Kaye's modesty ignited in her. She wasn't a stranger to humility, though it was a quality in short supply in her work at the club other than Preeda in reception. But she didn't know Preeda well and didn't care to know her any better. Kaye's handling of the vines reminded her more of the feeling she had when she spent time with the horses at the sanctuary. They too were sensitive and intelligent creatures. She checked herself and looked across the estate to focus on the furthest point for a moment and made a promise to visit the sanctuary again soon. It was a sufficient distraction to settle her pulse. "That's excellent. I can trust you with my vineyard now." Elodie cut another three bunches in quick succession and hooked them over her fingers.

She felt intensity in Kaye's gaze, then she watched Kaye's eyes narrow before she smiled a glorious wide smile. Kaye's laughter was as sweet as the juice of the fruit she'd just eaten. Elodie imagined her lips as soft, and warm, and as delicious as the grapes. "You have a pretty smile."

Kaye looked away instantly.

An overwhelming sensation of dread flooded Elodie. Her comment had clearly elicited discomfort. "I'm sorry, I didn't mean to embarrass you. Your smile, it suits you." Elodie turned and strode toward the Land Rover.

"Thank you," Kaye whispered as she followed Elodie. She climbed into the car and put on her seat belt.

Heat burned Elodie's face. She positioned herself in the driver's seat so as to create the greatest amount of distance between them, all the while feeling drawn closer. Kaye was smart and interesting, cute and funny. Elodie's stomach had knotted at the sight of her, and the thought of Kaye's transient visit sat like a lead weight in her chest. She had to drop the idea of getting to know Kaye better. That would be futile and dangerous, and nothing good would come of it. Kaye was a tourist moving through, and that made her the worst person to get close to. Elodie checked herself. She didn't get *that* close to anyone. She wasn't thinking of getting close. Thinking had nothing to do with feelings, and feelings like *these* were deeply disconcerting.

She placed the grapes on the seat between them, shifted the vehicle into gear, and set off toward the barn. “There’s a small lunch waiting for us so we can sample the fruits of our labour.”

The voice in her head taunted her. It was her mother’s acerbic tone. *You’re not good enough for her.*

6.

THE REDDISH RESIDUE OF the grapes stained her fingertips, and the sugary taste lingered on her tongue as she followed Elodie into the barn next to the factory building. She filled her lungs with the cooler air and the scent of new wood. The beamed structure inside the stone building gave a modern, spacious, and aesthetic appeal where she imagined the chateau to be much darker and oppressive.

As they walked through the central area, a large glass feature window to her left gave views across the vineyard and drew natural light inside. It connected the inside with the outside, creating a space that was at one with its surroundings. She imagined an artist with their easel standing at the window and recreating the vista. It would make a fabulous picture.

Within the large foyer space, a range of soft seating had been positioned to take full advantage of the expansive view. Chairs and couches were set out to cater for small informal groups with low tables. The smell of percolated coffee filtered from the pot on the table that also held a water cooler, a selection of bite-sized biscuits, and a variety of mini croissants on trays next to a drinks machine. On her right, glass-partitioned rooms housed computers, desks, and people in short sleeved shirts. One had a telephone pressed to their ear and gesticulated enthusiastically as they paced the room.

A mezzanine towered above her head that concealed the first-floor rooms. She'd noticed the dormer windows in the roof before entering the building, and from what she could see there must be a third level, maybe a stock room, or something else associated with the business. She had the urge to explore and find out more about the building's history.

Heat rose to her cheeks with her reflection. Elodie must think her a little strange after her behaviour at the vines. Her anxiety about the cost of wasting the grapes seemed ridiculous now, given the scope of the winery's operation. She'd felt even more daft picking the wrong bunch, because she'd known they weren't ready and hadn't trusted herself, and then anger had flared inside her at Sylvie for what she'd created in Kaye. There had been a time when she was more frivolous in her outlook and not obsessively concerned with making the wrong decisions. She'd never worried about money or waste when she'd been at uni and her family were always very generous on both fronts. Sylvie had controlled everything: their bank accounts, what Kaye wore, where she went, and who she was friends with. The years of being told she'd got this wrong, got that wrong, made a stupid decision and messed it up again echoed through her nervous system such that her innate responses were conditioned by her deeply negative experiences. In time, the imprint would fade. In time, she'd feel confident being herself in the company of others. Her ex's shrill voice resounded in her ear, an unpleasant intrusion from the past that encroached on this magnificent space. A surge of anger flared inside her again. She turned the image to black and white, remembering how her therapist taught her to desensitise a strong negative emotion, and the image became a silent screenshot in the background. Elodie was staring at her and smiling, as if waiting for her, but not impatiently, and for some strange reason it made her feel better.

She took a deep breath and followed Elodie beyond the stairs and into another partitioned space. It was set up as a formal dining area with a large marble-topped table and hand-crafted wooden chairs with black leather cushioned seats. She glanced at the selection of hors d'oeuvres on small individual white china plates, laid out in a perfect arc along the shorter end of the table. The half carafe bottle had condensation running the length of it and contained an opaque liquid that definitely wasn't wine.

Elodie poured from the bottle of mineral water into the two larger cut crystal glasses and handed one to Kaye.

"Thank you."

Kaye couldn't stop herself from staring into Elodie's dark green eyes, their shape accentuated by long lashes that curled upward naturally. In the brief moment that they both held the glass, Kaye's mouth parched. Elodie's tanned, smooth skin, unblemished and absent of any makeup, held her captivated by the desire to touch. The soft curve of her high cheekbones and the line of her jaw had the fineness of a more petite woman. Kaye felt assessed by her steady gaze, and Elodie's slight frown hinted at questions. Kaye didn't want to answer questions. "When was the barn built?"

"The original building was built sixty-two years ago. We renovated and extended it recently. You like it?"

"Very much. It's wonderfully light and spacious."

Elodie smiled, and a flood of warmth expanded in Kaye's chest. It wasn't just that Elodie was a beautiful and intriguing woman; she also had an appreciation of architecture and history, and she was...interesting wasn't the right word. Fascinating? No. Enchanting. Yes, enchanting, though not in any fairy tale prince kind of away. She knew nothing about Elodie, and there had been moments of awkwardness—the voice in her head had reminded her incessantly. But then there had been a look that had passed between them at the vines, and she'd recognised something of herself in Elodie's private world. The loneliness that she'd denied to herself had felt suddenly very real in that moment.

The chilled water soothed her dry mouth. "How many people work here?"

"Thirty-seven full time. We'll have a hundred or so extra people for picking though."

"Do you ever get bored of it? Doing the same thing year on year?"

Elodie smiled. "No. Every crop presents us new challenges, particularly with the weather. Yes, the work is driven by routine and processes, but it never gets boring. The vines keep us on our toes."

Kaye sighed as the effect of Elodie's smile rippled through her. Courtney would say that Kaye wasn't the best judge of character, that she was too caring and trusting to be able to see people clearly. Courtney may be right, but there was no other explanation for the ease and calm that Kaye felt around Elodie.

"It's your baby, isn't it?"

"I think everyone who works here is passionate about making the best wine."

Watching Elodie nurture the grapes, and the look of simple pleasure when she'd tested the fruit for its taste and texture, had put Kaye in awe. She'd tried to imagine what it was like to be able to identify the subtle distinctions in flavour and composition of the fruit, as Elodie did. The juicy flesh had tasted sweeter than a sugar cube, and the deep red skins were pleasantly softer than she'd anticipated, but that was the limit of her ability. Elodie's gaze was direct and unwavering, and Kaye felt exposed by the apparent assessment.

She went to the window and looked out across the plains. "This is spectacular." She had thought the agency she'd worked for had been a good business and having been valued at a little over five million for the purpose of the divorce settlement, it hadn't been too shabby. She would bet the vineyard alone was worth three times that and probably more if she included the chateau.

Kaye jolted when Elodie's arm brushed hers. Elodie stood close to her side and sipped her water as she looked out over familiar terrain. She must know every vine in every acre. Heat and the smell of sweet musk stole Kaye's concentration.

"Some of our appellation vines are almost a hundred years old." Elodie pointed in the direction of the vines that spanned the hills in the distance. "They produce our finest and most expensive wines. We have a rolling schedule to replace blocks of vines every thirty to forty years, depending on their yield."

Kaye cleared her throat. "Has the vineyard been in your family a long time?"

"Five generations."

"I can't imagine what it's like to know that level of history. I traced my family tree when I was at uni and couldn't relate to anyone beyond my grandparents. They were just names in a chain that led to me." She turned to face Elodie and was captivated by the intensity in her eyes. Kaye took a deep breath and looked out the window to recover herself. "It's odd, isn't it? Having a biological link, albeit distant, to someone in the past who is effectively a stranger to you. And yet, you have this wonderful vineyard that connects you all, even if you couldn't know your ancestors."

Elodie turned away from the window and went to the table, and Kaye followed.

"I've never considered it. I'm an only child, and I was destined to inherit the vineyard from my mother. My father left us when I was two. I never contemplated that I had a choice to do anything else."

Kaye thought she'd seen a flicker of remorse in Elodie's expression, but then she smiled and whatever it was had gone. She got the sense that Elodie guarded secrets. But who didn't? She took a sip of water. "I can relate to not thinking you had a choice. It's too easy to get stuck in our status quo lives. We forget to look inside ourselves to check whether we're happy living or just happy being comfortable." Kaye nearly choked on the wisdom that fell from her lips, the words she hadn't been able to heed until very recently. She was preaching a little, and the energy between them had tensed in the silent contemplation that they'd both retreated to.

Elodie poured Kaye a small glass of the cloudy liquid. "Here, try this."

The sweetness struck her instantly, and when she swallowed, the smooth nectar bathed her throat. "That's delicious." She took another sip, and the air between them seemed lighter.

"These are the fruits of your labour. Well, not from your labour exactly, but these are our grapes."

"It tastes so fresh."

"It is. Fresh from the vines earlier today."

Kaye finished the grape juice and placed the empty glass on the table.

Elodie refilled it. "Help yourself to food."

Kaye studied the labelled dishes. She leaned forward to take a mushroom stuffed with garlic and cheese at the same time as Elodie reached across her, brushing their arms lightly. Kaye inhaled the faint musk scent again. Elodie's shirt was soft and the warmth reassuring.

"Excuse me." Elodie plucked a piece of skewered chicken from the plate and took a pace back.

Kaye watched her put the morsel into her mouth and chew enthusiastically. She bit on the mushroom, and the garlic aroma stung the inside of her nose. "Crikey." She cupped her hand to her mouth. "That's strong."

Elodie chuckled as she handed Kaye a serviette. "We like our garlic, along with our rotten cabbage-smelling artichokes." Her laugh had a low and free resonance to it. She stopped laughing and narrowed her eyes. "Is it too much? I'll have the chef change it for something more to your taste." Elodie picked up the plate of mushrooms.

Kaye put her hand on Elodie's arm. "It's fine. Honestly. Please don't fuss on my account." She let go and created a little distance between them.

Elodie pressed her lips together. "It's no fuss."

The garlic mellowed in Kaye's mouth, and a rich nutty flavour replaced it. "It's very tasty. Odd after the fruit juice and the garlic's stronger than I'm used to, but please don't change anything. This is perfect." She couldn't remember the last time she'd felt spoilt and frivolous. Even though she'd paid for the experience, it felt more like a special occasion than a purchase. She took the plate from Elodie and ate another mushroom. "So, do you think I'll be good enough to pick?"

Elodie lowered her head a fraction and squinted at Kaye. Then a slight smile appeared on her face. "Let me think about that." She brought her hand to her chin, tapped her finger to her lips, and continued to look Kaye up and down.

The sparkle in Elodie's eyes resonated in the softness in Kaye's chest. She felt as if she were being undressed slowly and admired deeply. She focused on Elodie's lips and the insistent thought rolling around her mind. *I really want to kiss you.*

Elodie turned to the table. "Yes, our harvest will be safe in your hands." There was formality in her tone, and her smile seemed suddenly distant. Elodie picked up a sliver of cured ham, tilted her head back slightly, and lowered it into her mouth. She chewed as she nodded, then swallowed.

"The night runs from seven in the evening through to seven in the morning. We have two overlapping shifts. Seven until two and twelve until seven. There's a half-hour break. Which shift would you prefer to work?"

Kaye didn't need to think for long. "Seven until two."

"That's the best option. It's easier to get into the pattern of work and sleep. You'll get to see some of the day. Very good. We start tomorrow."

Kaye's stomach did a somersault. "Thank you so much."

Elodie shook her head. "You won't be thanking me by ten o'clock when your back is breaking. See how it goes. If it's too much, let me know."

Kaye smiled. She knew what genuine concern looked like. On the receiving end, it felt warm inside, as it did after drinking mulled wine. Gentle vibrations tingled through to her hands. She looked down to see they were trembling a little. She looked up and felt the intensity of Elodie's deep thought as if directed at her. It was harder to breathe. Her inner voice had stopped talking to her, stopped reminding her it was too soon to get involved with anyone. There was just a blankness in her mind, except for a strong sense of knowing she was likely to do something that her inner voice would try to tell her she might regret. She was on this trip to rediscover herself. All of herself. What better place to start than to listen to her body's innate needs? Elodie was still staring at her. "I'd better get going," she said, her voice barely a whisper.

Elodie's eyes lit up when she smiled. "I hope you enjoyed the taster."

"I did, very much. Thank you."

Elodie indicated the exit. Kaye couldn't get out of the place quickly enough just to be able to breathe and compose herself. Elodie seemed in no hurry. She appeared to move in slow motion, and the faster Kaye willed her to speed up, the slower she seemed to go. The voice in Kaye's head had returned before they reached her bicycle. *Get the hell out of here and take a cold shower. Don't do anything in haste.*

She grabbed her bike from the wall, threw her leg over the central bar, and put her foot on the pedal. She was about to push down and set the bicycle in motion when she realised she hadn't properly said goodbye. She stepped off the bike. Her dress had pulled up above her knee, and she tried to brush it down. "I…thank you for…everything."

Elodie took a pace toward Kaye, and her heart tried to break out of her chest.

"In France, it's customary to do this." Elodie took another step closer, put her hands on each of Kaye's arms, and leaned forward.

When Elodie's lips met Kaye's cheek, a quake moved through Kaye. Flames shot down to her core, and her cheek felt as if it was on fire. Maybe it was the years of repressed sexual appetite or the desire to reclaim the exquisite feeling of needing and wanting to be touched, but the softness of Elodie's cheek against her own lingered long after Elodie let her go. Elodie said something, then she smiled and started to laugh. Kaye felt caressed by the gentle amusement though she hadn't heard a word Elodie had said.

"I was wondering...would you like a tour around the factory some time? It's good to know how the wine is made."

Kaye could still feel Elodie's lips against her cheek. Processing the words was a challenge. She nodded. She walked along the track pushing her bike for some time until she realised she should put on her hat to avoid getting burnt and get on the bike and ride it.

By the time she reached the narrowboat, she was adamant about one thing. She needed that cold shower and an early night. The craving that had snuck up on her would be gone by the morning, or she would have better control over it.

7.

ELODIE SLOWED THE LAND Rover, leaned forward, and squinted through the windscreen. She recognised the bicycle that was resting upside down on its handlebars and seat on the side of the narrow road. Kaye moved from being bent over the rear wheel to standing with her hands on her hips. She looked cuter than ever in her hiking boots and short red dress.

Kaye turned toward the vehicle as it approached.

Elodie stepped from the driver's seat and studied the tyre. "Puncture?"

Kaye wiped her forehead. "I've been trying to get the tyre off, but I can't."

Elodie smiled. "With your bare hands?"

"Yes. I have a puncture kit." Kaye held out a small container of repair patches.

"You'd have to be quite strong to get this off without a lever."

"I don't have anything else." Kaye's fingers were black from the combination of chain oil and dirt.

"I have tools in the car." Elodie grabbed the kit from the boot and a bottle of water from the front seat for Kaye.

"Thanks." Kaye took a long drink. "Is it always this hot in September?"

The vibrant colour in Kaye's cheeks gave her a youthful appearance, but with her complexion Elodie feared there was a good chance of her getting bad sunburn and possibly making herself ill. "I think we have what you call an Indian summer. It's hotter than normal. You need to take care not to get burned."

"Yes." Kaye touched the tip of her nose.

Elodie pulled out two levers and gave her attention to the wheel. "You need to push the spanner between the rim of the tyre and the frame, like this. This one's a really tight fit."

Elodie glanced up at Kaye as she teased out the inner tube and pinched her finger between the rubber and metal rim. "Merde."

Kaye gasped. "Are you okay?"

"I trapped it." The embarrassment of knowing she'd been gawping at Kaye instead of concentrating on what she was doing was worse than the pain that shot through her finger. She examined her reddening finger and gave it a shake. Kaye took her hand.

Heat flooded Elodie's cheeks as Kaye gently massaged her fingers. "It'll be fine." Reluctantly, she eased her hand from Kaye's. Apart from the hiking boots and now the dirty mark on the end of Kaye's nose, Kaye looked dressed up as if she'd been heading to a party of some kind. Her dress was very well pressed for someone living on a narrowboat. Dainty white buttons ran the length of it from the centre of her breasts to where the dress ended mid-thigh. The freckles across the top of her chest had darkened from the sun. "That's a pretty dress. Were you heading somewhere nice?"

Kaye held out the pump.

"Thanks."

"I was heading to a craft fair. In..." Kaye frowned and looked skyward.

"Pouilly-sur-Loire?"

"Yes, that's it."

"It's very popular. We have some talented local artists. There's an excellent pottery stall there too, if you like that sort of thing. Were you heading that way?" Elodie pointed in the direction she'd been driving.

Kaye nodded. She flushed and a delicate film of moisture formed across the sunburnt skin under her eyes. "Yes."

"Lost again?"

"A little, maybe."

Elodie squinted up at Kaye and smiled. "You needed to take the first exit at the last roundabout. Pouilly-sur-Loire's in that direction." She pointed over her shoulder, directly across the fields.

Kaye released a puff of air. "Damn it."

Elodie chuckled. "You know you're very funny when you're cross with yourself." She watched Kaye smile slowly and noticed the laughter lines fan her eyes, and then Kaye's shoulders dropped. When Kaye laughed, warmth radiated through Elodie's chest, and she had the urge to take her into her arms and hold her tightly. She bent back down to the bike and pumped up the innertube. She moved the rubber through her hands looking for signs of a puncture and tried to ignore the slight tremor in her fingers.

"I've never been good with directions."

Elodie glanced up from the tyre, up Kaye's legs to the hem of the dress, and then up the line of buttons to her breasts. She blinked to reclaim her concentration from Kaye's body. "I can't see anything obvious here."

Kaye frowned. She looked up and down the long track road and then down to Elodie and sighed.

"Would you like me to take you to the craft fair?"

Kaye shook her head.

Elodie swallowed her disappointment and smiled.

"I can't trouble you."

Elodie stood. "Honestly, it's no problem. I haven't been there in a while. It'll be a nice break for me. And you can't use the bike until it's repaired. I can fix it at home."

Kaye looked down at her dirty hands.

Elodie held out hers. "Mine are filthy too. And you have dirt on your nose." She narrowed her eyes and pointed at the spot. "We'll go and wash up first." She shrugged, silently hoping Kaye would agree.

"If you're sure?"

"Of course." Elodie picked up the bicycle and worked it into the boot before Kaye could change her mind. "You'll love Pouilly-sur-Loire. It's very quaint. Do you like ice cream?"

Kaye got in the car. "I love ice cream, and I haven't had one here yet."

Elodie turned the engine. "Well, that's going to change this afternoon. They have an excellent place for gelato."

***

Kaye pressed her finger to her lips as she looked into the ice cream chiller. "It all looks wonderful. It's impossible to choose."

Elodie smiled at the frown that bunched Kaye's brow as she pointed from one flavour to another and mumbled. She'd never come across anyone quite as innocent and modest as Kaye appeared. She wondered what went on inside Kaye's mind that made it so difficult to choose between the triple chocolate and the double chocolate. "Have a scoop of both," she said.

"But that's eight Euros for an ice cream. Who pays that?"

Elodie usually wouldn't but with Kaye, she was behaving like a tourist and it was fun. "Me. I'm having two scoops of salted caramel, and this is my treat so please don't worry about the cost." Kaye's worry lines deepened and Elodie felt her joy dampen a little. She was determined to treat Kaye and spoil herself. Surely, that's what being on holiday, albeit for a day, was all about. "Shall I get you a surprise?"

Kaye tilted her head and smiled at Elodie. "I'll have the double chocolate."

"Two scoops?"

Kaye looked down and ran her hands down her dress and over her stomach. "I probably shouldn't."

Elodie widened her eyes. "You have a beautiful body." Heat blossomed inside her as Kaye flushed and glanced away.

"That's very kind of you, but I could do with losing a few pounds."

Elodie shook her head. "Not in my opinion." She turned from Kaye to the counter, despondent that someone so beautiful could be uncomfortable in her own skin. Kaye had gorgeous curves and Elodie wanted to touch every part of her and show her exactly how wonderful she was. She had the impression that Kaye didn't have a partner and that she certainly wasn't used to receiving compliments. If she was with someone, she would have surely talked about them already. Elodie wanted to ask but didn't want to offend Kaye by intruding on her personal life. Kaye hadn't asked Elodie about hers and that usually meant a woman either didn't want to know or they weren't interested. Either way, the conversation seemed to be off limits. "This afternoon is a rare treat for me. I'm having two scoops." She could hear the pleading in her tone. She really wanted Kaye to enjoy the experience without feeling that she needed to hold back.

Kaye smiled. "Okay. I'll keep you company."

"Excellent."

The woman behind the counter leaned toward Elodie and asked for their order in clipped tone. The queue behind them had extended up the street. "I'll have two scoops of double chocolate and two of salted caramel." The woman huffed as if to say, is that all. Elodie beamed at her. Within a moment the woman gave them two cones, each with a large scoop of gelato.

Elodie handed the cone to Kaye. "Do you like pottery?"

"Yes."

They crossed the cobbled street to the low wall opposite the gelato shop and sat with their backs to the small graveyard in the twelfth century church. Kaye's leg pressed against Elodie's as they sat. Elodie didn't move away from the contact and neither did Kaye.

Elodie enjoyed the cool sensation of the gelato on her tongue, salty and sweet, contrasted with the heat pressing against her leg. She probably should create a little space between them because she didn't want to create a wrong impression, but she didn't want to move. She turned her head to Kaye. The effect of Kaye sliding her tongue around the top of the cone to catch the chocolate gelato that trickled down the wafer caused a gentle vibration inside her. Cocoa and sugar clung to her tongue, resurrecting a distant and long since buried memory. Sister Mary's voice was always soft and kind, but Elodie had read the truth in the hollowness she'd seen in her eyes. "I'm sure your mother is on her way," Sister Mary had said. Her mother hadn't shown up to collect her that Christmas, or the next one.

"How's your gelato?" Elodie asked and sucked hers into her mouth. Kaye had chocolate on her top lip, and Elodie wanted to kiss it off.

"It's creamy and chocolatey."

"It's the best, isn't it?" Elodie finished her cone and wiped the corners of her mouth with her fingers.

"You'll have to come to England to compare," Kaye said and quickly went back to eating.

Elodie smiled. She would quite like to visit England, if Kaye was there with her. "Perhaps you should make a point of testing the gelato wherever you go. Italy, America, Singapore, Australia, Hong Kong."

Kaye nodded. "You know, I might just do that. And then I'll return home as big as a house." She finished her cone.

Elodie handed her a tissue. "You have to live."

Kaye gave a half-smile. Elodie tried to imagine what it would be like to travel the world with Kaye and eat gelato in every city and village. All she could picture was the silhouette of

Kaye in the distance, too far away to be heard and out of reach. That's what had happened when she'd committed her heart fully to a relationship in the past. The emotional distance, which should close between two people in the security of their love for each other, had always become wider and the possibility of closing the space was insurmountable. She would feel herself withdrawing and be powerless to stop the process until eventually *they* left her.

Days like today, taking a leisurely stroll around the fair with a gorgeous woman at her side, didn't happen in Elodie's world. She wouldn't allow it. It would give the wrong impression to any of the other women she knew, and it would imply that Elodie was more invested in a relationship with them than she was. She was being a host to Kaye, and the time they spent together would come to a natural end when Kaye moved on.

Today was like being on holiday, living as someone she wasn't, and she hadn't experienced a weightless feeling like this since before taking over the vineyard. The novelty of the soft warm sensation radiating from deep within her chest surprised her. Even in the past, the happiness she'd known with women at university had always been short-lived, and the joy of intimate moments had been effortlessly shattered by the depth of emptiness that always followed. Relationships ended before they had a chance to start, let alone bloom. It was the way of life that Elodie knew best, like the blood that flowed through her veins. The situation required no thought or analysis. It simply was what it was.

She had everything she needed close to hand in Sancerre—money, sex, status, the company of other women—and she'd never wanted for anything, or so she'd believed, until now? Maybe the flaw in her rationale to keep intimate relationships at arms-length had always been susceptible to change if the right person came into her life. But she had to be open to seeing someone as the right person. It was a catch twenty-two. The prospect that Kaye might be *the one* sat uneasily. It threatened the façade that she'd put in place, being desired and unreachable, that demonstrated to herself she was content. Elodie had never felt farther removed from *content* than she did now. Kaye had thrown a light into the fissure of her ungrounded reality and the desire to distance herself seeped into her poisoned mind. But Kaye's gentle manner and healthy respect stopped her withdrawing, caused her to pause, and she felt encouraged to spend time with her. She uncrossed her arms. She hadn't intentionally adopted the defensive posture, lost in thought, and she rolled her shoulders to loosen them.

When Kaye finished her cone, Elodie stood. "Pottery," she said, and stopped short of offering Kaye her hand.

8.

KAYE STOOD ON THE deck of the Papillion sipping her coffee. Even the flaking red paint on the Kanab's cabin had more depth and vibrance about it this morning. The windows looked as though they'd been cleaned too, and she thought she'd heard someone moving around inside the neighbouring boat. She'd introduce herself to the occupant later. It would be nice to have someone else to chat to in the evenings.

Kaye yawned and leaned on the deck's railing, watching the ripples that emerged randomly from the side of the boat. Bubbles popped on the surface from whatever was lurking below the murky water. Picking grapes was hard work, though she'd loved every minute of the experience so far. Everyone who worked on the vines was as dedicated as if they owned the winery. The locals saw it as part of their heritage and worked tirelessly with pride and passion. The feeling of comradery had carried her through the nights and helped her forget the aches and pains that had grown more irritating with each venture. She'd slept like a log last night and woken in broad daylight to the sound of a dog barking in the distance.

The bicycle she hadn't used since Elodie had repaired it rested against the side of the boat. Elodie had insisted that Kaye either take a taxi, for which Elodie would pay, or use the transport provided by the winery to move to and from the vineyard at night. She hadn't felt in danger but with increasing tiredness, she'd welcomed the transportation.

The bronze and gold glazed flowerpot she'd bought from the fair that she'd put on the flat roof—she looked at it often—was a constant reminder of her afternoon at the fair with Elodie. She took a deep breath, closed her eyes, and held onto the image of Elodie as she enjoyed the warmth of the sun on her face. She'd wanted to taste the salted caramel ice cream on Elodie's lips. Their thighs had touched when they sat on the wall, and she'd found it impossible to concentrate on anything else. She had no idea why she'd bought the pot—it was too big for her to take anywhere. With just a rucksack, she'd continue her trip without it. It looked good on the boat though and would be lovely filled with flowers in the spring.

The swifts that lived in the hollow of the tree at the edge of the towpath were chirping merrily. Her secret desire bubbled in her chest, and she had the urge to share her excitement with them.

"Something made you happy."

Kaye jolted at the voice. She looked toward the Kanab. "Oh, hello."

The woman's dark hair was contained beneath a baseball cap. She held a plane in one hand and a sandpaper block in the other. A light coating of sawdust lightened the skin on her hands and arms, and the flecks formed an intricate pattern on her cheeks and across her brow.

"You look pleased," she said with a thick French accent.

"Yes, it's very beautiful here." Kaye sipped her coffee.

The woman laughed lightly. "Your smile speaks of love, and now I apologise, I embarrassed you."

Kaye almost choked as she swallowed her drink, then she smiled. "Would you like a coffee?"

The woman smiled widely. "That would be welcome. Black, one sugar if you have it. I still have to get wood for the stove." She shrugged and shook her head. "And oil for the boiler, of course." She indicated the inside of the boat. "It will be a life's work."

Kaye started down the stairs and stopped. She turned back to see the woman still smiling at her. "I'm Kaye."

"Françoise," she said and pointed at her chest.

Kaye poured two coffees and took them to the deck of the Kanab. Françoise wiped dust from her mouth with the back of her hand as she took the drink. It made little difference to her appearance. She took a sip as she appraised her boat.

"Have you moored here long?"

"A few days. I may stay another week." It was already five days since she'd stopped at Sancerre. She'd stayed longer than intended already. The time had flown, and although Kaye still planned to head south to Nice, she was in no rush to do so.

"Travelling?"

"Yes, you?"

"I just bought her. I'm going to do her up and live on her."

Kaye wondered at the deep affection she saw in Françoise's eyes as she rubbed her hand across the bare wood that she'd just sanded. "That sounds exciting." Kaye couldn't imagine living on a narrowboat. It was fun for a holiday, but she enjoyed the comfort that came with having a little more space...even though she didn't have many possessions with which to fill that space.

She'd dreamed of living in a three-bedroom detached cottage with a little land, maybe a horse and a cat, and as part of a village community where people were friendly and knew each other. She'd left that dream behind when she got married, because Sylvie would never consider living in the countryside. Sylvie was a city girl by her own admission, and Kaye had accepted that. It wasn't that their neighbours in London had been unfriendly either. They'd just been busy working like she and Sylvie had. They'd never managed to find the time to socialise together in all the years they'd lived next door.

Perhaps a bigger boat would be okay to live in. But as she considered it now, her heart didn't agree. She would feel too isolated, especially in the winter months.

"It is a wish coming true."

Françoise couldn't have been much older than Kaye, a little over forty maybe. There was calmness in her demeanour, a humility, and she had a presence that Kaye associated with someone who embodied contentment and peace.

"What do you do?" Kaye asked.

"Do?"

"For work?"

Françoise held Kaye's gaze, her smile warm. "I help people."

Kaye frowned. "How?"

"I help them see their future."

Kaye widened her eyes. "Like a life coach?"

Françoise tilted her head from side to side. "I read hands and faces."

Kaye felt the heat rise inside her and immediately worried that Françoise was able to read her thoughts.

"It is not something I do, unless asked."

Something in Françoise's gentle smile said she read everything and only revealed what she knew when requested, but that there was nothing to be concerned about. Kaye sipped her coffee, caught between being excited to know her future and embarrassed that Françoise could see right through her, which meant she would know how she felt about Elodie. Kaye looked at the door on the boat to avoid eye contact. "How long have you done that?"

Françoise picked at something on the side of the cabin and then started rubbing it with sandpaper. "Since a child. Some say it is a gift, others a curse. I worked as a waitress until two years now and did readings for friends and some others. Now, I own this boat and will follow my dream."

Warmth expanded in Kaye's chest. She liked Françoise. "How wonderful."

"Do you follow your dream?"

Kaye wasn't sure if it was a question or that Françoise had gleaned something from her. "Kind of."

"Dreams are important."

Kaye sighed. She'd started to realise how much of herself she'd lost inside her marriage and what an incredible world existed now that she was able to see it. She needed to re-establish her dreams. A beautiful home, a loving partner, family, friends, and work that she was passionate about. "Yes. I'm rediscovering mine."

"I believe we create our future through our dreams. If we dream of nothing, we get nothing in return. When we have desire, we act to make the dream come to life."

Kaye pondered. It was true. She hadn't thought about travelling or studying, architecture or anything beyond the sliver of an existence with Sylvie. Freed by the divorce, she'd reincarnated some of her old ambitions, at least in thought. "So, you think our future is within our control?"

"Control, non. Not in the sense that you have power to make something happen, like God. Other things can stop us believing and stop us trying. We choose to work to overcome them or stop chasing our dream and settle for a different life. Without belief, we have an empty life, floating and waiting for the next good thing to happen. Negative emotion stops us too. When we feel an emotion we don't like, we first need to look inside ourselves for the answer rather than just blaming something that's happening on the outside. Blame stops us taking responsibility for the things we can control. It stunts our growth." Françoise held Kaye's gaze. Then she turned and rubbed the sandpaper along the window frame. "Have you visited the horse sanctuary?"

Kaye shook her head.

"Horses are very sensitive creatures. But it is also a good place to connect with yourself. I can introduce you to the woman who runs it. There is a nice café there too."

"Is it far?"

"Non. Four kilometres. I can meet you there late tomorrow morning and show you around, if you would like to go."

"I think I'd like that." She smiled, elevated and sobered in equal measure by their brief conversation. "Would you like a hand?"

Françoise looked at Kaye and nodded. "Can you sand wood?" She pointed to the side of the boat she was working on. "Or maybe you prefer to paint something?"

Kaye chuckled. She'd never done either. She didn't want to mess up the painting though and from what she'd seen of sanding, it didn't look too challenging. "Sanding."

"Here."

Kaye took the abrasive paper and started sanding the side of the boat. After a short time, her arms felt like lead, and she'd torn a fine layer of skin from her already stiff and sore fingers. Sweat trickled into her eyes and down her temples, and her cheeks felt sticky from the dust. She stretched and groaned. Wiping the back of her hand across her face added to the stickiness, and her eyes stung. "This is as hard as grape picking."

"You want something badly, you have to make it happen. Where there is effort, there is reward."

Kaye knew that from her divorce. She laughed at the sincerity and wisdom with which Françoise spoke. "And a broken body."

Françoise chuckled. "That's right. You can stop any time."

"I'm enjoying myself."

Kaye continued to sand at a steady pace. Feeling the change in the surface of the wood was satisfying. Having company and sharing the task with someone was nice too. Françoise was easy to be around, as was Elodie. Thinking about Elodie made her stomach flip and sent a quiver through her. Her lips were dry and rough. She smoothed them with her tongue and tasted salted...it wasn't caramel. It was salted wood. She brought her hand to her mouth then realized that too was covered in tiny particles of wood and paint. Françoise's light chuckle caught her attention.

"That look." Françoise pointed at her. "That is love."

Kaye's cheeks burned. She shook her head. "I..." She couldn't even begin to explain to someone who could potentially read her mind or her face. She tucked her hands out of Françoise's view, even though she was too far away for them to be properly read.

"It is a good love." Françoise nodded as she spoke. "A very good love."

Kaye shook her head. This wasn't love. It was way too soon for love, and she didn't want love either...not yet. This was passion and infatuation. And who could blame her? Elodie was attractive and intelligent, and Kaye had enjoyed spending time with her. She'd loved picking the grapes knowing that Elodie was close by. She'd wondered what she was doing in the barn as they'd worked in the fields, and on the occasions when the lights in the barn went out and the Land Rover wasn't in the drive, she'd wondered where Elodie had gone. She'd wondered a lot about Elodie, in fact, but the lingering thought of kissing her threaded desire through her veins and refused to abate.

9.

ELODIE'S HEART SKIPPED A beat as she spotted Kaye in the canary yellow dress she'd sewn the hem of just three days earlier, the hiking boots that were too big for the pedals, and the wide-brimmed straw hat that was being held down with one hand as she pedalled the bike into the yard. The unexpected sight of Kaye took her breath away and her heart thundered as if it was shouting to Kaye to take notice of it. She took a pace back to remain out of sight and lowered herself so she could just about see past Rolo's back. "Well done, old boy," she whispered, keeping a watch over Rolo's back as she brushed his hind quarters.

Kaye stepped off the bicycle, straightened her dress, and wheeled the bike to the wooden rail that separated the main yard from the other areas within the sanctuary. She glanced toward the paddock to her left, and Elodie ducked down behind Rolo. She was behaving like a teenager with something to hide. She was a grown woman. It was ridiculous and out of character, but her desire to avoid Kaye was stronger, and to add to it she now felt utterly embarrassed. She couldn't maintain her cover like this. Curiosity getting the better of her, she peaked above the horse again, Kaye was looking toward the café.

The impulse to talk to Kaye and see her soft smile was compelling, but she didn't want to intrude on her free time. Kaye might feel suffocated or worst still, think that Elodie was stalking her. She didn't want to get caught spying on her either. She felt guilty, even though she had no sound reason to, but still she struggled to take her eyes off of Kaye. Elodie had watched her a lot and become familiar with her idiosyncrasies, like how she always dressed for an occasion, no matter what she was doing. If she were mucking out the stables, she'd most likely do it in her best dress. She always fiddled with the hat that flopped around her ears, as if wearing it was a necessity and a mild irritation. She gave everything she came across her time, studying it with curious enthusiasm, and whatever activity she took on, she seemed intent on getting it right. She was like a child, exploring and discovering a world she'd never conceived of before and was blossoming with every new experience. She was as beautiful as spring on a sunny day and as fascinating as the stars on a dark winter night.

The breeze whipped at the brim of the hat, and Kaye pressed it to her head while her dress flapped and rose up her legs, and Elodie imagined Kaye had tutted. She stiffened as she resisted the urge to approach, which was against her natural instinct to want to be close to Kaye. She'd missed not seeing her since their last day together at the fair.

Kaye hadn't said she planned to visit the sanctuary, but then again, they hadn't had that type of conversation, and Kaye didn't owe Elodie an explanation for her comings and goings. A thought that had at one time bothered her, and that hadn't been important in a long time, caused a niggling feeling that burrowed into her chest. Elodie wasn't anything special to anyone. She took a deep breath and released it slowly as she watched Kaye walk across the main yard and into the office.

When Kaye came back into the yard, there was another woman at her side that Elodie didn't recognize. She wasn't a member of the main staff, though she clearly knew the sanctuary. She pointed at aspects of their surroundings when she spoke as if showing Kaye around. Maybe she was one of the support workers that helped out from time to time, as Elodie did. Kaye smiled and was animated. Kaye had an aura that radiated pure happiness, and she was sharing her experience with another woman. The way the two women interacted caused Elodie's gut to twist.

As the other woman took Kaye's arm and led her into a stable, Elodie's stomach hardened. She brushed Rolo with more vigour to release the tension, moving to his other hind quarter before she groomed him bare. Her memory of the time she'd returned to school to find that Mylene had left and wouldn't be returning became sharp and intense. Elodie had blamed her mother for taking her home that summer. *If* she hadn't had to work at the vineyard, *if* she'd been able to spend the summer at the convent with Mylene, Mylene wouldn't have been able to leave her without saying goodbye. They could have cried together, exchanged addresses, and promised to keep in touch. That might have made a difference.

Her thoughts turning to Claris surprised her. She'd been the only woman Elodie had truly cared about at university. Claris had never been to Elodie what Mylene was, she could never compare anyone with her first—and only—love, but she'd been the first person Elodie had trusted since Mylene. The hurt she'd felt when Claris told her she needed to be with someone who could be fully involved in a relationship hadn't been as bad as the devastation she'd endured after Mylene left her. Instead, Elodie had been angry at herself for being so foolish. She'd given all she was capable of, and it hadn't been enough. It would never be enough.

Some lessons were easily learned. Her attempts at a relationship before her mother had died might have been futile, but she'd tried. Her mother's funeral had sealed the coffin on her heart. The memory of that time was as consuming now as it had been back then. She'd stood in the snow at her mother's newly dug grave and felt nothing. And then, soon after, anger had surfaced and remained with her for a long time.

The light that Kaye had shone into her world was almost as painful as the isolation she'd endured in her efforts to avoid rejection. Head-spinning nausea challenged her to breathe deeply. She stood up from her crouched position at Rolo's leg, closed her eyes, and took as deep a breath as she could manage. The smell of horse manure cleared her mind.

"Elodie."

Elodie startled at Kaye's voice and opened her eyes. She turned to face Kaye, her heart thumping. "Oh, hello," she said, as if she hadn't just been watching her every move.

Kaye's cheeks were flushed, and she wore a smile that matched the brightness of her dress. "I thought it was you."

Elodie cringed and forced a smile, acutely aware of the heat that had crept into her cheeks. She stood taller, regaining control of herself and studied the woman at Kaye's side.

"This is Françoise. She owns the boat moored next to mine. Françoise, this is Elodie. She owns the Marchand winery."

Elodie felt quietly assessed by Françoise's dark brown eyes, which were hard to read, and her soft expression transmitted understanding. "Hello." She forced a smile that softened as Françoise approached Rolo and brushed his cheek.

"Marchand," she said softly. "The best Pinot Noir in the region."

"Thank you."

The discomfort of being caught off guard by Kaye's proximity had eased. At the vineyard and the spa and as the host, the roles she knew by heart carried her. She could command a performance like a well-rehearsed actor. Something about Françoise's familiarity with Kaye bothered her, though she didn't know what it was. She didn't look like a predator type. Elodie was familiar with those characteristics in others she knew. Those women were gauche and aggressive. Françoise had an ease about her manner, a gentle confidence that was intimidating in a different way.

Françoise turned to Kaye and smiled. "I'm sorry. I need to go."

Kaye widened her eyes and looked mildly surprised. "Oh. Okay. Thanks for the introduction."

"Thank you for your help earlier." Françoise looked from Kaye to Elodie. "Good to meet you, Elodie."

Elodie stroked Rolo's nose and felt calmer than she had moments earlier. "You too."

Françoise turned to Kaye and touched her arm. "Enjoy your lunch."

Kaye nodded. "I'll see you later."

Elodie pressed her lips tightly together and watched Françoise leave, then became aware that Kaye was frowning at her. She parted her lips and smiled. "Hi, again."

Kaye's gaze drifted down her body and back up again and left a trail of heat in its wake.

Kaye smiled softly. "I didn't expect to see you here."

Elodie glanced around the yard. "Likewise."

"Françoise recommended it. We were working on her boat earlier. She's renovating and going to live on it. Isn't that brave?"

Elodie cleared her throat, the words barely registering. "Yes." She didn't enjoy the feeling of jealousy or the destruction it caused. She'd known relationships crucified because of it. Trust was crucial in love, otherwise what did you really have? Love? It was another good reason she'd kept her lovers at a distance. Jealousy was an emotional timebomb that fractured everything that had the potential to be good. It was also a big red flag that she didn't want to acknowledge. She was getting too close to Kaye and powerless to stop herself heading deeper. Kaye was like a pleasantly hypnotic drug. More potent than wine, thoughts of Kaye had occupied her dreams at night and her musings during the day. She'd stared out of the mezzanine window into the darkness in the direction of the pickers and had stopped herself heading out there just to see Kaye. "She seems nice."

"She is."

Kaye seemed charmed by the woman, and Elodie's stomach clenched. "What do you know about her?" She couldn't hide her suspicion, though the fact that Elodie was as much a stranger to Kaye didn't escape her.

"Not much, I guess." Kaye looked at the horse. "Do you believe you can create your future?"

Elodie shook her head. "I don't know, why?"

"Françoise helps people. She reads hands and faces."

Elodie inhaled slowly. She'd heard of palm readers and the like and wasn't convinced by the science behind their claims. "She's a medium?"

"I don't think so. She just sees people differently and helps them believe they can achieve their dreams. If you believe you can, then you will."

Resistance wedged itself inside Elodie's mind as she recalled her unfulfilled childhood wishes. "I think we can want things to be different all we like, but we have no control over making our wishes come true. Things are as they are. Destiny is predesigned by heredity and influenced by conditioning. It's that simple." It wasn't that simple though, and she knew it from her own experience.

Kaye turned slowly toward Elodie and stared at her. "You don't think you can influence your future by what you desire and imagine to be possible? That having a dream can't lead you to take action?"

Elodie had read about the concept of universal consciousness as an exact mathematical truth, and the fact that there is a single intelligent consciousness that pervades the entire universe. That universal mind is absolute and all-present. When at the convent, she'd dared to believe she had some power to change her life. But over time, and after taking on the family business, she'd seen how difficult that was in reality. Risk, fear, and uncertainty held power far stronger than belief. Yes, of course, some things could be influenced. Elodie could choose when to harvest the grapes, but such decisions were still based on solid facts such as weather conditions and grape maturity.

Even if what Kaye was saying was true, something deeply rooted stopped her believing her life could be different now, especially when it came to love. “For most things in life, no. There are too many other factors involved.” The sticky silence gained weight, and Elodie’s chest tightened with the pressure. “You can’t force someone to want or love you, no matter how much you might desire that,” she said, her voice affected by emotion.

Kaye lowered her gaze. “I guess that’s true.” The silence resumed. Kaye huffed out a breath. “But you can find love if you’re open to it. Maybe you’ll never find it if you aren’t.”

Elodie swallowed. Her constricted throat burned. She couldn’t deny the logic, though resistance still gnawed inside her mind, asserting in her mother’s voice that she was different from the others. *Love equals hurt and hurt steals life.* What would be the point in looking if those you love are going to leave you anyway? A shadow formed across her heart, familiar and depressing, and blocked Kaye’s rays of sunshine. She stroked Rolo’s neck. “Maybe you’re right.”

Kaye smiled. “Anyway, I think we can create our future.” She shrugged.

Kaye’s optimism was a delight, and Elodie didn’t want to spoil their time together. There was a small opportunity to get to know Kaye better, and it was a welcome distraction. “So, you like horses?”

Kaye nodded. “I’ve always admired them from a distance.”

“You’ve never ridden?”

“No. My parents couldn’t afford for me to have lessons, and then I grew up. We never had pets either. I got Winston instead.”

“Who’s Winston?”

“My pet tiger.”

Elodie chuckled.

"He's a stuffed toy I've had since I was a kid. I sleep with him at night."

"Lucky Winston."

Kaye blushed and turned her attention to the horse.

Elodie smiled. At least Kaye hadn't slapped her for the comment. She stroked her hand along the line of Rolo's nose. "It's never too late to learn."

Kaye patted the bay coloured horse's neck. "Maybe I will, sometime."

"Well, this is Rolo. He's an old boy. He was rescued from a farm where he spent most of his day tied to a fence post."

"Is he yours?"

"No, I don't own a horse. I sponsor him so he can have a good retirement. Some of the horses here can't be ridden because they're not safe, but they get to enjoy the remainder of their life here."

Kaye was squinting at her. She looked totally adorable.

"I just met Needles and Jeronimo. They're so gentle."

"They're sensitive creatures."

"Françoise said the same."

Elodie thought she might lose the moment, that Kaye might jump on her bike any minute if she'd finished looking around and disappear off down the road. "Would you like to have lunch with me?"

Kaye revealed her slightly crooked teeth with a smile that made her eyes appear darker. She looked toward the café. "I'd like that."

Elodie held up her hands. "I just need to wash up."

Kaye held Elodie's gaze. "Do you like getting your hands dirty?"

Elodie laughed. "It seems I do."

Kaye brushed her hands down her dress, and her smile grew wider.

Elodie wiped her clammy palms together then indicated the café. "There's a great view over the fields at the back," she said as they entered the prefabricated building. She led Kaye through the small, covered area to a wooden bench table on the extensive veranda. Horses were dotted around the field, heads bowed, munching on the grass. A dappled grey horse approached the fence and puffed out through its nostrils, making a loud vibrating purr.

"That's Misty. She's excited to see you."

Kaye laughed. "How do you know that?"

"That's the sound they make when they're excited." She pulled out a handful of treats from her pocket and handed them to Kaye. "She'll love you forever if you give her those."

"She's easily bought then," Kaye said and raised her eyebrows.

"You could be right."

Kaye fed Misty the treats, and she puffed out another purr. Elodie rubbed Misty's cheek.

"Do you think you'll start riding when you get back to England?"

Kaye looked out across the field. "I don't know. I haven't thought that far ahead. There's so much to consider. What job I'll do, where I'll live." She blew out a breath a little like Misty's. "Do you ride?"

Elodie had never had to think about anything on the job or place to live front. As an only child, it had been drilled into her that she didn't have any choice in the matter. Imagining what it was like to have that kind of freedom, to not be tied to the expectations of others and the life you wanted to leave behind, she felt a twinge of regret for what might have been. It wasn't that she hadn't tried to have a conversation with her mother about her career early on, well more like an extended argument over a short period of time, when she'd talked about wanting to study astrophysics and work in the field of space science. The idea had been quashed in its micro-embryonic form and her academic path of business and finance had been mandatory. Even her grandmother had sided with her mother as a matter of principle. Elodie's was a life of obligation to the Marchand lineage of vignerons. She'd grown to enjoy her job and had worked hard to save the family business from her mother's incompetence, but now that felt like a shallow victory.

Kaye was looking at her. Elodie hadn't answered the question. "No...not anymore. I did, before I went to the convent. My mother sold my pony, because I wasn't home to help look after it." The gentle pressure of Kaye's hand on Elodie's arm soothed the reawakened memory.

"That's awful."

Kaye's eyes had watered. Elodie swallowed and headed back to the table. "They're such humble creatures. I come down here when I can, to say hi to Rolo and lend a hand. It's mostly staffed by volunteers."

"I think I'd like to sponsor a horse here too."

Kaye stroked Elodie's arm lightly and looked at her with mild concern and a faint smile that spoke of understanding and touched Elodie with compassion and adoration. The kindness she saw, she knew flowed through her own heart, and yet Kaye's open expression of emotion was pure, as if unaffected by whatever her past entailed, whilst her own was still tainted by the cruelty that had shaped her life and decisions. Elodie's heart ached with longing that she knew would remain unfulfilled, because it had always been that way...and maybe it always would.

10.

KAYE HAD BEEN TAKEN aback seeing Elodie at the horse sanctuary and surprised when Françoise had deserted her since they'd planned to have lunch together. Elodie had looked incredible, like a cowgirl in her jeans and shirt, though a little reserved in Françoise's presence.

Françoise was interesting and different to talk to, and Kaye had had questions she'd wanted to ask following their discussion on the boat, lots of questions about how she was creating her future and how to do a better job of it. It was exciting to think she might be able to achieve her dreams but also frightening to accept that level of responsibility. The fear outweighed the thrill, and she worried that her concerns might prevent her achieving her dreams. It seemed very complicated. She couldn't remember a time when she'd made a decision in her relationship with Sylvie, who had said Kaye wasn't capable of rationalising information accurately and if she'd ever tried, she'd always got it wrong. So she'd stopped trying, because she didn't want to fail and didn't want to upset anyone, especially not Sylvie. Did pondering the past as she often did guide her future? She had so much to learn.

Elodie led her into the factory, and the smell burned inside her nose and throat. She put her hand to her mouth. "What's that?"

Elodie pointed to the top of one of the open stainless-steel vats where a man stood on a ledge and pushed down on something repeatedly. "It's carbon dioxide. It burns off during fermentation. Working here, you get used to it."

Twelve vats about fourteen feet high formed a row along one side of the factory floor. A large hose led from the bottom of each vat across the room and into another vat. The smell of fermenting grapes was intense and nauseating. Kaye's stomach churned. "It looks like hard work."

Elodie nodded. "Yes. The grapes are cap-punched four times a day during the fermentation process, which lasts a week to ten days. That releases the tannins and flavour. Then the juice gets siphoned off into these tanks where it rests so the sediment can settle, and the wine is then pumped to the barrels. Every time a vat is emptied, it has to be sterilised to be ready for the next batch. Each container takes about thirteen tonnes of grapes."

"Crikey." Kaye marvelled at the tall structures around her, spotlessly clean and sparkling shiny steel. "How long does the wine stay in the barrels?"

"Between eleven months and two and a half years, depending on the wine. There's a lot of tasting that goes on during that time to make sure we get it right before the wine is clarified, filtered, and bottled."

"Do you taste the wine?"

"Some wines, yes."

She couldn't take her eyes off of Elodie's shirt, especially the point at which it fell open, just above her breasts. If she were honest, her interest in the wine-making process was a lot lower than her interest in the vigneron giving her the tour. She'd agreed to Elodie showing her around just to be able to spend more time with her.

The smell inside the factory was really quite disgusting. She preferred to be outside, picking grapes in the fresh air. Two workers scraping out the vat dragged the grapes through a large hole at the bottom and onto a conveyor belt that took them to another container. The work inside the factory was a lot more physically demanding than picking. "The grapes I pick will end up in one of these vats?"

"By the morning, yes. By next week they'll be in one of those containers and then a few days later, in a barrel."

Kaye had noted the rows and rows of racked barrels earlier in the tour. "I didn't realise it all happened that quickly."

"If we don't move quickly, we lose the wine. The process has to be carefully managed so the grapes don't—"

"Get stressed," Kaye said and smiled.

"Exactly."

Her stomach reminded her she didn't much like the smell. Elodie was frowning at her, one eye narrowed a little more than the other. "Would you mind if we got some air?"

"Sorry, I forget how intense it is."

Kaye took a deep breath of fresh air as they exited the factory.

"Let's get you some water." Elodie led Kaye into the barn.

Kaye slumped onto a deep couch and released a long breath. Her legs were heavy from being on her feet for the best part of the day, and her skin tingled from the sun. In a couple of hours, she'd be out there somewhere, picking grapes. Tired as she was, the thrill of the night ahead lifted her. She turned as Elodie approached, and her stomach flipped.

"Here." Elodie held out a glass of water and sat next to Kaye. She leaned back in the seat and gazed out the window. "Would you like to go on a trip with me tomorrow or the day after?"

"Are you with anyone?" Kaye blurted the question without thinking. Heat consumed her, and she inched away from Elodie and sipped her water.

Elodie smiled. "No."

Kaye sparkled from her head to her toes, so much so she felt that she might levitate from the seat. It was the strangest sensation, like fire dancing in the sky, full of heat and electrified.

"Would you like to come on a cultural visit?"

Disappointment dampened the fire. Delight seeped from Kaye, and she felt suddenly very tired. What on earth was a cultural visit? It sounded very formal. She sat quietly, sipping water, and gazed out the window without seeing.

"Are *you* with anyone?" Elodie asked.

Kaye swallowed hard. She'd not had a conversation about her relationship status with anyone outside her family and Courtney. Having asked Elodie the same question, she could hardly refuse to answer her. "I'm divorced." The phrase she'd normally associate with people of her parents age, sounded oddly distant in relation to how she thought of herself. She stared at Elodie for a long moment as her brain registered that wasn't the question Elodie had asked her. "No. I'm not with anyone."

"Divorced, as in husband or wife?" Elodie sipped her drink. "If you don't mind me asking?" She sat more upright in the chair and leaned forward.

"Wife." She sipped the water and stared into her mind, trawling for fond memories and finding nothing of any substance. "Twelve years married. I met her straight from uni and fell in love quickly. I'd known her for a little over two years before we tied the knot."

Elodie pressed her thumb against the glass in her hand.

"Fourteen years together," Kaye whispered. She couldn't believe how time had passed in the blink of an eye. "The best years of my life. Whoosh. Gone."

Elodie frowned. "Just out of university, you were still a kid. Looking back, I was naïve when I took over this place. Responsibility came to me too quickly. I had to learn and adapt before I was ready." She nodded as if reaffirming her thoughts. "Maybe the best years are those still to come."

Kaye shook her head. She had been naïve regarding Sylvie. Love is designed to make you blind, her mother had said later, once it was clear her relationship was over. *"You never see people clearly until a way down the line. If you did, you'd probably never marry them,"* she'd said. Courtney hadn't said I told you so out loud, but her friend had raised her concerns during the early years and stopped bothering as it became clear that Kaye didn't agree with her. "Maybe," she said.

"Are you on good terms with your ex?"

"No." Kaye sighed. "I got a good settlement, more money than I ever dreamed of, and Sylvie didn't take that at all well. I had to take her to court. Honestly, I think she hates my guts." She looked into Elodie's eyes and saw more empathy than she'd ever seen from Sylvie even when things were good. She noted the small twitch at the corner of Elodie's thinned lips and wondered if there was something she was holding back from saying. "I never wanted a divorce."

Elodie lifted her chin and nodded. "I think you were strong and courageous to go down that route."

"Staying was easy. Being honest with myself that it was over and recognising that I needed to take care of my own wellbeing was the hardest thing to accept."

She watched the small twitch persist at the corner of Elodie's mouth as her eyes narrowed, and she shook her head. Kaye wondered about the events in Elodie's life that might cause such a pensive mood. Whatever it was, her reflections seemed to trouble her, and Kaye didn't want to impose by asking questions that might cause any deeper discomfort. Elodie took a deep breath and swallowed, her gaze vacant, seemingly distracted by thought.

Kaye lowered her head. "I felt selfish, thinking about me and my needs over and above hers."

Elodie pinched her lips. She looked at Kaye and smiled a tight-lipped smile. "You need to look after yourself Kaye, because I think almost everyone struggles with something in their past."

"Unless we look after ourselves, we can't really be there for others."

"And by caring for others, we too nurture ourselves."

Elodie's body seemed to tense as her voice tailed off. She rolled her shoulders and pulled back a little and Kaye got the sense that Elodie didn't entirely believe her own words.

Elodie released a sigh and looked into Kaye's eyes. "Relationships are tricky, aren't they?"

Kaye shrugged. She'd never thought of them as tricky. She'd believed they just required selflessness, and effort, and a desire by both parties to make them work, but the selflessness had been turned against her with Sylvie and contradicted what her therapist had said about the need to look after herself first. "I just wanted us to be happy. We had committed to a life together, and it wasn't a bad one. I believe when you take a vow, you should try and make it work."

Elodie stared at the glass as she pressed her thumb into it until the colour drained from her skin.

The possibility that Elodie disagreed with her about taking a vow and making things work was more than a little disappointing.

Elodie strengthened her posture and when she smiled it was as if she had dropped the thoughts that had previously occupied her. "Did you have other lovers before her?"

Kaye smiled with light relief. "No. I was an ugly duckling and a history nerd, so no one was interested in me, and I spent all of my time with my head in a book." She hadn't intended to bring the conversation down with talk of her miserable marriage and pitiful experiences but opening up to Elodie seemed natural and effortless. She hadn't seen any critical judgement in her expression and conversation between them flowed easily. She liked that Elodie was thoughtful and interested. She liked that a lot. She'd had a wonderful day and didn't want to spoil it with intense conversation about something that lay in the past. "Anyway, enough about me. What about you?"

"Me?"

"Anyone special in your life?"

Elodie glanced away briefly. "No."

Kaye smiled. "Come on. I bared my soul. Now it's your turn. There's never been anyone special?"

Elodie seemed to look through her and she worried she'd pressed her on a sensitive topic. The silence stretched out between them for longer than was comfortable, and then Elodie sighed gently.

"My life hasn't been like yours. I had crushes at school and a few short-term relationships at university. But here…" She looked out the window. "Here, I don't get involved."

Kaye moved her head back and lowered her chin until Elodie turned to face her. "Why?"

Elodie pressed her lips together and looked away again. "I prefer to keep things simple, and relationships have always complicated matters for me."

Kaye allowed the disappointment to flow through her. She wanted to know what was working through Elodie's mind. She knew only too well how complicated relationships could be, that's why they needed dedication and commitment, but how did you stop yourself from falling in love? "But you've been with women?"

Elodie gave a faint smile. "Yes. A lot of women."

Her tone was quiet and reflective. Kaye's stomach fluttered, and a tingling sensation spread to her core. She didn't know what to say. She hadn't imagined that Elodie was a player. Courtney was a fan of one-night stands and had no desire to commit to a long-term relationship, despite Kaye's articulated misgivings that what she was doing would make her happy. Courtney enjoyed clubbing at the weekends and the buzz that she got out of having casual sex. It had never been Kaye's thing and at times, she'd despaired at Courtney for being selfish and a heartbreaker. That was before she'd learned that her own needs mattered. But Elodie didn't strike Kaye as being anything like her friend. She hadn't got the impression that Elodie was out on the town every weekend or the type to break hearts, unwittingly or otherwise.

"You're offended?" Elodie asked.

"No. I...um... You surprised me." Fascination drove her to want to ask more questions. "You didn't strike me as a player. How many women?"

Elodie shook her head. "I'm not like that." She closed her eyes and her lips thinned.

Kaye sensed hurt in the tense pause. She bit the inside of her lip and cursed the fact that she'd insulted Elodie. "That sounded wrong, I'm sorry."

"I don't know how many women. I never counted."

How many women exactly? Kaye felt suddenly very small. Their worlds were more different than she'd imagined when talking about history and grapes. She straightened her dress, conscious of her figure and how she compared to the many women Elodie had slept with. Elodie watched her with a steady gaze that drew her in. The longer she stared at Elodie, faster her heartbeat raced. The vibration in her stomach increased. "My friend keeps a tally," she said and felt odd about mentioning Courtney.

Elodie shook her head. "It's not like that for me. I belong to a club. If I want to enjoy the company of other women, then I meet them there. It's not a competition."

Kaye's body softened with the sense of relief that Elodie wasn't like her friend. That surprisingly meant something significant, and whilst it might not be a competition for Elodie, the idea that Elodie would have sex with other women, lots of other women, was both intimidating and thrilling to Kaye. She leaned forward her interest peaked by the prospect of being one of those women. "Where do you meet?"

"At people's houses, and dinner parties, and other events. We have rooms at the spa too."

"Here?" Kaye's gaze drifted to the mezzanine.

Elodie chuckled. It had a light resonance with a melodic ring to it that made Kaye smile, thankful the tension between them had shifted.

Elodie followed Kaye's gaze. "No. I never bring women here."

Kaye glanced at Elodie's shoulders, broader and stronger than her own, and imagined her toned arms beneath the shirt. She studied Elodie's slender fingers clasped around the glass and couldn't help but wonder how *exactly* Elodie pleasured the other women. Did she want to find out? "Oh."

"It's not terribly romantic," Elodie said.

"It's very sexy though." Kaye bit down on her lip, and desire flooded every cell in her body.

Elodie looked to be stifling a smile but failed. Her eyes radiated warmth and intrigue, and Kaye got the impression that Elodie would probably not say no if Kaye asked her to have sex. Kaye had sneaked a peek inside the Blue Room at the spa as a woman had exited. Together with the art and décor, and the way some women interacted in the chill-out bar, she'd wondered then whether there was something else going on in the quiet picturesque village of Sancerre. The sense of Elodie touching her and Elodie's soft lips against hers, was more breath-taking than the incredible views across the plains and far more tempting than any glass of wine could ever be.

"It's sex."

Elodie's deep tone and the word sex rolling off her tongue sent a tremor through Kaye. Suddenly hot, she stood and walked to the window.

Within a brief moment, Elodie was at her side, her arm touching Kaye's. "Is everything okay?"

Kaye cleared her throat and turned to face her. Elodie's warm breath brushed her cheek, and she blinked. Elodie had the twitch in the corner of her lip again, her breaths were short and shallow, and her eyes were dark. Kaye's heart thundered against her ribs. She wanted to be touched and held. She wanted Elodie to caress her, to make love to her in an unhurried lazy Sunday afternoon fashion. And she wanted to be taken to orgasm quickly, pressed against the window, right here and now. She blinked repeatedly for the images to go away and when they didn't, she stared out the window, trembling inside. She could feel the effect of Elodie touching her as if it were happening. It was terrifying but blissful. "This has been the nicest day I've had in a long while," she whispered.

She didn't want a relationship and neither, it appeared, did Elodie. It would be a perfect arrangement. She had nothing to lose by just having sex. She inched closer until her arm pressed firmly against Elodie's, and her breath caught when Elodie didn't move away. Kaye's heart raced. She turned to face Elodie. Electric energy fizzed across the narrow gap between them and tingled down the back of Kaye's neck. She willed Elodie to kiss her, and as she closed her eyes the musk scent became stronger. Her lips quivered.

The buzz of the phone jolted Kaye, and she opened her eyes. She withheld the moan that rushed to the tip of her tongue. Elodie cleared her throat and answered her phone.

Kaye took a deep breath and moved away from the window. A shiver floated across her skin, and she cursed the invention of mobile technology. She hadn't used her mobile for days and hadn't missed it either. There was freedom in not being compelled to respond to a notification or the ring of a bell.

"Sorry, I have to go to the club. It's Yvette, she's the owner." Elodie pointed at her screen as if that explained everything.

The quaking inside Kaye intensified at the thought of Elodie going to the club and having sex. She looked away to shift her thoughts. "I need to go and change for my shift."

"I'll drop you off. Maybe I can pick you up on my way back and save you cycling here?"

Kaye nodded. Elodie leaned forward until her lips touched Kaye's cheek. She closed her eyes and stifled a moan as fire coursed through her.

"Thank you for today. It was fun," Elodie whispered.

Kaye could barely breathe. The kiss on the cheek had lasted longer than the first time, and instead of the formality there had been an intensity to it, as if delivering an acknowledgement of a desire they shared for each other. Or maybe Kaye was imagining everything. Her breath faltered as she opened her eyes and saw Elodie's kind smile. She would be very happy if Elodie picked her up and didn't put her down for days. Her face was on fire, and the heat had nothing to do with the sunburn and everything to do with the pulsing sensation between her legs. And, no, she wouldn't turn Elodie away if she had the chance. Maybe she needed to create *that* future.

11.

THE SALTY TASTE OF Kaye's sun-kissed skin had remained on Elodie's lips and imprinted in her imagination while she'd attended to business at the club the previous evening. If she hadn't taken the call in the barn, they would surely have kissed. She'd told herself it would have been a big mistake and that Yvette had saved her from a problem, but she knew she was deceiving herself. She'd wanted to kiss Kaye, probably since she'd first seen her at the spa, and the truth that lay behind her want was the scariest thing of all, because it meant that kissing Kaye meant something. She couldn't deny her attraction to Kaye but attraction was usually easier to manage than this. Don't get involved and move on. With Kaye, she was driven closer by every conversation and interaction they had. She wanted to know more about her, wanted to share and show her things, and learn about things with her. She wanted desperately, more than she ever had with any other woman, to kiss her. *Merde.* She was in this deeper than was safe, if she wanted to keep her well-practised distance...and her heart, intact.

That Kaye had had a difficult and unfulfilling marriage made Elodie's heart ache as if it were her own pain. Everyone should know what tenderness feels like. Everyone was worthy of love. The incongruity of her words with her own experience clawed at her chest. You have to be open to being loved and not fearful of loss, she'd read in one of the books in the library at the convent. She hadn't understood then what it really meant. The logic was simple enough. It was the application that was a challenge. Elodie had raised the barrier to her heart so high after her mother's death that no one could scale it, and yet there was something about Kaye that had exposed her fractured life that made emotional detachment impossible to sustain. The wall that had guarded her fragile heart, for longer than she'd owned the vineyard, was crumbling while her protective mind looked on and laughed at her for thinking that she might be worthy of someone as wonderful as Kaye.

Fuelled by adrenaline after a fitful night's sleep was never the best way to start a long day. If she paced across the site much longer, she'd wear the soles of her deck shoes out. She'd not been able to take her eyes from the road leading to the estate, waiting for a glimpse of Kaye's wide brimmed straw hat and whatever flowing dress she'd chosen to wear for the trip. She shook out her hands and rubbed her palms down the hips of her chinos. She paced back across the yard and clutched her arms to her chest. Had she gone too far with the lingering kiss on the cheek and the personal questions? She had been so close to kissing Kaye, in front of her offices of all places. What was she thinking? She wasn't, and that was the problem. She'd seen the way Kaye had looked at her and felt the weight of Kaye's arm pressed against hers. She'd seen the spark of desire grow in Kaye's expression as she'd talked about the club and the other women. And when she dropped Kaye off at her narrowboat, she'd been a little subdued, already grieving the end of their time together. Elodie had felt it too. She hadn't wanted to leave. Thoughts of Kaye had distracted her from business, and she hoped Yvette hadn't noticed. But no matter what she felt, she couldn't be the one to make the first move. She clenched her hands into fists then released them and took a slow walk back to where she could get a better view of the road.

A blanket of warmth released the tight ball in her stomach as Kaye's straw hat came into view, its brim moving as gracefully as the wings of a kite. She blew out a few short breaths and strode to meet her. Her smile grew slowly. Kaye still made cycling look like hard work, though she was moving more quickly for the same level of effort.

By the time Kaye reached her, Elodie's cheeks ached. She thrust her hands deeply into the pockets of her trousers. Kaye's smile was as glorious as the bright sunrise Elodie had waited hours to greet this morning. She desperately wanted to kiss that smile. "Good morning." *God help me, I want you so much.*

"Bonjour." Kaye stepped off her bicycle and removed her handbag from the basket and slung it over her shoulder.

Elodie had chosen a loose-fitting soft-cotton top with a low neckline for comfort. They had a distance to drive and a long day ahead, and the last thing to wear on a day like today would be something tight fitting... but that was exactly the dress Kaye wore. "Here, let me take that." She took the bike and leaned it against the wall.

"Jade really looks good on you," Kaye said and smiled, though she looked toward her bike for a long moment.

"Thank you."

Elodie thought the tangerine orange dress that hugged Kaye closely and hung to just short of her knees suited her too. The tanned brogue shoes were purely functional, she assumed. "You look lovely."

Kaye pinned the hat to her head, though there was no breeze, and glanced down at her dress. "I wasn't sure what to wear. Where are we going?"

"A small village called Apremont-sur-Allier. It's close to the Burgundy region. Have you heard of it?"

Kaye shook her head.

"I think you'll appreciate it. Historically, it was a village of quarries. Between the two world wars, the village was reconstructed from the local rock to replace the original buildings because they were thought of as ugly. The main reason people visit now is for the landscaped gardens, though it's a bit late in the season for us to see them at their best. There's an incredible art gallery there too."

"It sounds delightful."

Elodie indicated her Land Rover. "Shall we go?"

As they drove, Elodie glanced across at Kaye. She sat stiffly with her hands clasped in her lap, her knuckles white and her focus firmly on the road ahead. She looked tense and distant, and Elodie hoped her change in demeanour didn't have anything to do with yesterday's almost-kiss or the conversation.

"Are you planning to travel for very long?" Elodie asked, hoping a change of subject might help Kaye relax.

"I don't know." Kaye looked out the passenger window.

Elodie noted the delicate beads of sweat that had formed on Kaye's brow, and her hands appeared to be trembling in her lap. She pinched her lips between her teeth and gave her attention to the road ahead, worried that something was wrong. The silence that became thick and prickly reinforced her concerns. She turned on the radio, keeping the music low. "What do you do? In the UK, when you're not travelling?"

Kaye continued to stare out the passenger window. She squeezed her hands together and fidgeted in the seat. The hat shifted on her head, and she took it off and placed it in the footwell with her handbag. "I'm in between jobs at the moment. My work was linked to my divorce."

"I'm sorry."

"My friend Courtney says I'm chasing my youth."

Elodie shook her head. "How?"

Kaye sighed and slowly turned to face Elodie, clasping her hands back together again. She looked close to prayer.

"I planned to take a gap year after uni and travel but ended up in London instead. And...well...time passed, I guess, and I forgot I'd once had that dream."

"What did you do? For your job I mean."

"I worked for my wife's interior design agency as a design consultant."

"Did you enjoy it?" Elodie hoped she wasn't firing too many questions at Kaye again, but she seemed a little more relaxed. She was talking, which was a good thing.

Kaye picked up her hat and fanned herself. "Yes, for the most part. I loved the challenge of creating a vision for the client. It's great to see their faces light up when you create what they can't." She rested the hat in her lap. Her cheeks glowed, and she bit down on her lower lip.

"And what's your dream now?" Elodie asked, hoping to lighten the conversation further.

Kaye smiled. "I always fancied the idea of building my own house at some point and studying architecture. Maybe I'll do that after this trip."

"I think you'd be good at that. You have an eye for details. Will you go back to England?"

The host on the radio station had a sing-song voice that easily occupied the brief silence with relaxing tones.

"I don't know. My friends and family are there, but I don't feel any particular draw to live in the UK."

Elodie chuckled. "It always rains there, eh?"

"A lot, yes. I like the rain and the cold. I love snow." Kaye smiled. "What about you? What's your ambition?"

Elodie's stomach fluttered and then her chest tightened as Kaye's focus seemed to drift to her mouth. "I don't have one. My future was always to be the vigneron here."

"Didn't you *ever* think about doing something different from your family?"

"No." She'd never dared to dream. If she had, she would have wished for her father to come back and for her mother to love her. Those had been her deepest wishes, the ones she'd stopped hoping for during her final years at the convent. She'd buried any idea of both wishes completely at her graduation when her mother hadn't shown up. Material wealth had always been a given in her life, but her mother had done a good job of almost taking it all from her before she then took her own life. "I had a privileged life. I was one of the lucky ones."

Kaye frowned. "You're very self-sufficient, aren't you?"

"What do you mean?"

"You seem very self-assured, like you know yourself well, what you want, and what you don't. I admire that. I'm only just discovering who I am."

Elodie felt as though the locks that sealed the doors around her inner world had become tighter. She had kept people at a distance, that was the truth. She knew how to run the business with clockwork efficiency, how to entertain and pleasure women, how to network for the club, and how to live the life she'd grown into over the past thirty-plus years. But she didn't feel as though she knew who *she* was beneath the confident façade she projected to the world, and her wounded inner child lay abandoned. She admired Kaye for her openness and her ability to start anew after a hellish experience. Elodie had never been that strong, and only now was she beginning to realise that.

"Do you have any family?" Kaye asked softly.

Elodie shook her head. "Yvette is the closest I have to a mother. I mentioned that I do business at the spa. I access funders for clients. It's something I enjoy."

Kaye raised her eyebrows. "When not having sex?"

Elodie smiled. Heat spread across her chest, up her neck, and into her cheeks. She never normally blushed when talking about having sex with women. On the contrary, she never normally felt anything other than a basic physical need and then a release. Conversation was different with Kaye: honest, and unguarded, and revealing. "Mostly, I do business there."

"So, the vineyard isn't busy enough for you?"

Elodie shrugged. "I have an excellent team who take good care of the day-to-day operation. I get more involved during peak season, keep my hand in with picking and tasting. But I also get to play. I enjoy helping people, and I'm good with numbers."

Kaye smiled. "Numbers of women?"

Elodie laughed out loud. "I mean business, money, investments...that kind of thing."

"I was teasing you. You're blushing. It's...nice."

Elodie glanced at Kaye and smiled. The earlier tension had slipped away, and she wasn't sure when or how that had happened. She enjoyed the playful side of Kaye very much, but she didn't want to talk about herself or the business anymore. She wanted to know about Kaye's life beyond her marriage and what her other interests were. "What about your family. Are you close?"

Kaye looked out the front window. Elodie appreciated the soft contours of her jaw and rosy cheeks, and the three freckles that looked like outcasts close to her ear.

Kaye smiled, and a fine line creased her cheek. "Yes, we've always been close. I have three older brothers and a younger sister. Mum and my sister are both nurses. My brothers work for themselves. Electrician, plumber, small scale construction. It was my father's business before he retired. I love them all dearly."

Elodie didn't know what that kind of closeness felt like. She'd only ever felt loss. The nuns at the convent were the closest thing she'd had to a real family until Yvette took her under her wing. She'd never gone back to the convent. Maybe one day she should.

Kaye's contemplative state was hard to read. Elodie had the urge to ask her about her thoughts but decided not to in case she inadvertently prodded a raw nerve. Maybe Kaye missed her family. Elodie had forgotten what that felt like. Relief and regret, maybe. "So, let me ask, are you a fan of cubism or impressionism?"

Kaye blew a half whistle. "Now there's a question. I like both. But I bet you can't guess my favourite though."

"A challenge. I like that. Let me think."

Kaye shuffled in her seat and clasped her hands together in her lap. She looked more excited than tense.

"You've chosen a trip on a narrowboat, so I'm going with minimalism."

"Funny you say that. The sum total of my belongings sits in a two-metre by two-metre warehouse space. But no, it's not minimalism."

An ache settled in Elodie's chest. "You really have nowhere to live?"

"I'll find somewhere when I'm ready. Another guess."

"Right. Neoclassicism because of the Roman architecture influence."

Kaye laughed.

Elodie shrugged. "It was a fair guess. Okay, how about Pointillism? I can see you having the patience to join thousands of dots together to create a picture." Elodie laughed. "Actually, no, I take that back. My last guess will be correct. Baroque, again because of its links with architecture."

Kaye shook her head. "I'm afraid I'm a classicist through and through."

Elodie laughed loudly. "No way. Me too. They have some incredible pieces at the gallery we're going to. You'll love it." Elodie's breath hitched as Kaye gently stroked across the back of her hand. Then a shiver moved swiftly up her arms and down her neck. She resisted the need to change gear for as long as possible. Then Kaye took her hand from Elodie's and rested it back in her lap, and Elodie breathed more easily and shifted gear.

As the town came into view, Kaye leaned forward and stared out the windscreen. "That's a stunning castle."

"It's fifteenth century, a Gothic Revival. It's now the residence of the novelist, Elvire de Brissac."

Kaye looked at Elodie through a narrowing of her eyes. "So, you *do* know your history."

"Not really. I looked it up for today. We have more castles in France than we have wineries. Did you know that?"

Kaye shrugged. "I enjoy wine and I like castles, so France is the perfect place for me."

"I think you are perfect for France too." She opened the window and turned briefly to catch the slight breeze on her face. She was pushing too hard. Kaye turned back to look out the windscreen and remained silent. Elodie noted Kaye's eyes close as she took a deep breath. When she opened them, she cleared her throat and sat taller. Elodie cursed the renewed tension she felt between them again as she drove them into the town. She parked up, and they headed into the village. The buildings looked taller for the narrow, cobbled streets that separated them. Their spires reached skywards like spears, casting shadows across each other and the streets below.

"I thought you'd appreciate the architecture and the history here. The castle garden is classified as a remarkable garden of France, and the village is one of one hundred and sixty of the most beautiful villages. You see those medieval houses?" She pointed. "They're actually twentieth century reconstructions."

"Wow. They look authentic."

Elodie smiled at Kaye's appreciation of the village's rich history. She matched Kaye's easy pace as they walked through landscaped gardens that displayed rainbows of colour and countless textures across an undulating green landscape. Trees clumped together formed dense parkland around a small, thriving, natural pond. As they sat on the grass, she spied Kaye staring at her with a look that sent a shiver through her, and Kaye's eyes didn't leave hers for a long moment.

"It's restful here," Elodie said and felt the intensity in Kaye's stare deepen. Kaye didn't respond. Elodie couldn't take that look for much longer, or she might end up doing something that would scare Kaye off completely. "Let's go to the gallery."

They headed out of the park and back into the village.

"Why is the silence in a gallery slightly eerie, or is it just me?" Kaye asked as they stood shoulder to shoulder staring at one of the smaller exhibits that took up a lot of space. "What do you think that is?"

Elodie shook her head. "I really have no idea. I don't get abstract art. I can appreciate constructivism because it's driven by mathematics and geometry, but something that looks like a white canvas with a white mark on it, I just don't get it."

"Me neither. A snowflake on snow is all I see. And tell me that's an exhibit number, not the price tag."

Elodie laughed. "Twenty thousand euros. It's a tag."

Kaye shook her head. "Not at any price." She wandered away from the exhibit and into the next room. "This is more my thing."

Paintings of houses in countryside settings featured on every wall. Elodie followed Kaye's lead. They stood in front of a watercolour painting of a stone barn with rows of vines set behind it and rolling hills beyond that led to a deep blue sky.

Kaye frowned as she pointed. "That could be your barn."

"It is, or it was before the renovations and before the factory was built. We have the first copy in the meeting room at the barn."

"Wow." Kaye's smile lit up the canvas.

"Do you like it?"

Kaye stayed silent for a long moment. "Yes. Yes, I do. I don't think I'd pay three-thousand-seven hundred for it though."

"It's a limited-edition piece. There are cheaper prints in the shop."

"Do you get commission on sales?" She winked playfully.

"No. I was thinking you might like a memento of your visit. Wine is consumed, but art remains with us."

"True."

They wandered into the next room and stood before the expressionist painting of a naked woman. Kaye stared at it, her eyes narrowed. "I think I prefer naked women in a Baroque or Neo-classic style. That just looks odd."

"It loses its eroticism for me." Heat rose to Elodie's cheeks. She'd love to see Kaye as the subject of the painting, naked, reclining, and liberated in expression. "Are you hungry?"

Kaye cleared her throat and turned from the exhibit. "A little."

Elodie wasn't hungry in the slightest. She wanted to stroll along the river with Kaye, hand in hand, and stand on the Pagoda bridge at the chateau and visit the museums in the stables there to see the restored horse drawn carriages. She wanted to share this incredible place with Kaye and show her everything. Then they would lay in the grass, side by side, until the sun lost its heat. Their drive back would be long and leisurely, and the night... She didn't want to think about the night, when Kaye would be picking grapes, and Elodie would be stood on the mezzanine, watching and alone.

"Let's go and buy a print for you and then eat."

Kaye smiled and nodded. Elodie's stomach fizzed. She could have sworn Kaye made a move to take her hand and then withdrew it. Kaye had opened her Pandora's box though, and Elodie had no power to close it. Unwittingly, she was standing inside the lion's den and when she should be on high alert and making a fast retreat, she wanted to snuggle up with the lion. She was falling more deeply for Kaye with every hour they spent together. There was danger here, she knew it well, but there was also the prospect of experiencing the deepest passion possible. The lure to love had become greater than the fear of losing it. Like an unfulfilled need, it would become stronger until satiated.

She moved closer as they walked along the cobbled street, brushing her arm against Kaye's just to feel the warmth tingle across her skin. Kaye edged closer and if Elodie wasn't mistaken, enjoyed their physical contact. When Kaye stopped walking suddenly and stood on the corner of the street, Elodie halted and turned to her. Her heart skipped a beat at the fire she saw in Kaye's eyes. The trembling inside Elodie was fierce, bordering on unbearable. "Is everything—" She stopped speaking. Kaye's breath was hot on her lips. She closed her eyes. Her core throbbed.

The thud against Elodie's shin jolted her, and she looked down to see a small child on a three-wheeled bicycle. The toddler had clearly been unable to avoid them and seemed determined to push straight through their combined solidity.

"Excuse me," Elodie said and smiled as she stood aside.

The child rode between them, closely followed by a woman with flushed cheeks who apologized profusely and chased after the child.

Heat flooded Elodie as Kaye moved closer and pressed her mouth to Elodie's, and Elodie had the sensation of warm silky softness at her lips and fire coursing through her veins. It was exquisite.

Kaye eased out of the kiss, put her arms around Elodie's neck, and smiled. "Sorry. I've wanted to do that for a while."

Elodie kissed the tip of Kaye's nose. "I'm very glad you did," she said, noticing that Kaye's smile had lost its earlier tension, and instead Elodie saw a stillness in her gaze that spoke of having time. "I was a little concerned about you, in the car."

Kaye ran her hand through Elodie's hair. "I was so nervous. I've never initiated a kiss before."

Elodie slipped her hand around Kaye's waist and slowly drew her closer. Kaye's lips were soft and quivered at her feather-like touch. She eased back and stroked Kaye's flushed cheek. "I've never been kissed unless I've already initiated it." *Except Mylene.* She was sure Mylene had kissed her first, though it was so long ago she wouldn't gamble on it. "I was anxious." With Kaye, she felt out of control and bizarrely out of her depth.

Kaye's smile broadened as she ran her fingertip down the line of Elodie's top to the lowest point between her breasts. "Would it be too forward for me to say I want to have sex with you?"

Elodie tilted her head. She tried to frown but her smile wouldn't let her. "I think that would be both forward and just fine with me."

"No strings sex."

Elodie stroked Kaye's cheek. "Whatever you want." Her stomach twisted and the ache in her heart deepened. Her head was silent on the matter, conceding in the back corner of her mind like a boxer already beaten. It was too late. Any strings Elodie had were already firmly tied to Kaye.

12.

THE DRIVE BACK FROM the vineyard had been long and slow, and a new sense of unease had afflicted Kaye. On the journey to Apremont-sur-Allier she'd been worried, knowing she was going to kiss Elodie and scared of messing it up. After being kissed back, she had wanted so much more when desire of the kind she'd only read about struck and overwhelmed her.

Everything about the day had been perfect and especially that kiss. In fact, it had been beyond her wildest fantasy. She'd never been kissed with such tenderness. It wasn't just the surge of electricity that had lit up her nervous system quicker than the lights on a Christmas tree in Trafalgar Square. Her desire to have sex with Elodie had reached stratospheric levels and was still climbing, and the thought of picking grapes couldn't be further from her mind.

As they pulled into the vineyard, Kaye's heart sank. Within minutes she would be heading back to the boat to change and get ready for her shift. She would return and maybe not see Elodie for the whole shift. *Again.* The thought was incomprehensible to her libido that seemed intent on claiming back years of repressed sexual appetite.

Elodie took her hand. The gentle pressure and the fiery heat just made matters worse. She wanted Elodie's hands all over her body. Elodie's eyes were dark and inviting, and she gave Kaye a half-smile that rocketed her lust along the same route through her that the shot of electricity had just taken. Her body was on overload. A silent moan lingered at the back of her throat. Elodie's smile was too tempting and unfair, given Kaye had to go to work. She held her breath and refused to budge from the car seat.

"Would you like to do a wine tasting with me?"

Kaye gave a short laugh, a release, that sounded as though she'd thought Elodie had lost the plot when in fact it was a resounding yes. Elodie was teasing her. Very unfair. "I have to get to work."

Elodie made a soft sucking sound. "And what if I asked you to take the evening off?"

Kaye traced her thumb along the lines in Elodie's palm. Her racing pulse made it hard to think of anything other than running her hands along Elodie's naked body. Elodie was her boss for now, and if she asked her to take the evening off, how could Kaye say no? Hell, she didn't want to say no. A rush of nervous energy trembled in her stomach. "I'd feel obliged to accept, I guess."

Elodie's smile broadened, and she lowered her chin a fraction. "You don't seem too keen."

Kaye wanted nothing more. "I'm very sure about wanting to have sex with you, with or without tasting the wine. But I..." She took a deep breath and squeezed Elodie's hand. "I haven't had sex in a while and...I'm a little apprehensive."

Elodie kissed Kaye's fingers. "Don't be. We don't have to do anything you don't want. I would like to spend the evening with you. Tasting the wine is the final step in the wine making process." Elodie shrugged. "After that, you will have had the full Marchand experience and be free to continue on your travels."

Kaye laughed though "continue on your travels" didn't sit well. She had to stay upbeat and not think about the consequences of having sex with Elodie, of what would happen when she moved on. "The full Marchand experience, eh?"

Elodie chuckled. She stepped out of the vehicle and met Kaye on her side. "Come."

The tremor in Kaye's stomach heightened as she followed Elodie into the wine cave. When she heard the clunk of the door being locked, Kaye could barely breathe. Something about the natural climate inside the dimly lit space and the white painted rock walls felt so utterly perfect. Kaye's heart ran a heavy beat. "I've never been inside a wine cave before." Her voice didn't echo around the room as she expected it might.

Elodie's smile touched Kaye with a steady flow of tingling vibration and dizzy excitement. She looked away, pretending to admire the room, which she was, in a way. She pressed her hand to the hard, cold, painted stone and inhaled. The subtle smell of fermented grapes, unlike the potent smell in the factory, formed an intoxicating blend of antiquity and expectation. Her heart settled with the feeling of anticipation. Her body might ache from the physical demands of grape picking and the long days exploring, but she'd never felt more alive than in this moment.

Elodie took her place behind the large, rectangular dark-oak table in the centre of the room which had two bowl-shaped glasses and several opened bottles of wine on it. The table looked small set against the stack of barrels behind it that filled the rear arch of the cave. To the left and right side of the table were six wooden crates piled two high. One crate was empty of bottles, the others were labelled—the wine, the year—and together they enclosed the space around the table. It was snug, and Kaye's overriding feeling was of coming home, which she didn't even think was bizarre.

Elodie pointed at the armchair opposite her. "Make yourself comfortable."

Elodie went to what looked like a fridge at the side of the boxes, opened the door, and pulled out a green bottle. She placed it on the table and cut the blood-red wax seal from around its neck. She lifted the bottle, held it by its base, and studied the label, even though she must know the details on every label of every bottle the winery produced.

"This is one of our midrange Sauvignon wines. It's five years old and from the block of grapes you're picking."

Kaye couldn't focus on the bottle, or the label, or the fact that she'd hand-picked grapes from the same vines that this wine came from. She was glued to Elodie turning the base of the bottle in her palm, the neck held loosely in her fingertips. Condensation trickled down the glass and onto Elodie's palm. She poured two small glasses of wine with craft-like precision and passed one across the table to Kaye. She picked up the other glass and slowly brought it to her nose.

Kaye felt Elodie's gaze, steady and enquiring. She noted the rise and fall of Elodie's chest as she inhaled deeply, the smoothness of her face, and the tanned skin between her breasts that led to the deep V of her top. Kaye had wanted to kiss that naked flesh since seeing Elodie that first morning in the spa, and it was so tempting now that she could barely draw her eyes from it. Elodie closed her eyes, and Kaye wanted to know what it was like inside her complex and beautiful mind. The delicate aroma spilled into the room. Hesitantly, Kaye picked up the glass in front of her and mirrored Elodie's movements.

"What notes do you smell?"

Elodie's voice, a little deeper, stole Kaye's concentration from the process. She closed her eyes to focus on the wine, lifted the glass, and inhaled the scent that came through with notes of Elodie. She forced her attention to the wine. "Can something smell zesty?" Kaye opened her eyes and her breath caught at the sight of Elodie's tender smile. Lips that she desperately wanted to feel against her own. Heat flooded her cheeks. "Lemon or grapefruit, I think."

"Very good. Now taste it and see what you think."

Kaye took a delicate sip and allowed the wine to rest in her mouth until the flavour of it came to life through her nose. "It's dry, not sweet, and it's soft on my tongue. The grapefruit is very light, not zesty as I thought."

Elodie nodded. "Do you like it?"

Kaye held Elodie's gaze. "Yes. I like it a lot."

Her voice was quiet, and her throat was steadily becoming tighter than the cork inside the bottle that Elodie had just popped. She couldn't break eye contact, though she told herself she should. Maybe she should go now, get on the narrowboat and head south, before it was too late. Elodie had made it clear she didn't believe in creating a future and clearly didn't do relationships. She couldn't afford another mistake like Sylvie, and yet she couldn't walk away either. The force between them was too compelling and beyond reason. They were going to have sex here, soon, and there was nothing Kaye could do to stop it. On the contrary, she'd never wanted to have sex with anyone as much as she did with Elodie. Whatever the fallout, she would deal with it later. No strings, she'd said, and Elodie had agreed, which was fine except that Kaye didn't know how to do the no strings thing. She only knew how to be in a relationship or be out of one. She sat, transfixed by overwhelming desire and absorbed by vivid imagination, experiencing the taste of Elodie's lips, the warmth of her mouth, the feel of her breasts, and her nakedness touching Kaye's body. She had already created that future in her mind. It had to happen.

Elodie collected clean glasses from a box at her side and poured from another of the bottles on the table. "Do you like red wine?"

Kaye nodded. She went through the same routine of appreciating the wine, identified a strong smell she couldn't name, and already feeling light-headed, sipped slowly. The rich taste of berries lingered on her tongue and as she swallowed, her throat became warm and supple. "That's beautiful."

"*You* are beautiful."

Kaye looked up. Elodie's smile was made more intense by the depth in her gaze that Kaye imagined saw directly into her. "I find you very sexy," she said. The pulse in her clit mirrored the beat of her heart.

Elodie put her glass down. She walked around the table, took Kaye by the hand, and drew her to her feet. "Can I kiss you?"

Kaye nodded slowly and hoped the somersaults in her stomach and the trembling that shook her hands didn't give away her nerves. "I want you," she whispered.

Elodie lifted her chin and brushed her thumb across Kaye's lips. Her smile conveyed patience. Kaye felt safe. She closed her eyes as softness, and warmth, and the taste of red berries that was richer than it had been before filled her. Elodie's lips caressed her with gentle kisses. She allowed herself to be tugged deeper into the kiss, and she wrapped her arms around Elodie's neck. Then she kissed Elodie harder.

Elodie pulled out of the kiss and bit down on her lip. "We should slow down."

Kaye swiftly pulled Elodie into a deep lingering kiss and explored her lips, her mouth, and her tongue, clashing their teeth. She didn't know how to slow down. She pressed herself against Elodie's palm, cupped against her breast, and moaned as Elodie's thumb flicked across her nipple. A bolt of lightning jolted through her and exploded in her clit. She pulled away and stared at Elodie as she encouraged the strap of Kaye's dress to slip from her shoulder. Kaye wriggled the garment to the floor.

Elodie removed her shirt and chinos and flung them over the boxes of wine. She undid her bra and slipped off her knickers and threw them too. Kaye laughed and tossed her underwear in the same direction. They stared at each other's naked bodies, and time stood still but for the racing beat that pounded in Kaye's chest, urging her on: a corporeal recognition that she was *very much* alive.

Elodie took a pace closer. She reached out and cupped Kaye's breast gently in her hand. She lowered her head and took Kaye's nipple into her mouth then stroked along the line of her breast and across her stomach. Kaye moaned as another surge of energy rose within her. Elodie's scent was stronger and more intoxicating than the wine. Kaye clasped her hands around Elodie's head, tugged Elodie to her, and kissed her. "You feel so good."

Elodie coaxed Kaye to lay back across the table. She gasped softly as her back touched the wood. Then there was the heat from Elodie's skin and the weight of her body as Elodie moved on top of her. Elodie was stroking and kissing the parts of Kaye that hadn't been touched in too long, and any concerns she might have had about Elodie desiring her died in the rise of her own longing.

"I adore your body," Elodie said, her voice slightly raspy.

Kaye jerked and stifled a giggle as Elodie explored a sensitive spot on the inside of her hip. "That tickles."

Elodie trailed her fingertip over the same spot and laughed when Kaye jerked again.

"Really, not helpful."

Elodie teased with a smile and raised her eyebrows. "Not good?"

"Too good." Kaye gasped.

"I like to see you respond."

Kaye moaned as Elodie kissed her lips and then her cheek, then her eyes and then the tip of her nose. Kaye could barely breathe. She wanted Elodie inside her, now.

"I want to explore you," Elodie whispered and kissed Kaye's ear, then kissed down her neck.

Elodie's breath on her skin drove Kaye close to what felt like insanity. And when Elodie moved her hand over Kaye's hip, along her inner thigh, and then slid her hand between Kaye's legs, she cried out softly and arched her hips beseechingly into her. Kaye watched Elodie pull her lip between her teeth and stare at her for a long moment. Elodie slowly entered Kaye and muttered something in French, and Kaye felt the ache in her heart and the pulse between her legs become one blissful stream of increasing arousal.

Kaye stifled a murmur as the tension built inside her. Elodie moved gently inside her, and it was as if she were talking to a part of Kaye that had never been heard. Kaye couldn't take her eyes off Elodie as Elodie watched her closely. The thrusts came deeper, and harder, and filled her more completely. She bucked beneath Elodie, who held her hips higher and penetrated her deeper until the trembling started. "I'm coming." She cried out in ecstasy and tipped over the edge, gliding free. She started to shake and then laughed as her body spasmed uncontrollably. "Oh boy. That was insane."

Soft kisses quieted her until she could no longer feel her pulse thundering in her chest. Elodie moved astride her and hovered over her with her hands either side of Kaye's head. Kaye trailed her fingertip across Elodie's chest, first one breast and nipple and then the other. She was so delicious.

Kaye lifted her head and took Elodie's nipple into her mouth. She sucked and bit, causing Elodie to pull back in response, and released a soft murmur. She cupped Elodie's breasts, one in each hand, and buried her head between them. She revelled in the soft warm skin against her cheeks and kissed and licked from one breast to the other. "I can't get enough of you," she whispered. "You taste salty and sweet. I want to eat you." She bit down on Elodie's nipple.

Elodie jolted and sat herself up, resting across Kaye's stomach. "Behave," she said and rocked her hips against Kaye.

"You're kidding?" Kaye tugged Elodie to her and kissed her fiercely. "I don't think I know how to behave with you." She trailed her hand down Elodie's body and stopped at her waist. She squeezed her hip and stroked along the outside of her firm thigh. "It's been too long, and now I know what great sex feels like."

Elodie took Kaye's nipple into her mouth. Kaye slipped her hand between Elodie's legs and savoured the warm, silky wetness that slipped around her fingers and into her palm. "So wet." Elodie's clit was firm beneath the softness that shielded its beauty. She responded to Kaye's gentle circling movements, and Elodie's utterances of pleasure and the gentle rocking of her hips whispered to Kaye for more. When Kaye entered Elodie, her breath stalled. She resisted the surge of desire that drove her on too quickly. She wanted to enjoy the softness, the suppleness, and luxuriate in the moment in case it would be their only time together. Elodie spoke to her again in French and bucked, as if seeking out Kaye's fingers. She slipped her fingers out of Elodie and returned them to her clit.

"You're a wonderful tease."

"Are you in a hurry?"

"No. I have all night." Elodie met Kaye's lips with a lingering kiss.

Kaye didn't want the kiss to end as the feeling at her mouth and her fingers became one continuous stream of bliss. And then Elodie was inside her again, and she entered Elodie. And the feeling was the most exquisite she'd ever experienced. Elodie was watching her, her lips quivering, her brow lined with tension. With every slow deep thrust Kaye experienced, she gave the same to Elodie. They mirrored each other, slow then fast, deep then shallow. The energy built inside Kaye too quickly even though she tried to resist.

Elodie closed her eyes. The frown deepened across her forehead and she tilted her head back slightly. "I'm coming, Kaye. Come with me."

Elodie's whispered voice released what felt like a burst of fire in a delicious quake that swept through every part of Kaye. Elodie spasmed against her fingers, and then Elodie lowered herself to Kaye and kissed her tenderly.

Kaye's heart thundered in her chest, and she panted to catch her breath. "That was insane."

Elodie smiled. "You're very responsive."

"I've never been *that* responsive...not like that at all." Kaye wiped away the light sheen of perspiration that had appeared above Elodie's lip.

Elodie kissed her fingers before she lifted herself from Kaye. She tugged Kaye to her feet and held her in her arms for a moment before she dressed her slowly.

The moment was over too quickly, and Kaye was left wanting.

"The night is still young," Elodie said as she walked back to her side of the table after dressing herself. She poured them each a glass of wine. "Try this one. It's our Grand Cru."

Kaye stared at the glass. It wasn't what she wanted. "I think I just sampled *your* Grand Cru." The depth of Elodie's laugh filled Kaye with joy, and she giggled like a child. "And it was excellent."

Kaye thought about the club and wondered what it would be like to have sex with Elodie in the Blue Room. She would delay leaving Sancerre by another week for a chance to hold onto this euphoric feeling a little longer. This thing they had would come to a natural end, because their lives were so different. Now though, she'd just unveiled a part of her she hadn't even realised existed, and she wanted to explore further. *No strings. I can do that.* She could do that now, because Elodie's modus operandi was no strings and Elodie would teach her how. "Tell me more about the club," she said and picked up the glass of wine. She took a long sip, every part of her radiating with the essence of Elodie.

13.

THE TEMPERATURE ON THE thermometer in the Lalla spa read twenty-two degrees, as it always did, and the long hand flowed in one seamless movement past the Roman numerals on the clock's face, as it always did. The marble surface in the reception area was as clean as it always was. But something inside the Lalla spa had altered almost beyond recognition. The radiant smiles of the women in the works of art on the walls were distorted by a change in her perception and Elodie saw, for the first time, the depth of loneliness that reflected her own in their vacant eyes. Their smiles were deceptive, and their bodies spoke to each other at a distance that couldn't be surmounted by physical contact. She felt that void acutely today, in an unfamiliar ache in her heart.

Preeda handed her a locker key. "Good afternoon, Mademoiselle Elodie."

She smiled as she took the key then strode through the chill-out bar without a glance to note the familiar faces and entered the changing room. Swiftly, she undressed and wrapped herself in a towel. She would soon get over the incongruous feelings that had kept her tossing and turning in bed for the best part of the last two nights. Having sex with Kaye had stirred something she hadn't expected to awaken. In truth, she'd known she was falling for her. The strength of emotion that had a hold over her had become stronger and she'd surrendered to it. The sex between them had surprised her though. It wasn't...*sex*. She should have backed away, damn it. But she couldn't ignore Kaye, even though part of her knew she should. And now Kaye had asked to come to the club and that left Elodie with a disconcerting feeling the likes of which she'd never experienced before.

She wanted to mean something to Kaye, the stranger from London with a kind smile, and curious eyes that held such deep concentration, and an innocence that made Elodie acutely aware of the preciousness of the time they shared. The lightness in her heart had become more intense and the draw to be with Kaye, alone, more potent. No other lover had obsessed her thoughts, except perhaps for Mylene. But Mylene was so long ago now that even that memory was likely to be an illusion, inflated by the ideology of the child she'd been back then. The intensity of emotion was too much to bear, and she had to find a way to pull back, to rethink, and regroup.

Mylene had been the first person Elodie had experienced a deep connection with, the first and only woman she'd ever loved. She'd been the sanity in Elodie's isolated world, an escape for when her mother had abandoned her at the convent. Kaye, like Mylene, had reached into her heart and left a piece of herself there. A big piece.

Kaye was a tourist on an adventure, like the hundreds of visitors who had stayed in the region before her, and she would leave without a second thought for Elodie as soon as she was ready to move on. That finality would come around all too soon. It had dawned on Elodie in the middle of the night, with only the lights from the vines for company and knowing that Kaye was out there picking grapes under the stars, that she didn't want Kaye to leave. But Kaye *would* go, and Kaye would create her future, and so Elodie needed to bury her newly kindled wishes and get back to what Kaye had called her "status quo life."

That's why she was at the spa today, to try to rid herself of the effect Kaye had on her. An effect that she couldn't afford to hold onto because if she did, it would fundamentally change her world. How could she consider making a commitment to someone like Kaye when she didn't trust herself to be able to deliver?

She had to get back to what she knew best, the relationships that required no commitment from her. No pressure. No expectations. No way to get hurt. Her unease derived from a feeling she hadn't experienced in a very long time, and it had first surfaced when she'd seen Kaye with Françoise: jealousy. Possessiveness had a fierce grip that was founded in fear. Again, she would lose someone who had surreptitiously become important to her. She had to try to entertain Kaye's desire to experience the Blue Room without worrying about who else Kaye might wish to join them and just hope that Kaye chose to be alone with her.

She lowered herself into the warm water and swam to the farthest point, away from the other three women in the bath and leaned forward over the edge. The cool tiles against her chest, her unease spoiling her intent to relax, she rested her head on her crossed arms and kept her back to the women.

Familiar moans of pleasure that would have previously been alluring were oddly disconcerting, and she had the experience of cheating on a lover. *Kaye is not my lover.* She wasn't even a friend. She was a stranger, a seasonal worker, a tourist. Kaye would leave her, as everyone Elodie had ever cared about had left her. The sting at the back of her eyes burned.

She turned and waded through the water toward the three women. The woman with long dark wavy hair pulled away from the others and waved Elodie toward her. Elodie stopped up short. The woman's nipples were dark, large, and inviting. Elodie sensed the texture of them at her fingertips, the taste of them on her tongue as a more recent memory.

The woman lifted her chin and slid her tongue over her top lip as she encouraged Elodie toward her.

Elodie glanced toward the other two women. One now lay back on the tiled floor, her feet resting over the shoulders of the other whose head was buried between her legs, making rhythmical rocking movements. The woman on her back cried out in pleasure.

She turned to see the lone woman moving toward her. The pulse that throbbed between her legs was a natural anticipatory response to the physical gratification and release that would come. Warm breath graced Elodie's cheek, and the woman cupped her breast. Elodie closed her eyes. A sharp sensation at her nipple gave way to a flood of heat that fed her core.

The woman's breath came again, hotter against her ear as she whispered, "Fuck with me."

There was no place for conversation inside the Blue Room, and only one word on Elodie's mind. *Kaye.* She flashed her eyes open and stared into the face of avarice. This wasn't the quality of passion shared by two lovers. It was a physical transaction, devoid of meaning, absent of connection. It was a physical fix to an underlying emotional problem that could never be solved through sexual gratification alone.

She pulled away, turned her back to the woman, and made her way quickly out of the Blue Room.

She put on her robe and slippers and went to the chill-out bar, ordered a coffee, and reclined in a chaise longue. She closed her eyes and noticed the leaden weight behind them.

"That was quick."

"Ça va, Yvette?"

"Do you mind if I join you? I have your coffee."

Yes, Elodie did mind, but she couldn't offend Yvette. "Of course, take a seat." She opened her eyes and sat up.

Yvette handed her the coffee and sat in the chaise longue next to her. "You look tired," Yvette said and sipped her coffee.

"A little, maybe. The nights are long." A sigh drew from her lips.

"Ah, yes, of course. All is going well, I hope?"

"It's an excellent harvest, yes." Elodie thought of Kaye and smiled. Kaye had found a picking method that suited her. She would never be as speedy or accurate as the seasonal pickers, but she could certainly hold her own with the newcomers and even when she had looked as if she might stop, she'd shown tenacity. Elodie had been impressed. Kaye's fighting spirit added another beautiful dimension to her already perfect being. Privately, Elodie had wagered on the first day that Kaye would flag by the third day, which was when most new starters felt the full strain of the job. Kaye hadn't. She had a unique pace, but she'd maintained it consistently and worked diligently. In fairness, Kaye could be the worst worker in the world and it wouldn't matter in the slightest.

Yvette wasn't talking about Kaye though. Yvette didn't know she existed even though she'd been there when Elodie had first met Kaye. Had Elodie lived with her eyes open all these years without truly seeing? Had her appreciation of a woman's beauty been tainted by her desperate need to feel loved? Yet she'd avoided emotional intimacy and in doing so, pushed the possibility of love away. It was logical and twisted by human design that she should want something and act in direct opposition to achieving it. Her fear of rejection had become more potent than her desire for love. She'd become an emotionally depleted soul, trapped behind a veil of heightened consciousness that instead of serving her had slowly sucked the joy of intimacy from her.

Yes, the past few nights had been very long.

"Baroness Carolina is hosting a dinner party in a couple of weeks and has extended an invitation to you," Yvette said.

Elodie was glad of the interruption to her thoughts. "She's accepted the deal?"

"Yes. This dinner is a small token of her appreciation for you bailing her out of a very difficult situation. Two weeks on Saturday."

Kaye would be gone by then. "Well, that's very good. Everyone is happy."

Yvette smiled. "Except you, it seems."

Elodie struggled to raise a positive response, even a fake one. "I'm working a few things through." She tapped her head. "And it's peak season, so there aren't enough hours in the night or day. Once the crop is in, I'll be happier." Elodie got the sense she hadn't come across as authentic when Yvette raised her eyebrow questioningly. "How's Jean?"

"He has created a bucket list that includes visiting the ten wonders of the world."

"You know most of them are mausoleums?"

"Well, he's decided he's going to die next year, so he wants to see it all before he does. Maybe he's looking for ideas." She chuckled. "He bought a pair of hiking poles and started walking around the estate this week to build up his physical strength for this...this adventure as he calls it. The man has never looked healthier."

"That's good."

"He wants me to go with him."

Elodie shared a frown with Yvette that confirmed that that was never going to happen. Elodie relaxed back in the seat. "It's encouraging that he's found a new lease of life."

"He needs another woman. Someone...not like me."

Elodie sighed. She reached out and squeezed Yvette's hand.

"It is true. I like my life here. The spa. Entertaining women. Why would I want to traipse around the world chasing his grand finale? We've barely spoken for forty years. He's complained for thirty-eight of them. I have no desire to try and find something of common interest between us now."

"And you wonder why I steer clear of relationships." The excuses that Elodie had lived by were evident in the shallow and ungrounded resonance of the words. She thought of Kaye, and the ache in her chest deepened.

"Women are different."

"Maybe. Maybe not when it comes to monogamous relationships." What did Elodie know about long-term monogamous relationships? Most of the women who frequented the club were married.

"Monogamy is overrated. You're young and free to enjoy your pick of any woman you desire. Look at you with your incredibly smooth skin—"

"That's because there's at least thirty-five years between us."

"And your hair, and you have all your own teeth, and a strong desirable body."

"I should hope I have all my own teeth, as do you."

"I have implants, darling, and Botox in places to make up for genetic weaknesses you clearly do not have in your genes. You have no deficiencies."

Elodie did have deficiencies. She just hid them well. "I remember. I took you to the Botox clinic."

"That was you?"

"Yes, that was me. Age is catching up with you."

Yvette frowned. She sipped her coffee and looked lost in reflection. The silence was a welcome reprieve from the uninvited conversation. Elodie studied Yvette closely and saw the same quality in her appearance that she'd seen in the women in the pictures in the reception. Sleep deprivation was having a serious effect on her ability to function properly.

"I want you to take over the running of the club," Yvette said.

Elodie shook her head. "Why?"

"You're the closest thing I have to a daughter, and I'd like to retire."

"And see the ten wonders?"

Yvette shook her head. "I want to reap the pleasures without the headaches. I intend to take full advantage of the fact that Jean is away, and no, this isn't my last hurrah. I'm bored of dealing with the baronesses in this world, and the club needs an acute financial brain behind it. I trust you. The added bonus is you're well liked. Every invitation we get has your name at the top of it."

Elodie lowered her head. A week ago, she would have been thrilled by the proposition. She would have walked taller, talked to clients for longer, and made a bigger effort to ensure she said all the right things to make each one feel as if they were her most valued client. Instead, it was as though a plug had been pulled from her, and her essence swirled its way down a gaping hole. "Let me think about it," she said, knowing she didn't want to accept. But who else could Yvette turn to? She couldn't think about the future of the club until the present—Kaye—was firmly in the past. Once Kaye had moved on, normality could be re-established. Then, maybe, she would enjoy stepping up and managing the club.

The image of the three women inside the Blue Room settled with a bitter taste. She ran her fingers through her hair. Sexual gratification without intimacy had worked fine until now. She'd slept alone and woken up alone. She'd worked to fill the hours that she didn't spend at the club. If something happened to her, other than Yvette, no one would really care. Detached hearts forgot in the blink of an eye. And what would happen when she was another twenty years older? What would happen when she lost her physical appeal? A chill flowed through her in waves of increasing coldness until she trembled inside and out. "I'll think about it," she said again, in a tone that sounded uncharacteristically fragile.

"And another thing. We need an investor for Lady Babberage. Eight hundred thousand pounds. Her husband died and left an unwanted gift of a significantly diminished bank account. She wants to sell part of her estate in Scotland to fund her retirement. Can you ask around?"

"Scotland?"

"I know. It's freezing and wet there. I'm not sure who would find it an appealing place to live. But apparently, it's also exceptionally pretty. They still hunt and shoot, and there's a disused whiskey distillery that could be brought back to life. The property part of the offer includes a small cottage. It isn't worth eight hundred on its own. But the deal is that she will retain ownership of the main house until she dies, and then the investor will have an option to purchase the entire estate at a significantly reduced price. It's an interesting option. She could go to one of those equity firms but would prefer not to. She's emotionally invested and wants someone to care about her estate as much as she does. Of course, she'll stop caring if she doesn't get the financial support soon enough."

Elodie nodded. "I'll see what I can do."

Yvette put her hand on Elodie's arm. "It would be really helpful if we could help her out and as soon as possible. She's an old friend of the baroness...small circles with high expectations and loud voices."

Elodie sighed. She thought about Kaye then swiftly dismissed the idea. Then Kaye's image came back to her again and wouldn't go away. Kaye had mentioned her settlement from the divorce, but Elodie had no idea how much that was, let alone whether Kaye was in a position to invest. She was looking to settle somewhere though. Maybe this would help Kaye at the same time as keeping Yvette in the baroness's good books. She should at least put the offer to Kaye and let her choose. She smiled and deep affection lingered in the warmth in her chest. "I have someone in mind, but I can't promise anything."

14.

KAYE ROLLED OVER IN the bed in the narrowboat, gripped the side to stop herself falling out, then rolled onto her back with a smile on her face. Every movement highlighted the fact that she ached from head to toe. It was a delightful kind of ache, if there was such a thing, a trophy in recognition of the tonne of grapes she'd picked. It was nothing by the standards of the seasonal pickers, but it meant everything to her.

She hadn't seen much of Elodie in the previous three days, not since their time in the cave, and when she'd spoken to Elodie, other than Elodie inviting her to the spa today, she'd seemed preoccupied and distant. She'd put the shift down to the pressure of work, which seemed to escalate as each day passed. There had been a threat of rain, and that wasn't a good thing. Tight deadlines sucked at the best of times, and in Elodie's industry there wasn't an option to slacken off. Every day made a difference to the overall harvest.

Reminded of their evening in the cave, she felt warm inside, and thinking about going to the club today, her stomach fizzed and tossed like the rush of riding a rollercoaster. It was a giddy feeling, and it had the potential to become nauseous if she thought too much about what she was about to do. There would be other women in there. What would they do? The thrill combined with a large dose of apprehension that came with her sense of recklessness made her feel quite weak.

She tumbled out of bed and made coffee. She took a bite out of a croissant left over from the previous day, and her stomach sent it back to her throat. She washed it down with a few sips of coffee. Her mouth still felt dry. She took another few sips of her coffee and paced the narrow galley.

She hadn't realised how much she'd repressed her sexual urges while married. She'd gradually lost interest over the years as her relationship with Sylvie deteriorated. She should have seen the lack of desire as a sign, but instead she'd wrapped herself up in her work and falsely labelled herself as asexual. She'd notice attractive women, like art, but never had the inclination to do anything about it. She'd been married, and she wasn't a cheat. Now she was divorced, and Elodie had opened her eyes to how wonderfully liberating sex could be. She would never have gone to the Blue Room alone though. She would have felt too self-conscious. But with Elodie, and the no strings thing they'd agreed to, it was an exciting adventure.

She had to call Courtney and tell her all about the club and how good sex was with Elodie. Perhaps not. What would Courtney say? Kaye was expressing her newly evolving self, but Courtney would be worried about her. In fairness, this behaviour was out of character for the old Kaye that Courtney knew. But that's why she'd come on the trip in the first place. She was simply putting herself first for once in her life and learning to express her needs without fear of criticism. Elodie didn't judge her, and what she felt when around Elodie was the most wonderful feeling in the world.

She went into the shower. She had a massage to get to, a treat to herself for all her hard work, and then she had a date with Elodie and the club. Her cheeks ached from grinning for so long. She shivered with excitement as the shower water trickled down her skin.

The sun dazzled lower and the air was fresh as she cycled into the village. She entered the spa and studied the pictures on the wall more closely. The tiles shone a brilliant white, and the textures were more vivid than she remembered from her first visit. She noted the woman ahead of her with red wavy hair that stopped just below her shoulders in a dress that stopped well above her knees. The woman turned to Kaye and flashed her a smile that came across as perfunctory, and her eyes didn't seem to register Kaye at any level other than her physical presence in the room.

Kaye went from the reception to the designated massage room, undressed, wrapped a towel around her, and laid face down on the massage table. The eucalyptus scent filled her nose as she rested her head over the carved-out hole and stared at the highly polished tiled floor beneath her. She became aware of the quietest movements around her, the slosh of oil being rubbed into hands, delicate footsteps moving around the room, and she sighed softly. She closed her eyes. Cool air graced her skin as the towel being lifted unveiled her body. Warm hands replaced it, smooth and firm, rolling over the tired muscles along the line of her back. It felt divine, and time passed all too quickly.

She opened her eyes at the cool towel against her back. Her body ached more evenly than it had before the massage. She lay still until the delicate footsteps quieted. She couldn't stop the heat behind her eyes building and couldn't explain the overwhelming sense of sadness that caused the tears to slide from her eyes and drip onto the floor. Sometimes repressed emotions can come to the fore after a massage, the woman in reception had said. The floor beneath her became blurred. She eased herself up and sat on the bed, waiting for her energy to return. She held the towel to her face and allowed the feeling to wash over her.

She had the desire again to talk to Courtney, but what would she say? That she felt sad, tense, because...because of what? The fact that she wasted fourteen years of her life in total devoting herself to a narcissistic woman who didn't know how to care about her. The fact that she'd allowed herself to be emotionally and mentally abused by that same woman who had professed to love her. The fact that she'd been too weak to walk away sooner. The heaviness in her body wouldn't lift. She didn't want another conversation with Courtney about her past. It was time to move on.

She took a long, deep breath and gazed around the room without really seeing. She had the sense of dust settling on the thoughts in her mind. If she stayed still, she wouldn't disturb them, wouldn't unearth the ugliness that lay beneath. Another wave of emotion rose up inside her, fierce and fiery. The pressure in her head tightened. Slowly, she made her way off the table. Though her legs were heavy and resistant, she wrapped the towel around her, exited the room, and found a chaise longue in the chill-out area. She would sit for a while before heading to the steam room to wait for Elodie.

She leaned back against the wet tiles and took a deep breath of hot damp menthol-infused air. Her nose cleared, her eyes stung a little, and her skin felt both cool and hot at the same time. She closed her eyes and inhaled slowly through her nose, her chest expanding more freely than it had before the massage. The clearing effect released the tension in her head, and her thoughts drifted to Elodie.

The door opened. She opened her eyes and lifted her head from the wall.

"Bonjour."

It was the woman she'd seen earlier in the reception. "Bonjour."

"Do you mind if I join you?" The woman looked toward the bench opposite Kaye.

She had an American twang to her accent and her posture exuded self-assurance. "Not at all." Kaye straightened her back, acutely aware of her own physical presence, which seemed deficient by comparison. The woman sat, facing her. Kaye tried to relax, smiled a tight smile, and tried not to fix her gaze on the woman's naked body in case she sent the wrong message. She closed her eyes and inhaled deeply.

The woman took a deep breath. "This feels so darn good, doesn't it?"

"Yes, it's wonderful."

"You're not from here," the woman said.

Kaye opened her eyes and couldn't stop herself from studying her. Her tanned skin was a similar shade to Elodie's. Her narrow shoulders, cheeks, and chin were fine-boned and her muscles toned, as if she worked out regularly. A narrow waist separated the natural curves of her breasts and hips. "England. Travelling actually. You're American?"

"I was born in France, but I'm touring the region on business. I live in London, recently moved there from the US."

Kaye felt overawed. Not only was she very beautiful, but she had also travelled. She had an ease about her and a presence as if she was a woman of standing. Kaye had felt similarly intimidated by Sylvie when she'd first met her, and equally, admired her. The feeling was intoxicating. Kaye never displayed that kind of presence, always fading into the background, because she'd never had the confidence. "What do you do?"

"I'm the wine buyer for the Belvere hotel chain. You may have heard of it."

She was clearly good at her job. It wouldn't have been easy getting such a prestigious job with the most exclusive hotel chain in the country. "Yes, I have." The hotel chain was renowned for its large country estates and listed properties. "Weddings and special events venues."

"We like to offer the highest quality dining experience as well as comfort, ideal for every special occasion." She beamed a smile. "That's the corporate line."

Kaye chuckled. "It sounds like a fun job."

"If the wine's good, it's great fun. I've tasted some god-awful wines, though."

"Chateau Marchand has excellent wine."

"Yes, I've heard." The woman closed her eyes.

"I've been grape picking there. It's very hard work," Kaye said, then wondered why she'd offered the information. "Where in France are you from?"

"Originally from Leon. I was schooled in Paris and then moved to California as a child."

"I've never been to California."

"It's a nice place. I worked for a winery in the Napa Valley. I moved to London last year for this job."

Kaye wondered what Elodie thought of American wines. "And wine brings you back to France?"

"French wines are still the best. But, hey, don't tell any Americans I said that." She chuckled. "Anyway, I could talk all day, and I'm disturbing you."

Kaye cleared her throat as the woman locked eyes with her. "It's fine. It's too hot for me now. I need to cool down."

"Enjoy the rest of your day."

Kaye stood and wrapped the towel around her. "Thank you. It's been nice talking to you." She closed the door behind her and shuddered as the cooler air brushed her skin.

"Hi."

Kaye recognised Elodie's voice and her heart jumped. "Hi."

"Sorry, I'm late. Yvette collared me."

Kaye drifted her gaze down the length of Elodie, whose robe hung loosely and revealed the centre line of her chest. "You look very sexy," she said, the throb between her legs becoming more persistent.

"Are you finished in here?"

"Yes."

"Shall we go to the Blue Room?"

Kaye's heart raced. She felt a moment of hesitation when her stomach tightened. She'd imagined touching and kissing Elodie in the bath inside the club as she'd drifted in thought with the massage earlier. Other women would be doing the same with their lovers. Her hands were clammy, and her heart felt as though it was about to burst free from her chest. "Yes, let's go."

Kaye stood just inside the door of the Blue Room, taking in the layers of blue. Blue lights made the ambience soft and enticing. The room had the feel of secrets waiting to be revealed. A layer of heat shimmered from the surface of the large rectangular bath. Arched blue mosaic-tiled walls gave way to smaller enclosed spaces with marble seating and shallow footbaths shrouded in steam. Four naked women entertained themselves within one of the alcoves and she turned away, though not completely unaffected by the sight of them.

Elodie held out her hand. Her smile was reassuring. "Come."

Kaye moved slowly, every step forward giving her eyes something new to feast on. The white marble statues in here were more explicit than the art that hung from the walls in the reception. The centrepiece at one end of the bath, of two women orally pleasuring each other, caught her attention. Admiring it evoked a sense of place. She followed Elodie, put her towel on the hook, and her key on the shelf above it and then stepped into the water.

Kaye watched Elodie duck under the water and swim to the end of the bath. Kaye lowered her body to the point of weightlessness, leaned her head back, and floated. Looking into the blue above her was like hovering beyond the clouds and becoming aware of the universe and nothing else. Pure, endless blue. Timeless. She closed her eyes, leaned her head back as far as she could until the echo of voices became muffled, and became one with the water.

A hand gently lifted the back of Kaye's head, and her stomach fizzed with the thrill of not knowing who it was, though she prayed it was Elodie. She blinked her eyes open, released a gush of air, and smiled with relief. Elodie's gaze was soft, and her lips begged to be kissed. Lightness bubbled inside her as

Elodie slipped her arm under Kaye's waist and led her across the surface of the water. She closed her eyes and had the feeling of soaring into space. Then the motion came to a stop, and Elodie guided her to stand, tugged her to her chest, and kissed her. Her touch was tender and for a brief moment, Kaye sensed hesitation in Elodie's tentative approach. She opened her eyes and thought she'd seen a quiver in Elodie's lips that quickly disappeared with her smile.

"Have you had a relaxing day?" Elodie asked and kissed Kaye's shoulder.

Kaye recalled the events. The overwhelming sadness that had surfaced after the massage and how inadequate she'd felt in the presence of the stranger in the steam room. "Very." She smiled to hide the truth, noted Elodie's unwavering curious gaze, and stroked Elodie's cheek. Honestly, she felt wrung out from the mix of emotions that the day had elicited.

Elodie's smile reflected Kaye's tension. "There are beautiful women here. You can play to your heart's content, if you wish."

Kaye swallowed hard. She didn't want to *play* with anyone else. The room itself was magnificent. There was art and history, revolution and emancipation, a culture hidden for too long, all at play in the hues and shapes that characterised the Blue Room. She connected with its earthy resonance through the beat of her heart, and she knew, like the other visitors no doubt, that she too would be freed from her past by her experiences here.

Elodie took her nipple in her mouth, and her mind filled with sensations that charged her. Sensations that were only Elodie's to give to her. She held Elodie's head to her breast, dug her fingers into her scalp, and buried her face into her hair. "I only want you," she whispered.

15.

ELODIE PICKED UP THE knife from the tablecloth, wiped an imaginary smear from it with a napkin, and replaced it at the right-hand side of the placemat. "I only want you," Kaye had said. Elodie held the crystal glass to the light, her hand trembling. She cleaned its rim for the umpteenth time and put it back on the table. *I only want you.* She had wanted to say the words, because it was the truth. She picked up the decanter of red wine, inhaled its aroma and nodded, then replaced it onto the centre of the table. Everything was perfect.

She walked out of the room, leaned against the guardrail of the mezzanine and gazed out of the large window. Floodlights across the landscape, where the vines were still being worked, cast a haze of light that dulled the clarity that came with pure darkness. Another couple of weeks and the stars would be clearly visible again.

She used to stare out at them from her bedroom in the chateau as a young child, through the leaded-glass windows, on those occasions when her mother had bothered to collect her from school for the holidays. She'd dreamed of travelling into space and star hopping. It wasn't a dream as in a desire, nor was it something she could set her mind on achieving. It was a fantasy to escape the feeling of loneliness that came with being at home with her mother.

She'd not lived in the chateau since her mother's death when she'd returned to manage the vineyard. It might be an architecturally magnificent building, but to Elodie it was austere, cold, and a reflection of a childhood that was absent of the love and comfort of a parent. That Kaye would find it an interesting study and maybe would be willing to redesign the interior for her to evoke new memories made the building a little more appealing to venture into. She would invite Kaye to look inside.

The headlights of a vehicle pulling into the yard caught her eye. Had Kaye come by taxi? It was too early. And Kaye had insisted she would cycle here though Elodie had no intention of letting her cycle back. She had no intention of letting Kaye return to the narrowboat at all tonight. She'd never slept with another woman in her own bed, in her own home. No matter how much she tried to tell herself to back off, she couldn't. Time would solve the problem for her. For now, she wanted to have sex with Kaye until they fell asleep together, wake up next to her in the morning, and watch Kaye as she stirred, drowsy from sleep. What if Kaye didn't want to stay overnight with her? Her stomach roiled. The vehicle stopped outside the barn, and the headlights went off.

She took the stairs to the ground floor as quickly as she could, strode past the empty offices, and swung the front door open. Her heart stopped for a beat. She blinked to register the wide, bright smile and the red hair she'd admired all those years ago. "No." She shook her head, leaning back into the barn, then leaned forward and squinted. "Mylene?"

"Hello, Elodie." Her voice was deep, mellow beyond her years.

Elodie's heart thundered. She ran her fingers through her hair and blew out a deep breath. "Well, well." Her thoughts tossed around, jumbled, and merged into an incoherent, inarticulate mess. "I...I'm...wow. Sorry, come in. You've thrown me. I was expecting someone else." She stepped back from the threshold.

"If this isn't a good time, I can come back." Mylene stopped just short of the doorway.

"No. Please, come in. I have a friend on her way. We're having dinner later. Would you care to join us?" Elodie re-ran the offer through her mind and felt a small twinge of regret at having extended it.

"I don't want to impose. I'm here on business really. I went to the chateau, but there was no answer. I saw the light on."

"You're not imposing at all. It's been..." Elodie did the maths quickly in her head. "Eighteen years."

"Too long," Mylene said in a soft tone and smiled. "And the world still hasn't come to an end."

Elodie gave a short laugh. "You remember our millennium debate?" She led Mylene up the stairs to the mezzanine and into the dining room.

"How could I forget it? You were right."

Elodie stared into the familiar blue-grey smiling eyes. Fine lines fanned from their corners. Maturity suited her. Her hair was the same stunning red as Elodie recalled from their childhood, only there was a lot more of it. She looked down her body, still shaped by beautiful curves. "You haven't changed a bit."

"Neither have you. You're still the same stick I remember."

Elodie laughed. "Can I get you a drink?"

"I hear you produce the finest wines in the Loire."

"So the authorities say, and I'm not going to challenge them."

Mylene laughed. "You're still good with numbers then."

Elodie watched Mylene as she looked around the room. The convent, their time together at the river, image after image flooded her mind. "You look good."

"You have a nice place. You always were going to do well for yourself."

There was no malice in her tone, just a quiet appreciation and maybe a hint of affection in her recollection.

"You should have let me know you were coming. You could have stayed here." She hesitated as Mylene half-smiled. "Or we could have done something together."

"You didn't write to me. I didn't want to risk you refusing to see me."

Elodie frowned. "I didn't know where to write. You disappeared. No one told us what had happened, just that your grandparents had taken you home."

"They took me to America. I wrote to you at the convent."

Elodie shook her head. "I never got a letter from you. Or anyone else for that matter."

"My grandparents must have forbidden the nuns to pass messages on."

Elodie's gut twisted. Mylene had written to her. It seemed incomprehensible and yet she knew it was true by the sincerity in her voice. A pounding in her ears began, and her pulse ran fast and fiery. The desire for vengeance gnawed at her mind unceasingly but what could she do about it now? Why would the people who professed to love and care about them both have stopped them from communicating? Had Mylene's grandparents found out about their relationship? Hate choked her: for her mother for taking her home that summer; for the nuns for adhering to their religious principles that just served to crucify the purest love as they saw it; and for Mylene's grandparents for breaking her heart when they took her away. How could they have been so cruel? She couldn't bear to think of how different her life would have been, the things they would have done together had Mylene not left, because if she thought about the depth of her loss, the desire for revenge would become overwhelming. She couldn't change the past, and she wasn't going to let this get in the way of her future. She turned toward the darkness outside the window and closed her eyes, biting back the tears, grappling for something positive from that time to hold onto. "Sister Mary wouldn't have withheld anything unless under strict instruction. She used to sneak us extra biscuits, remember? And she'd leave the main door unlocked late so we could stay out longer."

"When you didn't respond, I thought you didn't want to know me. I'm pleased you didn't get the letters. It would've been much harder to know you'd read them and hadn't responded." She took in a deep breath and puffed out. "I was actually very worried about coming to France, knowing you owned the vineyard and that our paths were likely to cross. I couldn't call in advance in case you refused to meet me. I wanted to see you, even though it was tough. It's insane, isn't it? After all these years." Mylene reached out and stroked Elodie's arm. "It's so good to see you."

Elodie froze at the contact. This was so confusing. She shook her head in an effort to rally her thoughts, to ground and calm herself. There was a time when Mylene's touch would have been more than welcome, encouraged even, but there was so much unspoken between them, and she couldn't think clearly. She craved the closeness they'd once shared and yet everything between them was different. *She* wasn't ready for this, she hadn't planned for this, though her heart hadn't forgotten Mylene. It thrummed now in a heavy longing beat, a fusion of love and loss. She moved toward Mylene and pulled her into an embrace that became stronger, as if grabbing hold of a potential that had been snatched from her before they'd been able to fully develop it. Mylene felt familiar in her arms and comforting, but she let her go and took a step back. The floral perfume that hung in the air triggered a memory of the soap they'd used at the convent and a shower they'd shared together. She cleared her throat. "Red or white?"

"Red, please."

Elodie became aware of the click of Kaye's heels on the wooden floor below them, becoming louder as she climbed the stairs. She turned to the door as Kaye entered the room, puffing, and heat flushed her cheeks. Kaye looked at her through a frown that quickly became a wide smile as she acknowledged the woman across from Elodie.

"Kaye, this is Mylene. Mylene, this is Kaye."

Kaye took a pace toward Mylene with her hand outstretched. "Hi. We met before."

Elodie became aware of similarities between the two women. They both had blue eyes that shifted in shade depending on the light, although Mylene's complexion was slightly darker than Kaye's. The curiosity and sense of adventure she'd known with Mylene as they'd explored the convent together, she'd also seen in Kaye. Both had a gentle and unimposing demeanour. Both were beautiful women who had claimed a place in her heart.

Mylene took Kaye's hand. "At the spa, of course. It's great to meet you again." Mylene looked from Kaye to Elodie. "Hey, look, I'm interrupting you guys. I should go."

Kaye shook her head. "Not at all." She turned to Elodie. "Do you two know each other?"

Elodie approached the table. "We do. A long time ago. Would you like red or white wine?"

Kaye glanced at the glasses on the table. "I'll have the same as you two, thanks."

"We were at school together, The Convent of the Sacred Heart in Paris, as kids," Elodie said.

"And you haven't seen each other since?"

"No," Mylene said. "Though I tried. But it seems my attempts were thwarted by my grandparents' desires to keep me from the sins of the devil." She laughed and glanced at Elodie through narrow eyes.

Elodie laughed. "It wasn't me who was the devil. And I wasn't the one who worried about not going to heaven either." Not going to heaven had been the ultimate threat the nuns levied at the girls when they'd run out of other punishment options. Elodie had known Sister Mary didn't believe in the threat, because she'd always delivered it whilst holding back an accepting smile.

"I gave up on the idea of going to heaven years ago. Too many sins under my belt," Mylene said.

Elodie laughed. Kaye looked from Mylene to Elodie and back again with a thin-lipped half-smile.

"Anyway, I must leave you to your evening." Mylene nodded to Kaye then focused her attention on Elodie. "I was hoping we could talk business at some point. My client is interested in buying your wine."

Elodie nodded. "Let's do lunch, then we can catch up on old times."

"Here's my card." Mylene placed her business card on the table and walked up to Kaye. She took her by the shoulders and kissed her on the cheek. "Enjoy your evening."

"You too."

Mylene approached Elodie. She hesitated, still locked into the shock that slowed her thinking, then she pulled Mylene to her. She kissed each cheek, and when they parted, she lowered her head and cleared her throat, fully aware that Kaye was watching her.

"I'll show you out," Elodie said and led Mylene down the stairs.

She could feel the heat radiating from Mylene across the short distance between them and was drawn back to the taste of cocoa and shortbread and a profound feeling of belonging. "I can't tell you how wonderful it is to see you after all this time."

Mylene reached up and ran a fingertip down her cheek. "I never forgot you," she said and stepped through the door.

A shiver passed over Elodie's skin as she locked the door. She hadn't expected to see Mylene again in a million years. She shook her head. The heavy feeling in her stomach had come from nowhere. Her pace back to the stairs was slow and deliberate. The past was the past and couldn't be recreated eighteen years later. There were too many years of difference that separated them. She knew the theory, but her heart still ached. Mylene had tried to contact her and tried to stay in touch with her. She hadn't known. Mylene hadn't abandoned her. Still, her thoughts seemed to merge and become incoherent. All this time she'd felt deserted by her first love when maybe Mylene had continued to love her all along. If she had known, she would have fought to be with her. And she would have won. It had never occurred to her that Mylene had been as abandoned by Elodie as she had by Mylene. Why would it? She swallowed down a bitter taste. She couldn't process her agonising thoughts anymore without them spoiling her evening with Kaye. *I cannot change the past.*

She lingered for a moment at the bottom of the stairs and looked up toward the mezzanine. Kaye was waiting for her. *Kaye will leave you,* the voice in her head said, and the feeling became solid. Mylene had returned. Even after all these years, she'd never really left you. She dismissed the crazy voice and took the stairs two at a time.

"I'm sorry about that. I haven't seen Mylene since we were teenagers. It was an unexpected surprise." She kissed Kaye. The warmth and tenderness of Kaye's lips lifted the fog that had formed in her mind, though the voice in her head persisted in taunting her. Giving Kaye her attention would help.

Kaye stroked her cheek. "She meant something to you, didn't she?"

Elodie picked up her glass. Her hand shook. She had to talk to Kaye, it was only fair to be honest with her. Filled with trepidation, the old wound reopened and raw, she slowly led Kaye to the couch. "Let me tell you about the convent."

16.

KAYE SAT ON THE couch, her mind in a fog. She'd picked up instantly on the connection between Elodie and Mylene. They had a bond that had clearly survived the test of time. She'd seen the depth of Mylene's feelings for Elodie in her gaze that lasted longer than the conversation between them, the gentleness in her lingering smile, and the slower cadence in her voice when she addressed Elodie. It shouldn't matter. Elodie was free to live her life, as was Kaye. No strings, right? She had to make it not matter.

The glass trembled in her cold fingers, and her stomach fluttered. She put the glass down but couldn't relax. The ache at the back of her throat was similar to the feeling she'd had moments before Sylvie had delivered the final blow that triggered everything that had followed. She curled her shoulders forward and pressed her knees tightly together. She couldn't let herself feel this way.

"Mylene was a long time ago. She was my first love, but you need to understand the context. She was special to me for lots of reasons."

Why did Kaye's heart ping at Elodie's admission of love? Everyone had a school sweetheart or a first crush that transformed their view of the world for good and sometimes for the better. It was a rite of passage, a natural part of growing into the teenage years. Kaye's had been Libby Hurst with her blonde curls and big front teeth that she could whistle through. Kaye was seven and Libby eight. They'd hung out together in the school playground, climbed trees, and rescued worms from the boys who would cut them up just to see what happened.

"Christmas, 1999."

Elodie drifted in quiet contemplation. Her hands trembled a little, and she let out a long sigh. Kaye had the urge to hold her but stopped herself.

"I'd been staring out the window for hours waiting for my mother to collect me, watching the snow deepen. It was very pretty. I like the snow." She smiled at Kaye wistfully then drifted back to her recollection. "I knew she wasn't going to come... She never did." Her eyes watered, and she looked down. "The nuns used to make us wear these stiff woollen skirts and blazers that itched like crazy, and our bedrooms were too dark to study in, and hot and stuffy. The radiators belched and the floorboards creaked. It was like a home that wasn't mine. I wanted to run away from it all and feel the cold air burn my cheeks, to calm the itching."

Kaye couldn't resist the urge any longer. She took Elodie's hand and enclosed it in her own.

"It was a nice enough place. We were governed by strict rules." Elodie wiped her eyes and then smiled. "Did you know, it is unbecoming of a lady to be seen cavorting in the snow?" She chuckled.

The gentle humour encouraged a fleeting smile from Kaye.

"Sister Mary was kind. She used to bring me cocoa and shortbread biscuits, and I'd dunk them. I can still taste them when I think about the convent. She always looked at me with sorrowful eyes. Every holiday, she used to insist my mother would come. I learned not to care. I'd been let down too many times to hope, though it still broke my heart. Until Mylene and I..."

Kaye shook her head, her heart aching with sympathy. Who would do that to someone they loved? To a child?

"My mother had wanted a son to take over the business, and she got me instead. She wanted a husband who would stand by her, and he left us both. Of course, it was all my fault. And while she was busy trying to gratify her own needs, she didn't give a thought for mine. Mylene's grandparents were her legal guardians, because her parents had been killed in a traffic accident. They didn't seem to want her around either, because she spent almost every holiday at the convent. We got close over the years and then one summer we discovered each other." Elodie looked up at Kaye and smiled, then her expression turned inward again. "When I returned after the holidays that summer, she'd left without saying goodbye. I had no way to get in touch with her. I felt utterly alone and broken."

Kaye rubbed her thumb across Elodie's hand. It sounded horrific. Kaye had brothers, and a sister, and a close-knit family. They would laugh together, play together, and argue with each other. But she had known what Elodie never had, a loving bond that transcended everything. Her eldest brother would fight to protect her and his other siblings, and she had stood up for her younger sister when she'd needed support too. Elodie had no one in her corner. She'd found a friend and that friend had been snatched from her without any explanation. She must have felt so lost, so scared. The ache in Kaye's heart intensified and she rubbed Elodie's hand harder, not wanting to let her go.

"My mother was drinking too much even before I went to university for my degree. When she didn't show up for my graduation, it wasn't a huge surprise. But then the police turned up as I was packing to come home and told me she'd taken her own life. She'd left the vineyard in a mess with debts of close to two million."

Kaye clasped her free hand to her chest. Words escaped her. Elodie squeezed Kaye's hand tighter. She huffed out a breath, and to Kaye it sounded like the noise a child might make trying to be brave while dismissing something that hurt them deeply.

"I used to love going to the library. It was my favourite place to hide away. I loved the smell of the waxed wood and leather. I used to read a lot. From ancient history to astrophysics, mathematics, art, and literature. I'm not creative like you, I've just stored a lot of facts and information. They had a section on woman's fiction too, and Mylene had hidden a book, *The Color Purple,* on one of the shelves. If the nuns realised it was there, they never said anything and didn't remove it. Reading about Celie's world made me feel a lot better about my own for a while. It gave me the courage to be me. You know, Mylene was so worried the world would end that Christmas with the millennium bug." She laughed.

Kaye leaned toward Elodie and kissed her cheek. "I'm so sorry."

Elodie stared at her. "I'm not as robust as you. I'm not even as strong as I thought I was. It's easy to hide weakness in comfort and familiarity."

"I think you're incredible."

"Business is easy. It's concrete or at least, the risks can be calculated. Business doesn't challenge my heart. Relationships have always been...difficult for me."

"In what way?" Kaye's heart raced, and the pain she saw in Elodie's expression she felt in her own chest, becoming sharper with every shallow breath. The sound of her own breathing became louder, Elodie's too. She looked down at her white knuckles, her hand firmly gripping Elodie's. It dawned on her that she was constricting the flow of blood to Elodie's hand, and she softened her grasp.

A sheen of moisture had formed on Elodie's cheeks and forehead, her skin had paled, and her hand was clammy and cold. She pulled her hand from Kaye's, blinked rapidly, and wiped the sweat from above her lip. She stared at Kaye, though Kaye didn't feel seen.

"I can't face rejection, so I stay out of relationships. It's easier for everyone that way."

Kaye released a long breath, her insides trembling. She didn't know how to respond to Elodie's admission, even though it wasn't news. The problem was the strength of her feelings for Elodie, the meaning of which had just hit her like a tonne of bricks. She wanted to be with her. But Elodie had confirmed that she couldn't be in a relationship. "I guessed as much," Kaye said softly, her heart aching. She took Elodie's hand in hers and brought it to her lips. "Rejection is never easy to take."

"I know. It's not that I don't want to try. I don't trust myself to not push the person I love away. Do you know what I mean?"

Kaye shook her head. Elodie looked diminished. "My marriage didn't turn out all that well, you know."

"At least you had the courage to try."

"And I'll try again."

"One day you'll find someone who deserves you, someone who will love you as you deserve to be loved."

Kaye eased her hand from Elodie's and cleared her throat. "Well, there's still time for you too. Mylene has come back. Maybe you could pick up with her." The words stuck in her throat. She didn't intend to say them to test Elodie's response or to gauge how Elodie felt about her by pitting herself against Mylene, but she still watched closely to see how the proposition landed.

Elodie stared at Kaye for what felt like a very long time. Her eyes were lighter, filled with emotion and weighed down by heavy lids. The lines that fanned from her eyes ran deeper, and her long black eyelashes were glossy and wet. Kaye wanted to hold her in her arms and never let her go. She wanted Elodie to be the one who deserved her...and loved her.

"You're very beautiful," Elodie whispered.

Kaye ran her fingers through Elodie's fringe, lifting it away from her face. "I don't feel it right now." A shadow had moved across Kaye's heart with the tone of the conversation.

She tried to smile but knew her expression had barely shifted, not just because of the wretchedness she felt for Elodie but because of the depth with which Elodie's comment about her finding someone had affected her. She put her trembling hand on Elodie's cheek.

Elodie held it there and closed her eyes. "Please don't say that."

Elodie's whispered voice created another jab to Kaye's heart. Elodie drew the palm of Kaye's hand to her lips and kissed it. Kaye's throat was unyielding as she swallowed. She had to ask the question etched on her mind since Mylene had turned up at the barn. "Do you still love her?"

Elodie looked skyward for a brief moment before settling her gaze on Kaye. She shook her head slowly. "Honestly, I don't know what I feel or what's real right now. She was a long time ago, and I'm a different person. She will be too."

Kaye willed herself not to let her tears spill. She wasn't sure when she'd made up her mind about what she was about to say, but she had to protect herself from getting really hurt, and there was only one way to do that. She stiffened her back and took in a deep breath. "I'll be leaving tomorrow." She said the words she didn't want to say, and her heart railed against them.

Elodie lowered her head. Her shoulders dropped with a long breath, as if the air had been sucked from her lungs. "Must you go so soon?"

The low tone in Elodie's voice ripped at Kaye's heart. No, there was nothing pulling her away. But she had to leave, because she wasn't going to sit in the middle of Elodie's unfinished business. Whether Elodie could see it or not, there was something unresolved between her and Mylene. And she got the impression it wasn't only from Mylene's perspective. "She still feels something for you."

Meeting Elodie had been more than Kaye had dreamed of, and she'd loved every second they'd spent together. More than that, she'd become closer than she'd expected. She felt Elodie's absence when she was alone in the narrowboat, and she'd been excited with the anticipation of seeing her again. The sex between them was mind-blowing, and her time in the Blue Room had been intense and almost overwhelming. It hadn't just been about having great sex in a place where others could watch, although that was novel for Kaye. There had been something in the ambience, and the history captured in the art inside the Blue Room, and the sense of women's liberation that spanned centuries. The whole experience had been made profound by being able to share it with a strong, beautiful woman like Elodie. It had been beyond her wildest dreams and something she would never forget. She'd felt an affinity with those women generations ago who hadn't been able to be true to their needs or had been vilified for doing so. She had come away feeling uplifted and appreciative of the freedom she had.

She'd always been vulnerable to the power of love, and Elodie had captured her heart. But she wouldn't stay in Sancerre and watch Elodie fall back in love with Mylene. That would break more than her heart; it would shatter her soul.

Yet the desire to make love with her one last time was more overwhelming than the logic which dictated she should walk away. The voice in her head became a whisper, silenced to her heart's yearning. Whatever she did, she would regret it one way or another.

Elodie leaned toward Kaye and traced her fingertip across her nose and under her eyes as she shook her head. "You have the most adorable freckles. They're so faint and look like tiny specks of pollen. I noticed them the first day I saw you."

The trembling built inside Kaye, and the last sliver of her imagined resolve seeped away. Elodie hadn't addressed her point about Mylene's affection for her, but the way Elodie looked at her now made Elodie's intentions clear. A few more days wouldn't break Kaye's heart any more than if she left Sancerre on Sunday. As long as she walked away soon, she could still recover herself. She had nowhere she needed to be and only one place she wanted to spend her time.

"Please don't go yet. I want to show you something."

Elodie's kiss was tender and pleading, and her lips quivered as she smiled. She ran her unsteady finger along the line of Kaye's chin, her thumb, and across her lips. Kaye leaned closer until she could feel Elodie's warm breath against her skin. At the hitch in Elodie's moan as their mouths barely touched, Kaye eased back and smiled. "What do you want to show me?"

Elodie ran her finger where Kaye had kissed her lips. "I'd like your creative advice for a project I'm working on."

Kaye burst out laughing, though her eyes burned. "You only want me for my creative input?"

Kaye saw mild concern in Elodie's expression.

Elodie traced Kaye's lips with the lightest of touch. "Well, I want you for this too." She trailed her finger down the cut of Kaye's dress and then followed a line across the flesh of her breast. "And this, too."

Kaye gasped. Her pulse raced. The intensity was undeniable and unstoppable. She wanted to feel Elodie's warm skin against her own, Elodie's fingers inside her. She kissed Elodie hard and tumbled on top of her. She moaned when Elodie lifted up her dress and moved her hand up her inner thigh. Elodie's palm was cool and firm against her sex, and the increase in pressure massaging her breast and nipple added fuel to the fire that coursed through her. "Do you know what you do to me?" Kaye moaned as Elodie entered her. "Oh, God."

"Yes," Elodie whispered. "I know this feeling."

The pressure built inside Kaye and slowly moulded to fill her, then touched her so deeply that she wanted it to never end. Suspended in the rawness and complexity of what they shared together, her heart stayed open, and she let Elodie in completely. She cried out as she orgasmed, and as she stared into Elodie's beautiful sparkling eyes, a tear slipped onto her cheek. Searching for an indication that Elodie felt remotely the same way, she found nothing. *No strings.* Elodie was better at that than Kaye could ever be.

Elodie put her hand around Kaye's head and coaxed her closer. "I love it when you come like that."

Kaye bit her lip and closed her eyes. *Love.* The word rolled from Elodie's lips so easily. If only she meant it in the way that Kaye wanted to hear it. The thought slid from her mind as Elodie's soft lips met hers, and she became bathed in warmth. She nipped at Elodie's lip and deepened the kiss. She slipped her hand beneath Elodie's shirt and enjoyed the texture of Elodie's nipple as it transformed at her touch. Elodie kissed Kaye harder. As she slid her hand inside Elodie's waistband and down into the wetness between her legs, Elodie moaned into her mouth. She would make Elodie come in a way that Elodie would never forget too, and she would stay and take a look at the damn project, because she couldn't bring herself to leave right now. She'd not had enough of Elodie to want to let her go. "When we have desire, we act to make the dream come to life." Françoise's words echoed in her mind. Kaye had desire for Elodie, and she was doing her utmost to act on it. She sensed Elodie's desire for her too. But was desire the same thing as love? "You can't force someone to love you." Elodie's riposte haunted her mind and her heart. No, she couldn't force Elodie to love her. But she couldn't stop herself from loving Elodie either. Until Kaye decided she was ready to move on, until she couldn't bear whatever might develop between Elodie and Mylene, she would enjoy her *no strings* relationship for the liberating experience that it was. She could always hope.

17.

A STRIP OF LIGHT squeezed through the shutters on the window and fell across Kaye's face. Her eyelashes flickered and her lips made small movements. Her cheeks had a soft golden glow, and the shadows that had once darkened her eyes had disappeared. She looked dishevelled and smelled of downy-warmth and sex. Elodie wanted to kiss every millimetre of her beautiful body, wanted to gently lift the loose strands of hair that lay across Kaye's face. She wanted to feel Kaye's soft lips against her own, their bodies pressed firmly together, and her sex sliding against Kaye's smooth firm thigh.

She rested her head on her hand and pondered, emotionally depleted from their discussion the previous evening. She'd managed to get Kaye to delay leaving and take a look at the chateau but at what cost?

Seeing Mylene had brought back old feelings from tender memories, and yes, there was unfinished business between them. They had had something special, and innocent, and it had been ripped from them both. Time had healed the hurt to a point. That Mylene had tried to contact Elodie and been prevented by whatever mechanisms had been put in place to stop them connecting with each other was both comforting and frustrating. Maybe, if their relationship had run its course, it would most likely have come to a natural end, like most childhood infatuations. That wasn't the point. This wasn't a rational matter, it was an emotional one, and her instinctive response was to want to cause pain to those responsible for pulling them apart. She did something she hadn't done since childhood. She took in a deep breath and let out a silent scream.

The vulnerability she'd felt confessing to Kaye that she couldn't do relationships was firmly etched in the gentle tremor that lingered beneath her skin. The veil to her inner world had been lowered, and the elements that would erode her could now reach her with ease. Other women would have walked away from her by now, if she'd allowed them to get close to her. Their wants would always been grander and more urgent than their tolerance for her Achilles heel. That's what she'd told herself to maintain her distance.

Kaye had held her and made love to her, complicating everything and reinforcing the link between them. Elodie feared the extent of the pain she would inevitably feel in Kaye's absence. She would deny herself the sadness, adeptly push it to the back of her mind, and then she would find her natural rhythm again. She took in a deep breath and turned to watch Kaye.

Kaye's chest rose and fell in a slow easy rhythm. Her mouth turned down a fraction and narrow lines settled across her brow. She wondered what dream would create that slightly troubled appearance. It didn't stop Kaye looking wonderfully edible. Maybe it was sleep that made Kaye look even more gorgeous than normal. Or maybe it was the fact that Elodie felt defenceless around her and safe in her arms. Kaye murmured, and Elodie had the urge to wake her. Having time, albeit limited, was something that hadn't been possible with Mylene. Even her dalliances at university had come to an immediate close as the other women drifted effortlessly into another's arms and didn't speak to her again. She would persuade Kaye to stay to help her with the chateau project and make every second count.

Kaye stirred, rolled her leg over Elodie's stomach, and mumbled incoherently.

Elodie tugged her into the crook of her arm and kissed the top of her head. She smelled almost imperceptibly of oranges, and...of Kaye. "Are you awake?"

"Kind of," Kaye whispered and wrapped her arm around Elodie's waist. "I think you killed me last night."

"You're still breathing."

"True. Morning seems to have come around very quickly."

"You smell delicious."

"I smell of sex."

"It's intoxicating."

Kaye moaned. Elodie kissed the top of her head again, the light growing inside the room, and snuggled into Kaye's soft, toasty body. Kaye moved her hand to cover Elodie's breast.

Elodie shuddered. She tugged Kaye closer. "Did you ever want children?"

There was a brief silence, and Elodie wondered why she'd asked such a question. Perhaps it was because it was another aspect of her life she'd denied. Did Elodie want children?

"Yes, I did. I realised I couldn't have them with Sylvie though. She wasn't very nurturing, and children should feel loved by their parents."

Elodie tightened her grip around Kaye. She knew that better than most.

"Did you never think of having children?" Kaye asked.

"No. I didn't have faith in myself to not turn out like my mother or my father."

Kaye lifted her head and squinted at Elodie. "You're nothing like your mother."

Elodie gave a light-hearted huff as she removed Kaye's hair from her face and tucked it around her ear. It fell back immediately. "You didn't know her."

"I don't need to have met her to know. You're kind and caring and...and no, you wouldn't abandon your children. So you're not like your father either. You're nothing like either of them." She shook her head.

The intensity in Kaye's eyes melted Elodie's heart. She kissed her tenderly. "Maybe you're right."

"I am definitely right."

She held Kaye's gaze. "What do you miss about being married?"

Kaye lowered her eyes. "Nothing right now."

"What would you do differently, if you had the chance?"

Kaye sighed. "Aside from not getting married in the first place, I should have challenged her behaviour. I prefer a quiet life, but I've learned that sometimes you have to fight for yourself. Fight for your sanity, fight for your life."

"Yes," Elodie whispered. She'd learned how to survive for different reasons, but the instinct was the same.

"Maybe in the future I'll miss something, but I can't think what that might be. I don't miss the bad stuff."

Elodie thought about her experience of leaving the convent to go to university. She'd been physically sick. She'd felt as if her life was coming to an end. Everything about being at the convent had made her feel safe, and it was being taken from her. The idea of being at university had also been exciting, but it would mean new people and new relationships, and she had been ready for neither. She'd missed the nuns dreadfully for a good six months or more. "What about comfort and security?"

"I was comfortable and secure in a dysfunctional relationship, because I couldn't see there was something better for me on the outside. It's too easy to slip into an illusion of happiness."

"Hmm." Elodie thought about the club. She'd been happy with being a part of it until recently. There had been other lovers she could have gotten closer to at university, but she'd never allowed her guard down long enough to let them in. She'd always known she was going to move on and return to Sancerre.

Elodie believed in love, because she'd experienced it, however briefly. Feeling love toward another, feeling loved by another, and holding onto love were all different aspects of love. What she'd felt the first few times she'd been abandoned by her mother, the last time when her mother left her for good, and when Mylene hadn't returned to school was powerlessness. She felt that now. Her chest tightened. She resisted and won.

Kaye eased out of Elodie's arm, leaned on her elbow, and stroked Elodie's cheek. "Are you happy?"

Elodie's stomach flipped. "In some ways." She wasn't lying. She held Kaye's soft gaze. "We don't know what we're missing until something or *someone* comes along to show us. I think you were brave, getting divorced and having no one else in your life."

Kaye's frown deepened. "You don't have anyone in your life."

"That's different. I've never lived with anyone, but I've had the company of other women whenever I wanted it. There's comfort and security in that. It's become my status quo. It's a bit like being married, I suppose." She wasn't sure what she was getting at because the comfort that the club provided, and the convent before it, didn't feel like it was enough to sustain her now.

Kaye chuckled lightly. "So, you see yourself as married to the club?"

Elodie's stomach dropped and she lowered her eyes. In a way, she was. She still hadn't allowed herself to dream of possibilities that didn't involve her working at the vineyard or the club.

"Hey," Kaye said softly and stroked Elodie's cheek.

"Sorry, I—"

"It's okay." Kaye inhaled deeply and rested her hand on Elodie's chest. "You've been let down by those you loved the most. That's hard for me to relate to. I was lucky, I had a supportive family. I think I'd avoid relationships if I were in your shoes. But how do you stop yourself from falling in love?"

You don't. You just don't deceive yourself that it will last. Elodie closed her hand around Kaye's. "Aren't you afraid of getting hurt again?"

Kaye looked away, beyond the bed, maybe beyond the room and into the ether of collective wisdom that Elodie had referred to. "Of course. I'm scared to death of falling in love again in case I lose that person. I'm worried about trusting someone and being taken for a ride. And I don't want to be in a relationship with someone who's going to try to control my every move and tell me I'm pathetic."

Elodie tugged Kaye closer and held her tightly. She would never do that to Kaye, not deliberately, not to anyone. They would stay good friends, and that would be better than hurting each other.

"But if I never take a risk again, if I close my heart, I'll never experience the most profound feeling of love possible. I think that would be more frightening, so empty and isolating. I need to express love and feel the kind of love that comes with commitment. If I don't, surely that's just an empty existence."

It was time to lighten the conversation, otherwise the day would be tainted by Elodie's inadequacies and she didn't want to be reminded. "Shall we talk about something else."

Kaye broke free from the embrace and slipped out of bed. She kissed Elodie firmly on the lips and smiled. "I need the bathroom, and yes."

Elodie studied Kaye's hips, swaying gently as she moved across the room. "You have a great ass."

Kaye laughed. "So, you don't live in the chateau?" she asked from the en-suite bathroom.

"Not since my mother died."

There was the sound of running water and then Kaye appeared in the doorway dressed in a robe and patting her face with a towel. "Has it been closed all that time?"

Elodie placed her hands behind her head. "Pretty much. A cleaner comes in every day and there's ongoing maintenance, but..." She was about to say she hated the place but didn't want to offend the historian in Kaye and hoped Kaye would offer her creative input to entice Elodie back in someday. "Would you like to look around?"

Kaye smiled. "I'd love to."

Elodie jumped out of bed, rushed over to Kaye, and kissed her on the nose. "Then it will be my pleasure, your highness." She made a bow and laughed. "I can't wait to see your design ideas...as well as the other things." She raised her eyebrows and smiled.

Kaye reached up and ran her fingers through Elodie's hair. "I'll do my best." She looked at her for a long time then pressed her thumb to her lips and looked away. "As long as you promise not to behave."

"I can do that." Elodie chuckled, though she was left with the impression that Kaye had wanted to say something as Elodie walked to the shower.

The shower felt cool against her skin. A shiver moved in steady waves across her skin until she trembled. She turned up the hot water, but it didn't stop her hands from shaking.

***

The chateau had two wings, with eleven en-suite bedrooms, three additional guest bathrooms, two kitchens that served the two separate dining rooms, five reception rooms, a library, an office, and a grand foyer.

"What do you think?" Elodie asked as they stood in the smaller of the two dining rooms.

The large table seated twenty-two guests with a half-metre space between each setting. As a young child, Elodie would sit opposite her grandmother, each with their own salt and pepper pot, and the distance across the table that separated them couldn't be closed even if they both held out their hands to each other. Not that she would dare to try. Etiquette dictated model behaviour even in the absence of guests. The portraits that hung around the room, dour looking faces of ancient relatives whose eyes had always freaked her out as a child, still made her skin crawl as if she was being judged by standards she could never achieve. There was a strong scent of freshly oiled wood and a musty smell that threatened its pleasant aroma. Elodie's stomach clenched.

Kaye looked around the room with wide eyes and a bright beaming smile. She was like sunshine casting light on the gloomy life Elodie had lived here.

"It's magnificent."

Elodie scanned the walls, up to the large ornate covings that seemed to dominate the ceilings. "It certainly has a history."

"More than that. It's remarkable. The craftwork on the dresser and table, the details in the Persian rug. Okay, the portraits are a little intimidating, and the walls are darker than they need to be. It needs a makeover, but those things are easily changed. It's a magnificent space to work with."

"My grandfather had the rug imported from India. It must be over a hundred years old. I never knew him. The portraits, I confess, I hate."

"The rug is bigger than the whole of Courtney's flat."

Elodie laughed for longer than was normal. She bit her lip. Who was Courtney to Kaye?

"I'm serious," Kaye said.

Elodie checked herself. "I didn't mean—"

Kaye smiled. "I'm teasing you. It's good. You have a wonderful laugh."

Elodie studied Kaye. "Who's Courtney?" she asked, trying to keep the question light though Kaye's answer could have heavy implications.

"We're good friends. We met at uni and worked in London together. She's the best friend I have."

Kaye's last sentence was delivered quietly and with a weary tone, as if she was pondering the nature of her relationship with Courtney.

She lowered her chin and narrowed her eyes at Elodie. "We've never been lovers, if that's what you've been wondering. She's not my type."

Elodie swallowed past the lump in her throat. "You should see the size of the bedrooms."

Kaye chuckled. "You're such a charmer, Elodie Marchand."

"I—"

Kaye gave her a look that said she was teasing her. Elodie felt warm inside. She'd forgotten what carefree felt like. Kaye didn't just light up a room, she lit up Elodie's world. "Would you like to advise me what to do with it?" She pulled Kaye close, and when their lips touched, Kaye flung her arms around her neck and kissed her firmly and deeply. When they stopped kissing, Elodie's heart was racing, and her breaths were short and fast.

Kaye smiled. "Bedrooms, you said."

Kaye hadn't answered the question. Elodie headed up the stairs at a pace. "There's something I think you'll appreciate."

"I'm appreciating your ass right now. I'm not sure much could beat it."

Elodie turned and smiled. "This will, I promise you." She took Kaye's hand when they reached the top of the stairs and led her down a long corridor with heavily patterned wallpaper and a tall arched roof structure. The carpet was threadbare in the places that had been well walked. One obvious trail led them to the room at the end of the chateau that Elodie now faced with a smile. It had been her grandmother's room. The door complained at being opened. In contrast with the darkness in the corridor, the expansive room with large leaded windows on all three aspects was bright, though the air was stale and the room had the same musty scent as the rest of the house. The four-poster bed, which could easily sleep four adults, and the large dressing table and chair failed to dominate the space. Elodie headed to the built-in wardrobes and opened the doors.

Kaye went to the central window and glanced out. "It's stunning."

Elodie rummaged through the clothes on the racks. "You can see pretty much the whole of the estate from these three windows," she said, her attention focused on her search. She opened the box she'd been looking for and lifted the garment. *Perfect.* She went to the window and held the dress up to Kaye. "What do you think?"

Kaye's gaze moved from the dress to Elodie and back to the dress again, her mouth open and her eyes wide. She took the material lightly in her hand as if it were fragile and allowed it to slip through her fingers.

"It's the most beautiful dress I've ever seen." The lightest of the blue tones shimmered, silver in the sunlight. "It's a silk sari, isn't it?"

"It was my grandmother's. My grandfather had it handmade for her. It will fit you perfectly."

Kaye cupped her hand to her mouth, shaking her head. "No. I can't possibly accept this."

"I want you to have it. My grandmother would be delighted if it was used. It's only been worn once. She hoped I might wear it at my wedding until she accepted that was never going to happen." Elodie rested the dress over her arm, the weight of it no match for the heaviness in her heart. "I'd be honoured if you'd take it. It will just rot here, along with everything else." She held out the dress. "Please? Would you come to a dinner party with me next Saturday? You could wear it."

Kaye shook her head and ran her fingers over the intricate design sown into the silk.

Elodie wiped a tear from Kaye's cheek. "There's nothing to be sad about. My grandmother would be delighted. You'll look stunning in it, and I'd like to take you as my guest."

Kaye nodded. Elodie folded the dress back into the box. She hesitated to speak. She didn't know if the right time was now or not, but if she didn't mention the Scottish investment opportunity, Yvette might raise the question at the dinner party, and she didn't want to spoil an evening with Kaye embroiled in discussions about a business proposition. Kaye might not be interested, or she may not have the money. She didn't care whether Kaye wanted to invest or not, though cutting a deal was always good for business. She just wanted an answer for when she next spoke to Yvette. "Have you ever considered investing? I have a proposition that's just come up, a property in Scotland, would you believe?"

Kaye blinked and frowned. "I don't know. I've never thought about investing."

"How about I give you the details and you let me know what you think? We can chat about it later, once you've had time to digest. If you want to?"

Kaye shrugged. "Okay."

She tugged Kaye to her and kissed her. "Come and tell me what I need to do with my old bedroom." She raised her eyebrows and smiled at Kaye, then took her hand and led her down the corridor.

18.

THE WOMAN'S POSTURE WAS familiar but totally out of place. Kaye narrowed her eyes as she cycled down the towpath toward the Papillion.

Courtney was standing with her hands in her jeans pockets, and she swayed from heel to toe as she talked to Françoise on the Kanab. She cycled closer and recognised the meaning of her friend's body language. She was chatting up Kaye's neighbour. Courtney turned and grinned.

Kaye pulled to a stop. "Wow, what are you doing here?"

"Hey, kiddo. Nice surprise?" She grinned at Kaye and then winked at Françoise.

"A surprise...Yes, a nice surprise. How come?" Hesitation stilled Kaye as she studied Courtney. She should be more pleased to see her but the weird feeling of being imposed upon dampened her enthusiasm. She'd been enjoying the freedom of being surrounded by people who didn't know her. Oddly, Courtney's unexpected presence felt like a threat, as if she represented the past that Kaye had moved away from. It was unfair. Courtney was her friend. She took a deep breath and smiled.

"Bonjour, Kaye," Françoise said. She dipped her paintbrush into the red paint and made sweeping strokes along the side of the boat.

"Bonjour, Françoise. I see you've met Courtney."

"Oui." Françoise smiled.

Courtney continued to grin as she eyed Françoise, squinting into the sun. "It was nice to meet you."

"It was a pleasure to meet you." Françoise acknowledged Kaye as she continued to paint. "Have a good day."

"See you around maybe?" Courtney asked.

Françoise lifted one shoulder. "Peut être."

Kaye tugged Courtney into a strong hug. The irksome feeling lifted a fraction. She took her by the arm and led her away from the boat, trying to control her bicycle with her other hand. "I can't believe you're here."

Courtney glanced over her shoulder. "You gotta love the way that accent rolls off their tongue. Makes me wonder what else she could do with it."

"Seriously. She's not your type."

"I don't have a type."

"Everyone has a type. Anyway, how come you're here? I thought you couldn't make it."

"I was worried. You haven't returned my calls."

Kaye's cheeks burned. "I've been busy. I didn't know you'd called." Kaye hadn't used her phone and forgotten to charge it. "How did you find me here?"

"With the greatest ingenuity, kiddo. I called the place you hired the boat from. Spoke pigeon Franglaise to them, pleaded a lot, and I think they felt sorry for me. They told me the last lock you went through. Don't ask me how they knew that. Probably got a monitor on the boat so you don't nick it. And here I am." She held out her hands. "Anyway, you look...wow...great, actually. The French air suits you." She turned and looked toward Françoise. "I think I could get used to it here too."

"Behave." Kaye sighed. "What if I hadn't been here?"

"I still would have met Françoise. It's not all bad." She slapped Kaye on the arm. "Nah, I would've tracked you down. My tracking skills are pretty hot, don't you know." She tapped her finger to her nose. "Anyway, are you going to invite me in or what? I've been waiting hours."

"You managed to occupy yourself." Kaye smiled though the fact that Courtney had already tried to hit on Françoise sat uncomfortably with her. She considered Françoise a friend and wouldn't want her to be the next heartbreak victim of

Courtney's. She stopped her thoughts. It wasn't her problem to solve. She set her bicycle at the side of the towpath, walked past Courtney's rucksack on the front deck, and opened the cabin door. The familiar smell didn't resonate as homely as it had done when she'd first taken charge of the boat. It felt thin, new, and transitory, which it was. Elodie's barn had character. Even the chateau, with its musty odour, had a charm. Of course, they both exuded the essence of Elodie and that made all the difference.

"She's just bought the boat and is renovating it. She was seconds off inviting me in for a glass of wine."

Kaye rolled her eyes.

"Don't bust my illusion. She's pretty though." Courtney glanced across to the Kanab. Françoise's rear end was sticking out from the back of the boat. "Nice ass."

Kaye dragged Courtney inside the boat. "Wine or beer?"

"You have Sancerre?"

She had the three bottles Elodie had given her to take away after the wine tasting. They'd been chilling in the fridge ever since, because she'd spent most of her time either in Elodie's company, grape picking, or sleeping. The facilities inside the Papillion remained almost as spotlessly clean as they had when she'd moored here. Kaye kept her back to Courtney as she located two glasses and uncorked the wine. Courtney would pick up on her feelings for Elodie, and then she'd be on at her to find out more, and Kaye didn't welcome that discussion. She was feeling raw and hadn't quite come to terms with reality. She cleared her throat. "I have this one from the vineyard I worked at."

"You survived grape picking. Not that I would have known, because you haven't called me."

Kaye poured the wine and handed over a glass. "I haven't used my phone. The battery must be flat."

"What?" Courtney frowned as she shook her head. "Who does that?" She sipped. "Ooh, that's quaffable." She sipped again and looked around the cabin. "This isn't too shabby either."

"No stinky water," Kaye said and sipped her wine.

"Smells like Christmas, with something missing."

"Yeah, Christmas is missing. It's only October. That's the potpourri."

"I guessed. It's pungent. Anyway, come here. I missed you." Courtney put down her glass, took a short pace to reach Kaye in the narrow galley kitchen, and pulled her into a tight embrace.

Kaye squeezed her back. "I missed you too," she said and felt a bit of a fraud. She had missed Courtney in the beginning but hadn't given her a second thought since spending more time with Elodie. Courtney let her go. "So, how come you got time off work? I thought you had deadlines."

Courtney waved her hand in the air. "I told them to stick their job where the sun don't shine."

Kaye widened her eyes. "Crikey." She recalled Courtney saying her job was under threat if she didn't hit the targets they'd set.

"Yeah. I thought I'd take a leaf out of your book."

"And travel?" Kaye raised her eyebrows. As far as she knew, Courtney didn't have the money to be long out of work.

"Well, just for a few days. I've got a second interview next week."

"Wow." Kaye released a burst of air that had been trapped in her lungs. Her sense of relief was greater than the topic of conversation warranted. Even though Courtney hadn't hinted at travelling with Kaye, for some reason the idea of Courtney's company for any length of time didn't sit well with her now. She'd worried when she left that her travelling might result in a distance between them that was more than physical.

She hadn't wanted to lose Courtney as a friend, but she'd changed, become stronger and more independent. She still cared about Courtney, she just didn't feel as close to her. What had previously felt reassuringly familiar between them now felt strained and forced. It was as though her experiences led her to see Courtney in a way that she hadn't before. In fact, she wondered if they had anything in common anymore. It wasn't Courtney's fault: she was who she was. But maybe that was the point, Courtney hadn't changed and Kaye had. "That's good news."

"Should be. The first interview couldn't have gone better." Courtney raised her eyebrows and smiled.

Kaye knew *that* look. "You had sex with a woman for a job interview?"

"Hell, no. What do you take me for? We had sex, then we got chatting over a few drinks, and then she offered me a job. The interview next week is a formality, but I can't tell you how ecstatic I was giving notice. I think I was being oppressed."

"By the woman or the job?"

"Ooh, look who's developed a sense of humour. I like it. You're back to your old self. Oppressed by middle-aged, white male, arrogant dominance."

Kaye smiled. She wasn't back to her old self, she'd discovered a new self which was much better than anything she'd been before. "It's been refreshing, getting away from it all. It's given me a new perspective."

"Who is she?"

"Give over."

"No. I'm serious. I can see it in your eyes. You never looked like this at any point married to Psycho—"

"You haven't come all this way to dig up the past that I'm over, have you?"

"Sorry. Come on then. Who is she? She must be something special to have this effect on you."

"What effect?"

"Ha. So there is someone."

Kaye's cheeks were on fire. "Her name's Elodie, and we're good friends."

"Kiddo, *we* are good friends, and I don't make you feel whatever it is that's put that colour into your cheeks and that sparkle in your eyes. No ships are gonna hit the rocks with your face as a beacon to direct them."

"I've caught the sun."

"You've caught more than the sun, that's for sure. Is she that woman you met at the spa?"

The term, *that woman,* grated on Kaye. She would have normally just let a comment like that pass because it wasn't particularly offensive, but something in Courtney's dismissive tone stirred her. Elodie was one of the most beautiful and kind-hearted people she'd ever come across. She was humble and considerate. She'd made Kaye feel...loved. Her heart raced. Cherished, she corrected herself. Special, like Kaye mattered. Elodie didn't deserve to be spoken about with such a cold and dispassionate term. "She's not *that woman*."

Courtney raised her hands and backed off. "No offence, kiddo."

"Sorry. That came out wrong." She was being overly sensitive about Elodie when she had no cause to be. The feeling of having her time invaded seemed heightened by her irritation with the situation. She needed to stop blaming Courtney for something that was out of her control, when really, Kaye was simply frustrated with the fact was that she was falling for Elodie, and Elodie couldn't commit to her. She took a deep breath. "She's just really nice. Come here." Kaye went to Courtney and tugged her into a hug. The narrowboat felt too small for them both. "So, did you book a five-star?" she asked, minded of Courtney's rucksack still on the deck and not wanting her to settle on the boat. When Kaye had invited Courtney after she arrived in Sancerre, she'd expected they would share the small double bunk. Now, something about the narrowness of the bed and the idea of sharing with someone that wasn't Elodie felt strangely uncomfortable. Friends should be able to share a bed together but not this bed and not with Courtney. She would hate to reach out in her sleep and touch Courtney. Courtney might think Kaye had been liberated and changed her mind about the status of their relationship, and that would be extremely awkward. Though she was sure they would laugh it off, she knew she wouldn't be able to sleep.

"I thought I might stay with you." Courtney looked over her shoulder to the dinette. "It's kinda cramped in here though."

Kaye filled Courtney's glass. "You've only got a few nights, why not enjoy them in style in one of the hotels? We can have dinner together, and you'd be closer to the nightlife."

"Are there any clubs then?"

Kaye thought about the Blue Room and shook her head. The Blue Room would be perfect for Courtney with so many women to enjoy casual sex with, but if she did it would taint Kaye's appreciation of the space and her experience there. She wanted to hold onto her memory and she certainly didn't want to be in the room with Courtney having sex with other women. It would be like watching her sister, and that was just wrong. Was she being selfish? Maybe, Elodie could arrange for Courtney to go there on her own. Courtney was referring to nightclubs though, and Kaye hadn't discovered anything like that in Sancerre. "There are just hotels, guest houses, and restaurants. They have live bands in the evenings...sometimes...I think."

Courtney raised one side of her lip and glanced around her. "This is tiny," she said.

"Give me your phone, and I'll ask Elodie if she can get you booked in somewhere. In fact, I'll stay the night with you, if you like?" A hotel would feel fine, and the bed would be a lot bigger. She refilled Courtney's glass.

Courtney unlocked her phone and handed it to Kaye. Kaye took a deep breath. Why did this feel so awkward? She called Elodie and for a taxi and handed the phone back to Courtney. "I'll just pack a bag."

"Sure. I'll be on the deck." Courtney tapped out a message on her phone.

It seemed odd not to feel the warm air on her face as the taxi made its way into the village. Cycling, she'd become used to the fresh air and got a lot fitter. She preferred it to the air conditioning that was too cold and the stale smell of tobacco and perfume that oozed from the fabric seat. It reminded her of a London black cab after a night out. She still couldn't explain her irrational unease, but it was tangible in the tightness in her stomach and the pressure in her head. It wasn't Courtney's fault. Françoise had said, "When we feel an emotion we don't like, we first need to look inside ourselves for the answer rather than just blaming something that's happening on the outside." She sighed softly, smiled at Courtney, and leaned into her arm. "It is great to see you, sweetheart. I'm sorry, I was a bit thrown by you showing up."

Courtney linked her arm through Kaye's. "It's okay, kiddo. I should have told you I was coming."

"You tried." Kaye said, mindful of Mylene trying to contact Elodie at the convent.

The boutique hotel was a hidden jewel. Its three-storey façade scaled skyward from a single lane street that had no footpath. What few cars passed did so slowly and from one direction. It was inconspicuous as a hotel. But for the small sign above its door and the symbols that identified it as an acclaimed five-star accommodation, its front entrance mirrored the shorter residential properties either side of it. Inside, the lounge had a beamed low ceiling and large off-white stone fireplace within which an aga stove featured. The hotel had an earthy feel. It was clean and with only six guest bedrooms, a sanctuary of tranquillity.

"This is quirky," Courtney said as she snuck a peek into the lounge.

"Elodie says it has one of the best reputations in the village."

Kaye smiled as she took the key from their host, a woman who reminded her of a tiny bird with small dark eyes, a narrow, pointed nose, and a thin wiry frame that made her look frail.

"Your room is on the third level. Dinner is at eight. We wish you a pleasant stay. There is wine in the fridge and spirits in the cabinet in the lounge. Help yourself to drinks, and please let me know what you take."

"Thank you," Kaye said and gave another smile to make up for the fact that Courtney, who was still poking around in the lounge, had failed to acknowledge their host.

"They just let you help yourself?" Courtney whispered as they climbed the stairs.

"Yes. It's called trust. Isn't it wonderful?"

"That would never work in a London hotel."

Kaye thought about the incident in Paris as she opened the bedroom door. "Wouldn't work in Paris either. Things are different in the villages. It's more relaxed and community based, I guess." The bed was at least twice the size of the small double bed on the boat even though the room was still tiny by comparison with the bedrooms in Elodie's chateau. She could manage to share for one night, and then she'd leave Courtney and go back and sleep on the boat, or maybe back to Elodie's. The thought of sleeping at Elodie's sent a pleasing tremor through her. She put her overnight bag on the bedside table.

"Very natty." Courtney dropped her rucksack on the floor and went to the window. "Tidy view."

Kaye went and looked out. It didn't compare to the vista from Elodie's barn, but it was pleasant enough, overlooking the street below and the cobbled square just a stone's throw away. The church's spires poked at a deep blue sky, and the plains extended beyond the outskirts of the town's rooftops to the horizon.

"Fancy a drink?" Courtney asked.

Kaye didn't particularly, but her friend was only here for a short time so they should celebrate. "Sure." They wandered back down the stairs and into the lounge.

"Hello, again."

Kaye held Mylene's easy gaze and heat rushed to her cheeks. "Oh, hi."

Courtney glanced from Kaye to Mylene and back to Kaye.

The air became thick for a moment, and then Kaye's thoughts caught up with her. "Courtney, this is Mylene, a friend of Elodie's. Mylene, this is my friend from London."

Mylene held out her hand. "Great to meet you."

Courtney grinned. "Yeah, you too."

"Can I get you both a drink?" Mylene made her way to the cabinet.

Courtney nodded. "Sure. Thanks. I'll have a vodka and Coke, if they have it."

Kaye sat on the couch. "You're staying here?" The answer to the question was blindingly obvious, but in the moment the obvious seemed too complex to process.

The can popped and fizzed as Mylene opened it. She mixed Courtney's drink and gave it to her. "What can I get you, Kaye? Red wine?"

"Thank you."

Mylene's smile was warm, and though she must have changed over the years, Kaye could see why Elodie had been attracted to her. It wasn't just her physical appearance. There was a softness in her eyes that conveyed kindness and compassion. She was the sort of woman Kaye could easily spend time with and would like to know better. She wanted to ask her about Elodie and their time at school together. She wanted to know her intentions toward Elodie, but she wasn't brave enough to ask something so personal. She took the glass of wine and leaned back on the couch.

"You're from London?" Mylene asked Courtney.

"Yeah. You're American?"

Mylene shook her head. "I lived in California for a while, but I was born in France. I live in London now."

"Where?"

"I have a place in Kingston. You?"

"In the city. I rent a flat the size of a postage stamp. I used to work three-hundred metres from my front door, but I'm in between jobs."

"What do you do?"

"Branding, marketing campaigns, and messaging. I'm what they call a creative analyst. What about you?"

"I'm a buyer. Wine." She held up her glass.

"Now there's a job I could do, eh, Kaye?" Courtney laughed.

Kaye smiled and took a small sip of her wine.

"Maybe you could show me some of your work while you're here," Mylene said to Courtney. "I might be able to introduce you to a few people. I can't promise anything, but you never know. It's a tough recruitment market at the moment, but things are still moving through networks and contacts. If I can help, I'll be happy to."

Courtney flushed. "Thanks. Are your folks still in the US?"

Kaye saw a flash of something in Mylene's eyes. It lasted no more than a couple of seconds but in that moment, she'd looked sad.

“No. I lived with my grandparents. My parents died when I was a child. I was my grandmother’s primary carer until she died. Her passing gave me the impetus to take a new job.”

Kaye could see how Mylene and Elodie would have been good friends, how easily they would have been drawn together. Mylene clearly cared deeply about her grandmother, as Elodie had for her own. “That must have been difficult.”

Mylene sipped her drink and smiled with warmth. “It was.”

“So, you’re not with anyone then?” Courtney asked.

Kaye cringed. She glared at her friend who shrugged and wiggled her eyebrows.

Mylene gave Courtney a gentle smile. “No, I’m single. I was dating before I left the US. I’ve just never found anyone special to settle down with.”

“I know what you mean,” Courtney said.

Kaye almost choked on her wine—Courtney who wasn’t the settling down type. Kaye imagined Mylene was referring to the fact that she’d never found anyone as special as Elodie. Mylene was the settling down type too. Did Mylene think that Kaye was with Elodie? Anyone could read the attraction between the two of them.

“So, you don’t have someone special?” Mylene asked Courtney.

Courtney blushed. Kaye smiled to herself. It was amusing to see her friend flustered by a good-looking woman who wasn’t going to fall for Courtney’s cheap lines.

“I’m with someone now, actually,” Courtney said.

Kaye frowned. “Really?”

Courtney glared at her. “I haven’t had the chance to talk to you about it.”

Kaye smiled and studied Courtney. Was this the woman she’d had sex with and then got the job from? She hoped not. A shiver crawled down Kaye’s spine as she recalled her own job interview with Sylvie that had led to their first sexual encounter soon after. The rest was history. She hoped Courtney hadn't done something she might later regret.

Mylene looked at Kaye. "What about you, Kaye? Are you and Elodie lovers?"

Mylene's bluntness took her by surprise, and she flushed. Courtney grinned broadly at her. "We're..." Yes, they were lovers without a future. "We are. We've not long met though. I'm travelling, and I'll be moving on soon." She didn't know why she'd felt the need to tell Mylene that she would be leaving, but she monitored Mylene's response very closely. Mylene's expression barely shifted, and she didn't know whether to feel relieved or even more confused.

"She doesn't seem to have changed much," Mylene said.

Kaye saw affection in Mylene's eyes as she mused, and she knew they shared a similar connection. One of them in the past, the other in the present. She couldn't think about the future without the weight of emptiness depressing her, because Elodie wouldn't feature in her future. *You will find someone who deserves you.* Elodie's words still stung like ice. Why couldn't Elodie see that she was deserving of Kaye? If she did, would she want Kaye as much as Kaye wanted her, or did Elodie still secretly feel more for Mylene than she had admitted? Mylene was lovely, Kaye couldn't deny that. How could Kaye *make* Elodie see that Kaye wouldn't abandon her? If Elodie believed that then maybe they could be together.

19.

SHE'S FLOATING AND THERE'S no telling whether the warmth comes from within her or from the outside. It doesn't really matter, because it's all the same thing to Elodie. Where one source of energy ends, so the other has already begun. She's inside the collective consciousness, the stored knowledge of everything that has ever happened that lies in the ether. She knows that her life could be different, but she can't work out how exactly to change things, because the shadow inside her taunts her about being undeserving of love. Love as a concept is intangible, and the enduring nature of the feeling is out of reach. Others can have someone who will stay with them, who will look after them and care for them, who will love them and protect them. God gave her a taste of love only to take it away again.

God is great, she's been told, but like the voice that talks to her of a love she cannot have, she can't see the greatness in God either. He's cruel because He made her like she is, and He's unrelenting because He makes her see the beauty in other women and shows her that she cannot have with them what she should have with a man, and that's why Mylene was taken away from her. She knows God isn't going to let her into heaven, because she doesn't follow His rules. She's okay burning in hell though. She likes the heat more, unless she's wearing her school skirt and blazer, in which case, she'd rather be rolling in the snow to rid herself of the irritating itch.

She spreads her arms and makes gentle waves that glide her slowly across the surface of the lake. Her hips rise as she leans her head back, and Sister Mary's face appears, cotton-wool white in the cloudless sky, which is odd because her face doesn't belong there. It's almost as round as her breasts, she has a rosy mark on each puffy cheek, and her blue eyes sparkle like sapphires when she smiles. Blue is Elodie's favourite colour, blue like the sea and the sky. Blue is the colour of love. It has so many different shades, and she imagines the collective conscious residing in the blue. Blue is a constant in which everything belongs, including her. Sister Mary is smiling at her, and the look in her eyes conveys secrets. It's then that Elodie notices that Sister Mary is naked, her breasts large and taunting. She's been sent by God to tease her or by the devil to encourage her. She can't quite decide.

Elodie's mother is sat in an armchair in the corner of the lake. It's the antique chair from the small reception room in the chateau, the one with a high carved wooden backrest and hard arms. The seat was very bouncy once but the last time Elodie sat in it, it sagged in the middle through the round hole in the wood seat. Her mother doesn't seem to notice that it's uncomfortable. She looks older than Elodie remembers her, her hair hanging in lifeless clumps, wet and unkempt. Her cheeks are puffy but not like Sister Mary's. They're a bloated kind of puffy, and there's a grey pallor to her skin that should be tanned because of living in the sun. She looks sickly. The blue doesn't come through her eyes. They're dark brown like the earth, and she imagines secrets buried beneath them. Shadows fall low down her cheek, and there's a red rim like lipstick that has been used as eyeliner. Her mouth is cast at an angle as if in a half-smile, but then her nose is turned up as if in disgust. Her lips are thin and bright red, closer to purple. She wears her nightgown, a faded peach colour that makes her look scrawny. She takes a long drink of the red wine from the glass that wavers in her hand. The glass crashes to the floor and she slouches. A policeman appears behind her mother. He's laughing. Her mother's eyes are closed, and her skin becomes paler, and the shape of her mother's skull slowly appears from beneath the disappearing veneer that was her skin. Her mother shouldn't be there, not with Sister Mary being naked.

Elodie allows her hips to drop and dives down to where the light can't reach her, into the darker blue. It's cold and shadows move beneath her. They too are laughing. It's not the joyful sound that children make because the voices have a richness that comes with maturity, and there's a mocking tone to them that is familiar and linked to the stabbing pain in her chest. She keeps diving, beyond the voices, and makes her way to the cave that can only be reached from the bottom of the lake. This is the cave that she alone has discovered. It's a magical place. Her happy place.

As she brings herself to the surface of the water inside the cave, the warmth comes again, and the water here is crystal clear. She shouts out "I love you" just to hear the echo and imagines the words are meant for her. Tears burn her eyes. She lays back in the water and stares upwards. She smiles up at Aquarius who appears in the opening at the apex. His leaning back body with his arm thrown out to the side is the brightest she's ever seen him, probably because it's October. The reds in the rock take shape, and she smiles as Mylene's face forms, and then Mylene comes closer.

She reaches up and cups Mylene's breast in her hand. The puckered nipple grows at her touch and soft encouraging moans fall from Mylene's lips. Lips that Elodie is desperate to kiss. As she moves closer, she wraps her arm around Mylene's waist. Their stomachs are touching, breasts too, and they're floating together. Mylene's eyes close and her lips part. Then there is just the softness of Mylene's mouth against her lips. There's tenderness and warmth in the silky wetness as their tongues collide and explore. Elodie is immersed in the sensations at her lips. The softness of Mylene's mouth and face is sensual, there's a lightness of pressure and then a heaviness, a depth and then the barest of contact that passes between them. Shivers slip down her neck and shoulders. She's trembling inside and out, and the warm water ripples in red waves, away from her trembling body. The image transforms and for a moment she feels nothing.

A dusting of freckles appears across cheeks that are now pale, and her hair becomes a light brown. The softness of her smile and the lightness in her eyes is that of Kaye's. Elodie's heart races as if it will soon burst into a thousand stars. Kaye is smiling down at her. Sweet, sweet Kaye. Kaye's lips are moving but she can't hear the words. She's laughing, not at Elodie, but with her and holding out her hand. A light feeling bubbles up in Elodie's chest, lifting her from the water. She's on her way to heaven, with Kaye, and she knows she's loved.

"Elodie."

Elodie blinked and rubbed her eyes. Her heart calmed as her focus slowly returned. Yvette hovered above her with a glass of champagne in her hand. "You disturbed the weirdest dream just as I got to a good bit."

"You had a sappy smile on your face I have not seen before. Who is she?" Yvette sipped from her glass.

Elodie sat up on the chaise longue. The essence of the dream echoed through her nervous system, more disconcerting than pleasant. Mylene appearing in her dream had been comforting, like a path to a known destination. And although the sensual feelings Elodie had as an adolescent hadn't completely faded, and maybe they never would, she was confident that she didn't feel as strongly attracted to her as she did to Kaye. She had no inclination to reincarnate their relationship, but she would treasure the fond memories she held of their time together without regret. The Mylene piece of her puzzle had been put in its rightful place. But Kaye's image had also stirred something in her that was both enticing and terrifying. Its name? Love. "Who is who?"

"Kaye. You mumbled the name twice. I came to wake you up about ten minutes ago but that look on your face stopped me."

Elodie looked at the glass in Yvette's hand. "You'd have drunk that by now if you'd been waiting that long."

Yvette sat in the chaise next to Elodie and sipped her drink. "This is my second. I had to get a refill. So, who is Kaye?"

She's wonderful. "No one. She's just a woman from England who's been picking for us." Elodie's gut twisted at her unfair dismissal of Kaye. She bit her lip and avoided Yvette's gaze. "I've been like a cultural guide while she's here. She's an interior designer and has an interest in architecture. Maybe you should commission her to do this place up."

"Well, I was hoping you'll take over the club, in which case you can commission her."

"I'm really not sure about that."

Yvette's hand trembled as she rested it on Elodie's arm. "Jean is dying."

Elodie blinked. Yvette's tone matched the genuinely subdued look in her eyes. Elodie shook her head. "Oh, no. I'm so sorry."

Yvette put her glass on the table. "He's got a few months at best. Grade four brain tumour, would you believe? He's refusing treatment."

Elodie puffed out a breath. Yvette's eyes teared, and Elodie's heart ached. Yvette's hand trembled on her arm. "I'm so sorry."

"Turns out he's known for months. He got the sticks to help with his balance. Bizarre, that you can live a lifetime with someone and not see what's happening in front of your eyes." She pulled her hand from Elodie's grip and wiped a tear from her cheek. "I need to be with him in his final weeks. He is going to need full-time care and stubborn as he is, he's refusing to allow the nurses into the house."

Elodie nodded. "I'll take care of the club."

Yvette sighed and leaned back in the seat. "Thank you. You know the baroness's party is next Saturday."

"Yes."

"Why don't you take Kaye? It will give the women someone different to talk about and be an interesting cultural experience for your friend."

"I've already asked her to join me." She didn't want to get into a discussion with Yvette about Kaye. Like a good mother, she would ask a string of questions that Elodie wouldn't want to answer.

"Good. Did you get anywhere with an investor for Lady Babberage?"

Elodie appreciated the change of topic. She'd explained the offer to Kaye. She hadn't been averse to the idea and was going to take advice first. "I'm still working on it."

"I might not go to the party. It depends on Jean. Is Kaye the *sociable* type?"

Elodie shook her head. Not sociable in the club sense that Yvette meant.

"I am quite sociable, I think. Hello, I'm Kaye."

Kaye came into Elodie's focus, along with an unfamiliar woman that Elodie assumed was Courtney.

"And I'm Yvette." She looked Kaye up and down, then nodded at Elodie. "Well, sociable is fun. We were just talking about the baroness's party." Yvette smiled briefly at Courtney then gave her attention to Kaye.

Elodie's stomach dropped faster than a lump of concrete dropped down a deep well. How long had Kaye been within earshot of them? Heat flushed her face as she retraced their conversation. She turned and smiled to Kaye and Courtney avoiding direct eye contact with both women. Courtney stood closer to Kaye than was necessary and seemed to occupy her personal space with her arm touching Kaye's. There was a predatory nature to Courtney's expression as she lingered her attention on one woman and then another, scanning the room as if hunting down her next prey. Everyone had a background that breathed life into their motivation and Elodie wasn't in the best position to judge Kaye's friend, though something about Courtney's manner galled Elodie, and she couldn't put her finger on what specifically that was.

Kaye smiled at Yvette. "I'm looking forward to it. I have a beautiful dress to wear."

"Excellent," Yvette said.

Courtney cleared her throat.

"Sorry, I should properly introduce my friend. Courtney, this is Elodie...and this is Yvette, who I've only just met too."

"Bonjour," Yvette said. She glanced briefly at Courtney and gave a tight smile and Elodie got the sense that she hadn't warmed to Kaye's friend.

Elodie straightened her back and looked directly at Courtney. "It's a pleasure to meet you. I hope you are enjoying the hotel."

She'd thought about heading into the village and checking they'd settled in but had dismissed the idea as intrusive and unwarranted. Kaye had said that Courtney was only staying a couple of nights, and she hadn't wanted to impose on their time together. She'd missed Kaye and now just wanted to get out of the spa with her and back to the barn. Elodie prayed she hadn't overheard her dismissal of Kaye to Yvette. It had been a flippant response and not the truth of what Kaye meant to her. "It will look stunning on you," she said.

"The hotel is the biz. Thanks for hooking us up. And your friend, Mylene, is super cool. We're meeting up to talk about work when she's back in the UK."

Yvette looked from one woman to the other with a deepening frown. She settled her focus on Elodie. "I feel I've missed a lifetime of gossip in less than a week. Who is Mylene?"

"Mylene's an old school friend."

"Is she of good standing? A potential investor?"

"I don't know. She's here on business. I can ask her when I see her." Was she the only one feeling awkward? Arranging a meeting with Mylene was still on her to-do list. "Can I get you both a drink?" she asked and stood swiftly to avoid further questions.

"Cheers," Courtney said and winked at Kaye.

Elodie avoided Kaye's gaze as she'd walked past her. The messages in the dream had been deeply unsettling. As wonderful as she'd felt when Kaye had entered the dream, she felt twice as bad seeing her here now. This wasn't about her casual dismissal of Kaye, though that still jarred, and she wished she'd had the courage to tell Yvette how she felt about Kaye. She wanted the dream with Kaye, but something deep-rooted stopped her from reaching out and making it happen.

She ran her fingers through her hair, the sounds in the room becoming distant and indistinguishable. Her mother's image came back to her. She'd never understood why her mother had been so unhappy. The prescribed medication hadn't helped, other than to facilitate her end. Sometimes the sadness she felt when thinking about her mother's sorry life was too quickly overshadowed by anger at having been repeatedly let down. Elodie had never truly grieved. Maybe she was angry with herself for not being able to help her mother. She'd tried to forgive her, but she hadn't been able to let go of the hurt and cruelty she'd suffered. Parents had a duty to take care of their children and hers had failed spectacularly on that front. Then she felt guilty, because she was wealthier than many people who'd had harder lives and had nowhere and no one to turn to. But still, she felt cheated by what had happened in her own life, as if she'd missed out. She just wished she'd known another side to her mother. There had to have been one. No one was all bad. She wished she'd been able to ask questions and get answers. She wished they'd been closer and that her mother had forgiven her. *Forgiven me for what though? What did I do that was so terrible?* For being so unlovable that her mother's only escape was to abandon her completely. The memory of her first day at the convent invaded her mind: her mother's laughter, a shove in the back accompanied with, "Be a good girl now." She rubbed her eyes and swept away the image. She ordered a bottle of champagne and hors d'oeuvres. She knew how to be an excellent host. Status quo life, as Kaye had said. No one gets hurt that way.

20.

"REMIND ME WHY I agreed to pick grapes in the dark?"

Kaye nudged Courtney as they walked towards the floodlights. "Because it's your last night here, and you can't possibly come all this way and miss out on the fun. Anyway, you need to apply what you learned from the taster."

"Honestly, the only thing I'm missing out on right now is sleep."

"It's ten-thirty. You wouldn't be back from a club until gone three on a Friday night."

"Don't remind me. What kind of place doesn't have a nightclub?"

Kaye nudged Courtney again and chuckled. "You can't be out on the town now you've got a girlfriend."

Courtney stayed silent as they ambled toward the vines, where the lights got brighter and the voices nearer. "Where are you going from here?"

Kaye sighed. She felt torn. She didn't want to leave, but there was little point in staying much longer. Every time she saw Elodie her stomach tied in knots, and she'd sensed her withdrawing from her little by little since their paths had crossed at the spa. "Maybe across to Italy and down to Sardinia." The names of the places might as well have been related to a quiz she had no desire to win for the lack of interest they stirred. Her excitement for travel had been replaced by apathy and her sense of adventure had been dulled.

"Sounds great, so why the pancake face?"

"I..."

"Elodie."

Kaye nodded.

Courtney stopped walking and put her hands on her hips. "Look, I get that she's stunning and sexy. Hell, even I'd go there, and she's not exactly my type."

"You said you didn't have a type."

Courtney glanced toward the lights. "Everyone has a type."

"That's what I said."

Courtney blew out a breath and frowned. "Look, it's great that you've had an awesome time here and you look incredible, so it's clearly done you a world of good. Maybe we can go clubbing when you get back. You know the best way to get over someone is to start up with someone else." She shrugged.

The thought of clubbing increased the dullness and weight of the ache in Kaye's chest. The last thing she wanted to do was try and find a partner at a nightclub. "That's just not me."

"Kiddo, look at the facts. She gave you a beautiful dress that must have cost a mint then immediately asked you about shedding a load of dosh in some scheme you've got no idea about."

"It wasn't like that." She'd never got the sense that Elodie was trying to buy her or con her.

"Well, it sure sounds something like that." She waved her hand around. "All this could be on the verge of folding for all you know. You never know what's going on behind closed doors. Why do you think I'm out of a job?"

She felt small, as she had done before leaving London, oppressed by someone who thought they knew about everything better than she did. "Because you told them to stick it where the sun don't shine, I think you said."

"I did, but only because the business was going under."

"You didn't say that."

"You've been a little self-absorbed, and we haven't chatted about me much."

That stung. Elodie had used the same phrase when talking about her mother. Elodie had said that her mother left the business with significant debt, but she hadn't ever even hinted that she might need money from Kaye. On the contrary, Elodie had been very generous. And whilst she'd mentioned that she'd taken on a loan to save her business, that had been years ago. She worked as an investment broker of some sort for the club too, which must surely generate an income, and with the renovations she planned to undertake on the chateau, Kaye had never got the impression that the business was doing anything other than thriving.

This was Courtney trying to protect Kaye and all she felt was sucked back into the world she'd worked so hard to extricate herself from. Not once had Elodie tried to persuade Kaye to think in a particular way, in the way that Courtney seemed to think it was her place to do so. That was another of the qualities that made Elodie different from anyone else Kaye knew.

Kaye wished she hadn't said anything to Courtney about the investment opportunity. She'd told her in a fit of frustration after seeing Elodie with Yvette, saying that Elodie could stick her investment, even though she didn't mean it. She'd felt dismissed by Elodie at the spa, hurt by the coldness she'd sensed from her and the lack of intimacy that she'd known in the way Elodie normally looked at her. She'd become accustomed to the softness in her gaze and the kindness in her smile. Elodie had been distant and distracted on and off during her visit, but she'd not felt it more acutely than at the spa, even though Elodie had been the perfect host to them all. Kaye couldn't stop herself from thinking that Elodie would never be able to give her what she needed. Love wasn't enough. She wanted the vows and the stable relationship that came with such a commitment.

"Sounds like she's after your money to me. Maybe, she's just smarter at getting it than some of the street-crooks out there. She's not going to rip you off for a few quid. The toffs deal in big bucks."

Kaye closed her eyes. Money. Crook. Ripped off. The words tightened every sinew in her body, and she wanted to scream at Courtney to shut up. She didn't want to think of Elodie that way. She *knew* Elodie wasn't like that. The assault ricocheted through her mind and fired up anger and frustration, but any significant verbal retort died before it reached her lips. "She's not a toff."

"And then there's her friend that shows up, blast from the past, who you said she clearly still likes...a lot. And who wouldn't?" Courtney shook her head. "I can see how you got drawn into this one. She's hot and she's charming."

"Stop it." Kaye rolled her shoulders to free the tension. Who was she mad at? Courtney, for her relentless digs at Elodie's character when she didn't know the first thing about her and for her apparent lack of awareness of the distress she was causing. Or was her anger related to Kaye not being able to entirely dismiss some of the points Courtney had raised, especially about Mylene turning up. Kaye might be confused by the depth of feelings she had for Elodie, what with her being on the back of a divorce and in a glorious setting that was so refreshing, and her thoughts were conflicted, but she wouldn't accept that Elodie was a crook. "You don't know her like I do."

Courtney shrugged, still apparently oblivious to the turmoil she'd elicited in Kaye. "I know you, kiddo."

Kaye shook her head and stood a little straighter. "No, you don't. I'm not who I was," she said calmly, trying to keep her anger in check.

Courtney nudged Kaye and smiled. "Look on the bright side. You've not signed your life away."

Kaye didn't smile. The gulf between her and Courtney couldn't be any wider. She had tried to enjoy her time here with Courtney, but she really did remind her too closely of her ex. She was quick to judge based on unfounded theory and would put two and two together and come up with sixty-five. Kaye was glad Courtney was leaving in the morning.

She could see how it might look from the outside. She couldn't *not* trust Elodie though or maybe her heart didn't want to find fault. Elodie had been true to her word. Kaye's financial advisor told her the investment was a sound proposition, as long as she didn't need it to mature before the current owner passed away. The "small property" on the estate was a four-bedroom detached cottage with its own gardens and stables, just the kind of place Kaye had dreamed of owning one day. It was a genuine offer that she intended to give serious thought. Right now, something like that would give her the opportunity to get away from everything and everyone, including Courtney, and she could truly consider what it was she wanted from the rest of her life.

She would create her own destiny, even though Elodie thought that wasn't entirely possible. The idea of more travelling had lost its appeal. It was as if she'd already found what she'd needed, and the search had come to an end. Courtney might mean well, but slating Elodie's character had created a rift between them that Kaye had no desire to close. For the first time in a very long time, she missed the comfort of being near her family. Perhaps she'd go to her mum's first. "Can we talk about something else?" she asked.

Courtney shoved her hands in her pockets and started walking. "So, you're seeing a real baroness tomorrow night?"

"Apparently." It didn't feel much like a change of topic.

"I mean, a real one. Like royalty."

Kaye sighed. She acknowledged the foreman with a weary smile, and they went to the section of vines they would be picking. "Yes, she's a real one."

"No shit. That's like the craziest thing ever. What do you say to a baroness?"

"Hello, I guess."

"Hello is a good place to start any conversation, I believe."

Kaye turned away and looked across the rows of vines. Her heart skipped a beat and her pulse raced when she saw Elodie. Bitterness rose in her throat.

Elodie smiled. "Hi."

The small word landed so softly, with a power that melted her. "Hi."

Elodie made her way toward them. Kaye's knees became weak and her head dizzy. Stars appeared before her eyes. She bent over and blinked, and a rush of blood filled her ears.

Elodie rushed forward and sank to her knees in front of Kaye. "What's wrong?"

Kaye shook her head, consoled by Elodie's touch on her arm. "I just came over a bit woozy. I'll be fine."

"Are you okay, kiddo? We should go."

Courtney placed her hand on her shoulder, but Kaye stood slowly, brushing off her contact.

"I'm fine, honestly." She wasn't. Her head was spinning, her heart was aching, and her legs were struggling to cope with the increasing weight that came from the stress of seeing Elodie and potentially having to endure Courtney's next assault. "What are you doing here?"

Elodie looked concerned. "I wanted to check you hadn't forgotten what to do."

Kaye smiled weakly, a reflection of her despair for Courtney rather than her tenderness for Elodie. She hadn't come out to the vines to check on her during the week she'd picked. The excuse was endearing. She saw faint humour reflected in Elodie's broadening smile and the faintest discomfort as Elodie ran her fingers through her hair.

"Are you sure you're fit?"

Kaye strengthened her smile. “Yes, I’ll be fine. Just give me a minute.” She took in a few deep breaths. She couldn’t deny the soothing effect Elodie’s presence had on her and her yearning heart.

“Are you picking?” Elodie asked Courtney.

“Yeah.”

“Good. We’ve got a lot to do tonight. There’s rain coming.” Elodie held up a pair of clippers. “If you two take one side, I’ll take the other.” She indicated the row of vines.

“You want a race?” Courtney asked.

Elodie’s laugh had the effect of Baroque music, lifting Kaye’s mood instantly. Lightness moved through her, her stomach felt warm, and she calmed.

“If it means we get the rest of this crop in tonight, then yes. I’ll race you both.” Elodie’s gaze lingered on Kaye for a long moment. “If you’re up to it?”

She nodded. Yes, unfortunately her heart was still up for Elodie, and yes, she was ready for the challenge. She ducked down and clipped four bunches in a row before Elodie had made her way back to the other side of the vines. She placed the grapes carefully in the bucket and continued to clip. She found her rhythm, and as long as she concentrated on the grapes rather than on the scent of Elodie that wafted across her path from the other side of the vines, all would be well. At least Courtney had stopped talking at her. Courtney was wrong about Elodie, and Kaye had never been more certain of anything.

“This is breaking me,” Courtney said after a short time. She stood and rubbed her back.

“Don’t stay bent over for too long. Make sure you stretch regularly,” Kaye said and heard Elodie chuckle at the repetition of her own advice. Kaye’s chest bubbled lightly. She’d be willing to pick all night if it meant she could stay closer to Elodie, and she would breathe a sigh of relief when Courtney left.

21.

SHE BLINKED HER EYES open to the thumping sound at the barn door and squinted at her phone. Ten past four. She'd been asleep less than an hour. The vines were shrouded in darkness and rain tapped out a heavy rhythm against the window. Lights from inside the factory spilled out to form a halo around the building. It would be unlikely that there was a problem that needed her input at this time of the night. She threw on her robe and went down the stairs. She couldn't see a vehicle in the drive. The thumping came again. She unlocked and opened the door.

"Kaye."

Kaye's wet hair streaked down her face and her arms were wrapped around her body as she shivered. Her bike lay against the side of the barn. "I couldn't sleep."

Elodie's initial shock and concern that after the incident in the field earlier that something might be wrong with Kaye gave way to a smile. Rain trickled down Kaye's face, dripped from her nose, and clung to her eyelashes. "You cycled here to tell me that?"

Kaye's teeth chattered, and her eyes shifted as if to avoid looking directly at Elodie. "Yes, I did."

Elodie resisted the urge to pull Kaye into her arms and stood back from the door. Kaye stepped unsteadily across the threshold and brushed against her. Elodie shuddered with the intensity of the brief touch, desire tempered by concern. "Is something wrong?"

Kaye held Elodie in an unwavering gaze. "Yes. I mean, no... I mean, I don't know."

Elodie's chest thundered and her stomach dived. She closed the door, turned to Kaye and held her gently by the shoulders. The shivering seemed worse, and her eyes were slightly bloodshot, like she'd been crying. "What's happened?"

"Will you hold me, please?" Kaye whispered.

Elodie drew Kaye to her and held her tightly. She tried to figure out why Kaye was distressed. She'd sensed friction between Kaye and her friend. Even though she hadn't warmed to Courtney particularly, she seemed nice enough, and Kaye wasn't the sort of person to make friends with distasteful people. Kaye had seemed fine when Elodie had dropped her at the narrowboat just an hour and a half ago. She was a little subdued maybe, but Elodie had put that down to tiredness. Kaye's head felt heavy against her chest. She squeezed Kaye lightly and kissed the top of her head. "Has something bad happened?" she whispered and felt Kaye's head rock against her.

"I don't..."

Elodie closed her eyes. "You can talk to me."

Kaye wrapped her arms around Elodie. She must have sensed the fear that coursed through Elodie's veins, because now she held Elodie, and it was as if she didn't intend to let go. "Please tell me what's wrong."

"I'm sorry," Kaye muttered as she buried her face into Elodie's chest.

Elodie eased her grip, creating a sliver of space between them. Kaye's eyes were dark and her breaths hot and fast, and the tight ball in Elodie's gut burned like hell. Kaye was leaving.

Kaye ran her fingers through Elodie's hair and released a soft sigh. "You're so beautiful."

Elodie couldn't read the look in her eyes. Kaye stared at her for a long moment, absent of a smile or the fine lines that hinted at her happiness. Her breaths were short and shallow.

"Can I stay with you tonight?"

A gush of air rocketed from Elodie's chest. She'd misread the signals. "Of course." She moved out of their embrace and slowly lifted Kaye's chin. With a slight tremble in her hand, she lifted the errant strands of hair that had stuck to

Kaye's face and looked deeply into her eyes. She traced the line of freckles across her cheek with the lightest touch. "You're cold," she said. Kaye looked striking and sad, like a portrait, and she couldn't capture the reason for the ache in her heart. Kaye shook her head though she shivered, and her dress was sopping wet. The quietness that appeared in Kaye's expression stole Elodie's breath. She took Kaye's hand and led her up the stairs. The silence, heady with anticipation, gained potency with each step to the top of the mezzanine.

"Can I get you a drink or something?"

Kaye bit her lip. "I just want to spend the night with you."

Elodie swallowed hard to alleviate the tightness that clamped her throat. The trembling that coursed from her chest to her hands drew her back to her time at the convent when she first touched Mylene. Why did this situation feel so very awkward, so oddly intense, and yet so deeply captivating? "I need a drink." She never *needed* a drink, but she poured two glasses of red wine from the decanter. She left one on the table and sipped the other, staring over the top of the glass at Kaye.

Kaye went to the table, picked up the glass, and sipped. "You don't want me?"

"Of course I do," she said and Kaye smiled faintly. The glass pressed to Kaye's quivering lips increased the throb in Elodie's core.

Kaye gazed at her with her head on a tilt as she often did. It was too much to take.

Kaye slowly closed the space between them and lifted her glass to Elodie's lips. "You need Dutch courage to make love to me?"

Elodie took a long slug from the glass then took it from Kaye's hand and placed both their glasses on the table. She tugged Kaye firmly to her and when their lips met, she released the wine into Kaye's mouth. She continued to explore Kaye with her tongue, sharing the wine between them. She eased back, swallowed, and licked her lips. "You like this?"

Kaye pressed her finger to Elodie's mouth, teasing Elodie's lips apart. Elodie licked and drew Kaye's fingers into her mouth and kissed down to her palm.

"You taste so good," Elodie whispered. She took Kaye's hand and brought it to her breast. The electric sensation at her nipple reached her core instantly. She teased Kaye's dress from her shoulders, cupped her breasts inside the cotton bra, and kissed them. "So perfect." She eased Kaye's bra off her and kissed the soft flesh beneath, then slipped the robe from her own shoulders. She slid Kaye's silk briefs to the floor. Her scent was musky and sweet, like nectar. She lifted Kaye up in her arms, and Kaye wrapped her legs around Elodie's waist. Warmth and soft hairs brushed her stomach, and she buried her head between Kaye's breasts as she walked her to the bed.

Kaye let out a soft moan as Elodie lowered her. Her fingers trembled as she ran them through Elodie's hair and pulled her into a lingering kiss. Elodie eased back and crouched over her and regarded her leisurely. She trailed her fingertips through the fine curls between Kaye's legs. "You smell so delicious." She knelt on the bed and separated Kaye's knees and revelled in her beauty and the slick shine that coated her sex. The line of Kaye's inner thigh was silk to her tongue, the scent of her intoxicating as she moved closer. She tucked her hands beneath Kaye's back to lift her hips, nuzzled into the warm wetness, and inhaled deeply. Pressing her tongue into Kaye, she kissed and licked her. Kaye bucked her hips into Elodie and moaned. She dipped her tongue deeper then trailed a line directly across Kaye's clit.

Kaye arched and tensed. "Don't stop."

Elodie freed her hands, and teased Kaye wider, and pressed her tongue deeper. The throbbing in Elodie's core intensified. She reached down to her own clit and made small circles, increasing the pressure to bring herself closer to orgasm. She drew Kaye's clit into her mouth as she entered her. With slow deep thrusts she found the deepest, softest part of her and then held her there with a gentle massage of her fingers.

"Yes," Kaye screamed as she shook.

Elodie stayed inside Kaye and moved on top of her. She placed tender kisses on her closed eyes, lashes wet with tears, and continued to make tiny movements inside her.

"Oh, God."

Kaye had barely stopped shaking before she tensed around Elodie again. She stilled inside Kaye and watched her orgasm for the second time. She kissed her trembling lips, then down her neck toward her breasts. She eased out and lay on top of her, her legs parted around Kaye's, her clit gently rubbing against Kaye's thigh.

Kaye opened her eyes and stared at Elodie, who couldn't smile through the sadness.

"I love you," Kaye whispered.

Elodie smoothed the hair from Kaye's face and smiled. The words pleaded to her heart but the deeper association, the fear of loss and the acceptance that Kaye was leaving hung like a guillotine above her head. She didn't need to see the silver shine of the razor-sharp blade to know the damage it would inflict on her. She couldn't cope with being abandoned again. She trembled inside, knowing she owed Kaye the truth. *I love you.* She felt it in the ache in her heart, but the words remained a thought.

Tears slid down Kaye's cheeks and Elodie felt her heart fracturing. Tiny splinters, sharp-edged and harsh, scarred her but she couldn't offer Kaye what she considered would be false hope.

Kaye closed her eyes and tugged Elodie to her chest and held her tightly as she began to cry. Elodie wrapped her arms around her and held her tightly, fighting her own tears. She blanked her mind to the truth, the sharp blade stabbing her repeatedly in the chest. Kaye was leaving.

"When are you going?" she asked into Kaye's chest, her voice broken.

"Sunday. After the baroness's dinner party."

A spiralling darkness drew Elodie down at racing speed. Spinning, beyond the bottom of the lake, beyond the sanctuary she'd discovered and into a void. Emptiness brought with it an absence of thought. She wanted to cling to Kaye but held her gently. She wanted to plead for her to stay but silence claimed her voice. She wanted to not feel and yet she felt everything. Sadness, loss, anger, and fear stood like a line of foot soldiers before her, each ready to claim her soul and send her to hell. To finally steal love from her. Joy and happiness were nowhere to be seen. They'd retreated to the hills, defeated before the battle had even begun. Love sucked, precisely because it hurt like this. Kaye was moving on, as she was always destined to do, and that was exactly what Elodie deserved. She'd known this moment would come, but she'd never anticipated the way she would feel. It was as if every buried memory of desertion that she'd ever experienced had coalesced and created this single moment of pain.

The back of her eyes burned, and she closed them. Her throat twisted, and she swallowed hard. Her heart ached. She had to do something, *say* something. She moved from Kaye and looked into her damp eyes, which spoke of the deepest love. "Please stay."

Kaye blinked then stroked Elodie's face. "I can't."

"Why?"

"I want more than you're able to give."

The words landed like a slap across her face. She couldn't deny the truth. "I'll try." Her tone sounded unconvincing.

Kaye leaned toward Elodie, bringing their lips to connect with a whisper of a kiss. She moaned as she moved back, her eyes remaining shut.

"The risk is too high, for me." She opened her eyes and her smile reeked of regret.

A tear slipped onto Elodie's cheek, and Kaye thumbed it away.

"This is hard for me," Kaye said. "I want to be with someone who wants to be with me. I need that commitment, the family, the promise of a future until death do us part."

Nothing Elodie could do or say would change Kaye's mind. She had already tried during their time together. But the closer she got to Kaye, the more she pulled back. Part of her wanted to leap in and take the biggest risk of her life, but the other part, the strongest and darkest part, felt like a clamp around her entire body, restricting her movement and limiting her options.

She had to let Kaye go and not make the situation any more difficult than it was. They would attend the party together, and she would wish Kaye well. Maybe they could stay friends at a distance. She ridiculed the idea before giving it voice. Once Kaye had gone, Elodie would get back to her life, run the club, and give the fallout time to settle. She imagined the scissors in her hand, the blades either side of the strings that attached her and Kaye together. She closed her eyes, squeezed the handles, and the blades sliced through the cord.

22.

KAYE SMOOTHED THE TURQUOISE silk dress across her stomach. It was elegant and fitted her perfectly, not that she could look at herself, because there wasn't a full-length one in the narrowboat.

She would give the gown straight back to Elodie after the event. Her eyes still looked a little puffy, even though she'd applied a slice of cucumber on them for half an hour and used the natural face pack the spa had given her. Whether she actually looked dreadful or just felt it, she couldn't tell.

It had dawned on her as she cycled home that she'd used Elodie to satisfy her own needs. She detested herself for that, but her desire had been so intense that she hadn't been able to stop herself. She'd intended for that night to be their last time. The reality had panned out differently once she'd decided to stay until after the baroness's dinner. The rainy days had passed slowly, and she'd seen very little of Elodie, who'd been busy finishing the harvest, other than to show her some ideas for the chateau. The nights they'd spent together had felt short, tinged with the inevitability of an ending she didn't want to come. She'd declined another visit to the Blue Room, and Elodie had looked relieved. Kaye didn't know how long it would take for desire to fade, but it would happen more easily with distance between them and no contact.

She'd been relieved that Courtney had returned to London. She wouldn't hold her comments about Elodie against her, but the shift between herself and her oldest friend was unlikely to change. They would never be as close as they once had been and would have to redefine their friendship if they were going to salvage it. Whether Courtney was right or wrong about Elodie, and Kaye was sure she was wrong about Elodie's motivations at least, Courtney's assertive opinions about how

Kaye conducted her life, and with whom, had to stop. She wanted a friend in Courtney, not a counsellor or protector.

Kaye needed something different in her life now, and last night she'd questioned the impact of that difference on Courtney and on her family. Either way, it was time to move on in more ways than one. She had made the decision to leave Sancerre not because Courtney's theories stacked up, but because she wanted to be with a woman who wanted to be with her, and by Elodie's own admission that was something she was incapable of. Maybe Elodie would feel safer and more able to commit to a relationship being with Mylene. After all, she hadn't deserted Elodie. Reality sucked.

She rearranged the pins in her hair then made her way to the galley and poured herself a glass of wine. Butterflies fluttered in her stomach as she thought about the dinner and the type of women who would be there. Wealthy women, beyond Kaye's comprehension, who held positions of power and standing. Elodie had said it would be a casual affair, though she had no idea what that meant within these social circles. The sari dress she wore certainly wasn't casual. She turned to the knock and opening of the door.

Her breath caught as Elodie slowly descended the narrow stairs. She took in the jade cummerbund around Elodie's waist, the dark grey trouser suit with jade lining, and the brilliant white shirt, which she wore with its collar open. The tanned skin she'd kissed was so tempting. She took a long, deep breath and willed the pulse between her legs to calm. "You look stunning."

Elodie looked her up and down as she approached. "You look striking. Your hair looks amazing done up like that. You have a beautiful neck." Elodie bit her lip and turned her eyes away from Kaye.

Kaye didn't try to stop the trembling that affected her hands and danced in her stomach. Elodie stared at her, as if undressing her slowly, and she felt delightfully seduced. Elodie would always be irresistible, which was hugely frustrating. Kaye wasn't the only woman to have fallen under her spell, and for a time it had been just the tonic she'd needed. Her breath juddered as she inhaled. She turned away swiftly and plucked a glass from the cupboard. "Wine?"

"A small one. How are you...about tonight?"

Kaye poured slowly with two hands to ensure the wine made it into the glass. "I'm looking forward to meeting some of your friends."

Elodie huffed lightly. "Acquaintances. And they will love you."

Kaye smiled. "I hope so."

Elodie glanced around the galley and the dinette. "This is quaint. I've not been inside a narrowboat before." She took a sip of her wine.

"It's tiny." Kaye wasn't sure why she'd stated the obvious.

"It's meant to be." Elodie smiled.

Kaye felt a fool. It was the sort of inane comment Courtney would have made. She didn't think the boat was particularly small at all, apart from the bed. She'd be happy sharing the space with Elodie though, no matter how small the mattress.

Elodie put her hand on her hip. Heat flooded Kaye's cheeks as she thought of slowly undoing the buttons on her shirt and running her fingertips across Elodie's hot skin and to where that might lead them.

"Shall we go?" Elodie asked and put her glass down.

Kaye left the last of her wine. She followed Elodie upstairs onto the deck. Elodie's perfume and their closeness was exhilarating and alluring, and Kaye wondered how she would get through the evening without wanting to have sex with Elodie...one last time. How many times had she said that? But there had always been another time, and another after that.

That situation would change for good tomorrow when she unmoored the boat and headed back home.

Elodie held out her arm and Kaye took it, clasping her hand around her firm bicep. They ambled along the dark towpath up to the parking area just off the main road and got in the car.

"It's only a half-hour drive," Elodie said.

Sitting was a challenge and not just because of the tight fit of the dress. The throb between Kaye's legs was electric. Half an hour would be purgatory. She needed a distraction. She sat upright in the seat and fitted the belt carefully around her. "Tell me something about yourself that I don't know."

Elodie pulled the car into the road and drove. "There isn't anything you don't already know."

Kaye laughed. "You've not told me your whole life story. There must be more."

"Pretty much. I don't have any dark secrets, if that's what you mean."

Heat consumed Kaye's cheeks. That wasn't what she meant, but the idea of Elodie having secrets was thrilling, like a child excited by the idea of discovering something new and potentially dangerous.

"What about you?" Elodie asked.

"I had to do ballet as a child, and I hated it."

Elodie chuckled. "Sorry, I'm not laughing at you. I would have hated ballet too. I was more into lacrosse, if anything. I wasn't really a team player. I preferred solitary activities such as reading."

"I preferred studying. Is that odd?"

"I don't think so. I used to enjoy astronomy. I have a thing about the stars."

"Do you believe in heaven?"

"No. Do you?"

Something in the certainty in Elodie's tone called to Kaye while she pondered her own views. "I went to a church school as a child too. Most of our village schools are affiliated with the churches. I never quite related to their teaching, though I don't know why. I think I found what I needed studying history. The origins of our existence seem too distant for me to comprehend. It's a bit like thinking about the future. It's too vast and incomprehensible. And yet, the idea of God has stayed with me. I don't really know what that God is though."

"I believe in energy and universal knowledge that we can all tap into if we're open to it."

"Are you open to it?"

Elodie didn't answer for a long moment. "I think I was when I was younger, but I've never allowed myself to explore that part of me fully. Maybe I'm too scared of what I will unearth now."

It was sad. Elodie had held back from creating a different life. From the outside she looked as though she had it all, and yet inside, beneath her skin, her mind had been poisoned by erroneous beliefs. For all that she owned, her life in the detail had been unfulfilling and absent of the love that she'd craved but couldn't hold onto. Kaye believed Elodie had the power to change all that. Maybe one day Elodie would believe she could too.

"You're not a bad person, you know."

Elodie smiled. "Deep down, I think I know that."

Kaye slipped her hand onto Elodie's thigh and squeezed. "It's very sad that the terrible things that happen to us can have such a devastating impact."

"We guard ourselves against being hurt to survive."

"I think so."

They travelled the remainder of the journey in contemplative silence.

Elodie turned the car down a private road and through an electronically controlled gate. A kilometre must have passed before the trees that lined the road came to an end. In front of them stood a period Renaissance style chateau at least twice the size of Elodie's childhood home. Two whitewashed turrets climbed majestically either side of the main entrance door, and two further turrets formed the outer corners of the extensive stone building. A row of eight sash style windows were set out in a symmetrical pattern on the first floor and parallel to the windows on the ground floor. Seven pitched roof windows made up a third-floor level, and each of the turrets had a smaller, fourth-level window. It was majestic. The front of the chateau was bathed in soft white light that made it look like a fairy-tale castle, like something Disney might use for one of their productions.

Tyres crunched on the gravel driveway at the front of the chateau. Someone in a red gown exited a white Tesla at the front of the mansion and walked toward the entrance. The vehicle moved away. Elodie parked the Land Rover to the left side of the main building next to a large stable block.

She leaned toward Kaye, pecked a kiss on her nose, and smiled. "Ready?"

"I'm nervous."

"Don't be. You look gorgeous, and they will all be very jealous." She lifted her hand to Kaye's face, stopped short of touching her, and brought her hand down. "I'd keep religion off the agenda though. There will be a few staunch Catholics in the room."

Kaye laughed. "I know that rule. Religion and politics are a no go."

Elodie exited the car and straightened her jacket as she walked to the other side and opened the door for Kaye. She held out her hand and Kaye took it. "Interior design is always a good topic. And they love talking fashion and wine."

"Thanks. I'll bear that in mind."

Kaye smiled at the man who greeted them at the door. With white hair neatly cut, clean-shaven, with eyes that had seen life, and a cheery smile, he looked like someone's chirpy grandfather.

"Madame Marchand, good evening."

"Good evening, Thomas."

"Madame Sykes, welcome." Thomas dipped his head to Kaye.

"Thank you." Kaye tried to breathe inside the dress that had taken on a vice-like grip around the tension in her ribs. She needed to relax, but that was proving impossible with a racing heart, trembling hands, and heightened senses. Acutely aware of being watched, even though no one in particular was looking at her, she stepped across the threshold.

"The baroness is in the Louis XIV reception room." Thomas gestured to his right.

Kaye scanned the foyer. The Venetian chandelier looked like a crown with flowers in multi-coloured glass paste, three tiers, a multitude of decorations, and transparent purity in the crystal. Kaye stood, breathless for a long moment. It was the most beautiful thing she'd ever seen. Supported by an ornate metal rope structure and hanging from the high vaulted ceiling above, it spun coloured stars and bright white light into the expansive space. She felt Elodie's hand in the small of her back and looked at her. Elodie's smile landed softly, and Kaye felt caressed by her warmth.

"Spectacular, isn't it?"

"I've never seen anything like it."

"Come."

As Elodie led Kaye toward the reception room, the muffled sound of voices became more distinct. A burst of laughter from inside the room made Kaye smile though her insides turned like a washing machine on full spin. She was totally out of her depth. She'd worked with rich clients before, but their wealth was significantly less than the level of affluence here. Understated beauty lay in the minimalist design. Each piece of art, even the paper on the walls, had been carefully selected to create the desired atmosphere in each space. Perhaps this was the difference between old wealth and new wealth. Old wealth was a culture, a way of life ingrained in the fabric of a long ancestral history. New wealth didn't always come with the grounded sense of entitlement that Kaye sensed here.

She reached out and took Elodie's arm and immediately felt a sense of relief. *Please stay close to me.*

23.

ELODIE SMILED TIGHTLY AS they entered the Louis XIV reception room. Her heart heavy, she would rather be anywhere else with Kaye than here. Somewhere alone preferably, where she could hold onto the illusion of their connection for one more night. She'd worked hard to maintain a physical distance from Kaye in the narrowboat. She looked incredible in the silk gown with her hair tied up and bangs that hung loosely around her ears. The essence of Kaye tingled unbearably across Elodie's skin and radiated heat.

Kaye would steal the attention of every woman here tonight, and Elodie would take pleasure watching her. Kaye's warmth against her side and the unique scent of Kaye teased her senses. It was going to be a long night. She released Kaye's arm and took two glasses of champagne from the offered tray, handing one to Kaye and holding her own glass up in a toast.

"Santé," Kaye said and raised her glass.

Transfixed, Elodie's heart raced, and she sipped her drink. "You look very beautiful," she whispered. She turned to Yvette who was waving her hand at them as she approached with an unfamiliar woman at her side.

"Elodie. Kaye. Let me introduce you to Lady Babberage." Yvette held out her arms in a welcoming gesture. "Lady Babberage, this is Elodie, who I hope has some good news for you regarding an investor. And this is Kaye, a good friend of Elodie's."

Lady Babberage acknowledged them with a broad smile. Her height and stiff posture gave her a forthright presence, and her ruddy cheeks suggested either heavily weathered skin or that she liked her drink. Her eyes were small and round, and her smile resonated joy.

"Call me Helena. I willnae be doing with formalities."

The last thing Elodie wanted was for Kaye to think she was being set up on her last evening in Sancerre. Heat rose swiftly from her stomach, expanded in her chest, and tension prevented her from greeting Helena with her usual interest. "It's a pleasure to meet you," she said. Helena's enthusiastic grip gave the sense of a determined and genuinely agreeable person.

"It's an honour to meet ye all too."

Kaye held out her hand. "Hello."

Helena's smile broadened as she turned her attention to Kaye. "And where in England are ye from."

"London, but I was born in Wiltshire."

"Och, a southerner. Have ye nae been to Scotland?"

"Once, on business. Edinburgh."

"Aye. Edinburgh's bonnie. I live near Melrose. We have the Melrose Abbey, founded in 1136 for the Cistercian Order, beneath which lies the heart of Robert the Bruce. Did ye know that?" She stood taller and nodded as she spoke.

Elodie smiled to herself. Little did Helena know the history of Melrose would be of great interest to Kaye. They would get on like a house on fire. Kaye nodded.

"And Abbotsford House is where Sir Walter Scott lived. It's an architectural wonder, if you're into that sort of thing. We're surrounded by bonnie countryside. If ye like rugby of course, Melrose is the home of the Rugby Sevens. Do ye like rugby, Kaye?"

Kaye smiled. "Not particularly. You?"

"What, nae. It's far too rough." Helena tutted as if the sport was most disagreeable to her.

Elodie watched Kaye's cheeks colour and felt warm inside.

"Ye should pay me a visit," Helena said, apparently picking up on her enthusiasm.

"I'm sure it's very beautiful," Kaye said.

"Aye, that it is."

Kaye smiled. "Perhaps you can tell me more later."

"I'd be delighted." Helena sipped her drink.

Yvette widened her eyes and indicated toward Kaye with a slight nod. It was a look that begged the question whether Kaye was interested in investing.

Elodie shrugged. She hadn't had any further conversation with Kaye since passing the information to her, but Kaye had definitely seemed interested as Helena had talked. She'd rather not engage in business on their last evening together, which was feeling more precious as every moment passed.

"Kaye's an interior designer with a passion for architecture," Yvette said. "You two should talk more."

"Is that so?" Helena widened her eyes. "In that case, I have tae steal you away for a wee while and tap into your creative wisdom."

Kaye nodded. Helena linked her arm through Kaye's and led her deeper into the room.

Yvette gave a tight-lipped smile. "I think they get along very well. I get a good feeling."

Elodie turned from watching Kaye as she disappeared beyond a small gathering of women. "How's Jean?"

"He's conceded to having a nurse, which is progress, but it's only going one way."

Elodie lowered her head. "I'm sorry to hear that."

Yvette tutted. "C'est la vie, n'est-ce pa."

"Oui, c'est de la merde."

"Life's not all bad, Elodie, but I suppose good things will always come to an end."

Yvette was staring in the direction Kaye had walked, the poignancy of her words evident. Elodie smiled weakly, following her gaze, then turned her attention to Yvette. "True."

"Well, good evening, ladies."

Elodie turned toward Mylene as she approached with a raised glass in her hand. "Hello. I didn't expect to see you here."

Mylene smiled. "Yvette invited me. We got chatting at the spa, about you actually." She winked at Yvette.

Elodie sighed.

Yvette lifted her hand in a submissive gesture. "It was a coincidence. You mentioned Mylene the other day and our paths happened to cross. We were talking about wine, and it turns out she drives a hard bargain." She chuckled. "It is not like you to cut such a good deal with a supplier. I think we need to review the contract for the club."

Elodie groaned inside. "It's a time-limited offer, and you already get the best deal for the club." Her tone was gruff. She questioned why she was justifying herself to both women who were standing shoulder-to-shoulder and smiling broadly at her.

She'd cut the deal with Mylene on a one-year supply contract with an agreement to guarantee rates for the following years, only for as long as Mylene worked for the company. If Mylene left, the deal would cease. It wasn't a favour so much as a gift for the times they'd shared—and maybe missed. She spotted Kaye in her peripheral vision and wondered what she and Helena were talking so animatedly about.

"And it's an offer I'm deeply grateful for. My budget would've forced me to sign up a lesser winery, so thank you again."

Elodie held Mylene's gaze. She looked as though she'd consumed a few glasses of champagne already. Her full lips curled into a wide smile and revealed perfectly aligned white teeth, and her laugh, which came from low in her chest, landed with affection. She was stunning, and someone would sweep her away this evening if she let them. One thing Elodie was certain of was that there was nothing unresolved between them, not from her perspective.

"Did Elodie tell you, she has agreed to run the club?" Yvette asked.

Tightness formed slowly in Elodie's shoulders and made its way down her arms. Yvette must have told Mylene about the Blue Room. Why wouldn't she? It was part of their role to introduce women with money and status into the club, especially when those women were attractive and seeking sexual gratification. Fortunately, Mylene would be going back to London soon so the situation would be short-lived. With Kaye gone, if they ever met in the Blue Room, Elodie would be tempted to enjoy the pleasure of Mylene's company. Why wouldn't she, once her status quo life had been restored? So why did that feel as though she would be cheating? A shiver slid down her spine, though she didn't know why, and then she turned around. Kaye had returned.

"I'm sure Elodie is always the perfect host," Mylene said. Elodie turned and smiled at Mylene who made no effort to hide the fact that she was admiring Elodie's body. She pressed a kiss to Elodie's cheek. "It was good to see you again," she said. She backed away and turned to Yvette. "What a fabulous event, thank you for inviting me."

Yvette sipped her drink. "Come on. I'll introduce you to the baroness."

"Yes, I'll catch you later," she said as the two women moved away. Kaye smiled at Elodie from across the room. Elodie rubbed her cheek where it tingled from the brief contact and willed the night to be over quickly and headed toward the buffet table.

"Hello, stranger."

Elodie turned to the unfamiliar voice and forced a smile at the woman with dark skin she knew from the Blue Room. Heat prickled across her skin. "Hello."

"I haven't seen you in a while."

Elodie fought the desire to evade the woman's gaze. Her pulse thudded, and a trickle of sweat made its way down her spine. "It's a busy time of year."

The woman's smile was brilliant white against her ebony skin as she looked Elodie up and down. "Ah, yes. The harvest. My name is Patrice, in case you wanted to know."

"Elodie."

"Yes, I know. Marchand. The vigneron. I enjoyed our brief time together."

"You're new to the club?" Elodie hadn't seen Patrice at any previous events. She'd not seen her before that time in the Blue Room either, but she got a strong impression from the way Patrice's gaze swept across her body that she'd be a new regular. The thought stuck in her throat and her chest cramped.

"The club wasn't an option for me before. I'm recently single and enjoying myself." Patrice ran her tongue lightly across her full, dark red lips.

Elodie cleared her throat. "Well, it's nice to see you again." She turned to look at the spread on the table though she wasn't hungry. "Are you eating?"

"Hmm, well, that depends. What's on offer?"

Shutters closed inside Elodie's mind as she studied the selection on the table. Patrice was a beautiful woman, that much hadn't changed since they'd had sex. What had changed was Elodie. She took a deep breath and glanced around the room. Kaye smiled back at her. Heat rose in fiery flames from her stomach. Had Kaye picked up that Patrice was making a pass at her? What did it matter? Kaye was leaving in the morning, and Elodie was free to engage with whomever she wished. There was just one problem. She didn't want to have sex with anyone other than Kaye. That realisation wasn't new. The compression in her chest was unyielding.

"The food looks excellent." Elodie cleared her throat and glanced around the room again, taking in the other women.

"Other than that, I'm not sure what else is on offer." Without selecting anything to eat, she gave Patrice a tight smile. "If you'll excuse me." She turned and walked away, feeling the heat of the gaze at her back until she'd exited the room.

At the end of the evening as she and Kaye walked back to the car, Elodie inhaled the fresh air deeply, forcing her lungs to expand. The feeling of impending finality that balled in her stomach wouldn't shift. She'd talked to Kaye only twice over the past four hours. Most of her night had been taken up being pulled into quiet conversation about investment opportunities, wine supply and distribution, and the club. She'd had to work hard to remain passionate and to curb herself from giving clipped responses. "Did you enjoy your evening?" she asked

"It was wonderful." Kaye smiled, linked her arm through Elodie's, and leaned into her. "Thank you. I've never been to anything like this. I now know what a royal banquet is like."

Elodie smiled. Lightness prised through the tightness that had been with her since they'd entered the baroness's residence. "It wasn't too much?"

Kaye squeezed Elodie's arm. "No. It was refreshing to talk about design with people who can actually afford to pay for what they want."

Elodie laughed and the vibration relaxed her. "Yes, I suppose it is."

"I know they have a budget, but most clients I've worked with aspire to something their bank account can't support. So design is often about finding a compromise. It would be incredible to work with someone where the budget isn't a major driver, within reason of course."

Elodie opened the passenger door before returning to the driver's side and getting in. She turned the engine, pulled slowly out of the long driveway, and drove them back toward the narrowboat. Kaye's chatter about her evening faded as

Elodie's thoughts turned to a last attempt to persuade Kaye to stay a little longer.

"Would you be interested in helping me do up the chateau and the spa?" She sounded as desperate as she felt, and Kaye's silence caused her gut to twist. "Sorry. I shouldn't have asked you, knowing you're leaving tomorrow. That was unfair of me."

Kaye remained silent, a frown forming and then disappearing again. "I could take some measurements for the spa first thing in the morning."

Warmth started to blossom inside Elodie.

"And then send some ideas through to you when I get home. You could contract someone locally to do the work. I can consult with them or manage the project if you like."

A dull ache formed in Elodie's chest. *Merde.* "Whatever you prefer." She parked the Land Rover and walked Kaye to the narrowboat. The night, filled with stars and a cool breeze, had the potential to be romantic. She smiled to eclipse her heavy heart and shortened her stride. "I'll miss you," she said.

Kaye squeezed her arm. "I'll miss you too."

They reached the Papillion too quickly and when Kaye turned to Elodie and held her gaze, sorrow consumed her.

"Thank you for showing me so much." Kaye bit her lip and looked away. She cleared her throat and looked at Elodie. "This trip has been perfect." She pressed her lips to Elodie's.

Elodie savoured the sensation but kept her eyes on Kaye. She looked back at her through heavy-lidded eyes.

"I have to let you go," Kaye whispered.

The deeper intended meaning didn't need clarifying. Kaye wasn't referring to them not spending the night together, she was talking about something bigger and more depressing. Kaye wouldn't be staying to measure the spa. Kaye was stronger than Elodie and determined to move on. Elodie wasn't ready to let go, and yet she was powerless to change the course of events. Kaye had made her position clear. She nodded. “Goodnight, Kaye.” She turned swiftly, unable to watch the tears as they fell from Kaye’s eyes and slipped down her cheeks. She increased her pace along the towpath, fighting the blurring of her vision. Steel tightness hindered her movement, and her mind was unwilling to process Kaye’s final words. She sat in the car and let the tears come.

24.

"HOW WAS YOUR EVENING?"

Kaye stood from leaning against the guardrail and staring at the shimmer on the water and turned toward Françoise. "Very lovely."

Françoise frowned. "That is a very special gown."

Kaye lowered her head and looked away. "Thank you." She needed to get the dress back to Elodie. She would have liked to have it dry cleaned before leaving, but there wasn't time to do that. Elodie would understand. Her discomfort had nothing to do with the soft feel of the silk against her skin that reminded her of Elodie's tender touch. The mild irritation came from the unfairness in life. Falling in love with a woman who was emotionally unavailable hadn't been the smartest move. Maybe if it hadn't been for her experience with Sylvie, she could have been tempted to try to make a future with Elodie. She might have been brave enough to take a risk.

"Would you like a drink? Herbal tea? I have port and rum."

"Herbal tea would be nice, thank you."

"Come in. I'll put the water on to boil."

Kaye went inside the Papillion and changed from the gown into her favourite dress. She folded the gown, traced the intricate pattern of the neckline with her fingertip, and placed it carefully back in the box. She swallowed hard as the memory of her arrival at the vineyard on the bicycle reminded her of the first time Elodie had kissed her on the cheek. The softness of her skin and the lingering warmth had been an awakening. Heat filled her aching heart. She bit back the tears and stepped off the boat. As she entered the Kanab, Françoise poured tea.

"Why so sad tonight?"

A tear slipped onto her cheek. "I'm leaving tomorrow."

Françoise frowned. "Then surely, you should be happy, non? Have you not had a good visit?"

"It's complicated."

"Ah, oui. Love, n'est-ce pas?" Françoise handed a cup of tea to Kaye and led her back onto the deck.

"How did you know?" Kaye rested against the guardrail and took a sip of tea.

"That love is complicated? Of course." Françoise shrugged. "How could it not be? Different worlds collide, driven by forces so powerful that our mind cannot make sense of it, and everything we learned about how to live and how to survive goes to war with our heart. It becomes impossible to know the future with absolute certainty, and so we shield ourselves from the inevitable pain we predict. When we don't trust love, we stunt its growth before it has time to flower. It's a self-fulfilling prophecy. We attract that which we fear the most."

Kaye wiped the tears from her cheek. "Do you think some people are so stuck they can never change?"

"Non."

Kaye turned to face Françoise. She hadn't expected her to say no and something about the conviction in her tone flickered a ray of light in a fleeting moment of hope.

"But a person has to believe they can change, otherwise they won't behave differently to create that change."

Could Elodie change? By Elodie's own admission, she didn't believe one could create their future, and Elodie had a lot of pain too. Her past had been so cruel, and she was living in it, unable to let it go. "I don't know whether change is possible."

"She loves you."

Kaye stared at Françoise, stemming the urge to challenge her, knowing that she was right. Françoise had watched Elodie's interaction with her when they'd visited the sanctuary, and the reason Françoise had left so suddenly had been to give them time together, she was sure of it. "I know. But that's not enough, is it?"

The darkness felt heavier in the silence.

"Love is all we have. It is what connects us to everything. It is only through our capacity to love that we know how to be kind to each other." Françoise stared up at the stars.

Sylvie wasn't kind. "Some people like to control and hurt others they love though, don't they?"

"Some people project their pain onto others, even though they love them."

Kaye shook her head. "What's the difference?"

Françoise's smile was gentle. "Consciousness."

Kaye sipped her tea. Elodie talked a lot about universal knowledge, the fact that everything that had ever existed was stored in the universal energy field. It was as far-fetched to Kaye as the concept of the universe itself. "I don't understand."

"Whatever has happened to us in our lives, we have the capacity to do the same to others. If you cannot conceive something, you cannot know it. If you do not imagine that the world is round, you will never explore it for fear of falling off the end. So, if we experience rejection, we can also reject others. Without awareness, that process cannot be stopped."

The words circled around inside Kaye's mind in an increasingly fuzzy and irritating spiral that created further confusion. She thought she'd grasped some appreciation of being able to design her own path and create her own outcomes. Now, she seriously doubted she'd understood anything from her conversations with Françoise. She wanted to argue against her but didn't have an alternative proposition. "So, because I was hurt by someone, I hurt others?" She shook her head. That couldn't possibly be right.

"You have the capacity to inflict on others what you have experienced. If you become conscious of your power, you can stop yourself before you act in a way that hurts that person."

"And be the doormat I became in my marriage?"

"Non, definitely not a doormat. That would be a wrong interpretation of the laws of the universe. When you see clearly, you don't allow others to hurt you anymore, because you can see those behaviours happening and walk away. If you are not aware, you are blind to the way you are being treated and even if others tell you, you can only deny it."

Kaye felt a leaden weight move through her, as if her whole world was crumbling and being consumed by the earth, and she was powerless to stop it. "So, that's how we create our future? By seeing those things in ourselves we haven't noticed before. Then we can choose to behave differently."

"Yes. It's hard. Emotion is stronger than reason. We guide our behaviour to the pleasant feelings and to the familiar. Though we settle for what we know even if it is uncomfortable when we fear the change." She leaned against the railings and stared up at the stars.

Françoise looked like she didn't have a worry in the world, like she understood this game of life and how to play it. "Like avoiding love?"

"We crave connection. But we learn to avoid connection, to push it away, because of the pain that we associate with a loss of love. We disconnect to avoid hurt."

Kaye thought about how Courtney had only ever engaged in meaningless one-night stands or casual friends with benefits arrangements. She'd never sought out a significant relationship in the time Kaye had known her. Françoise's words were starting to make sense. "So, by only choosing to be with people who are unavailable, perhaps because they're with someone or they're emotionally detached, we can avoid rejection? It's like we can have the feeling of being loved, but at a distance that's safe?"

"Yes. A lot like that."

Kaye thought about how Elodie lived with the club, the independent life, and avoiding commitment with anyone. Elodie buried herself in her work and could play the role of the perfect host. She had made Kaye feel special, and yet if Kaye wanted something more, Elodie wouldn't be able to give it. She understood the roots, the reasons why, the abandonment, and having those she'd loved taken from her. It must have been so devastating for Elodie as a child. And now, she'd created a lifestyle that supported her needs well enough. Kaye's heart ached for the journey Elodie had taken. She couldn't expect her to be willing or even able to give up all that she'd created to gamble on love with a stranger. Kaye couldn't promise forever any more than Elodie could. The difference between them was that Kaye could cope with the disappointment of losing love better than Elodie. "So, forcing someone to change—"

"You cannot force change. Change has to be desired above all else that exists. At that point, there is no fear. Sometimes, traumatic events or near-death experiences trigger such a shift. Most often, we make a lot of mistakes along the journey before we wake up. And sometimes we never awaken, because the darkness on the inside is more concentrated than the grey world in which we live."

Kaye stared at Françoise, her mind processing the words in slow time, her heart racing. Maybe she couldn't force Elodie to change, but she couldn't leave without sharing with Elodie the wisdom she'd just learned. And she didn't want to be the one to abandon Elodie. After all, it had been Kaye who had decided to leave. She'd never asked Elodie if she would change. Elodie had said she would try, though try what hadn't been discussed, because Kaye hadn't let Elodie explain herself. Kaye should give her the opportunity to speak. She was scrabbling at straws now, to keep what they had alive, but she had nothing to lose that she hadn't already lost in her decision to walk away. "Thank you. I need to go."

Françoise smiled. "Good luck."

Kaye pedaled as hard as she could, the dress in the box perched precariously in the basket at the front of the bicycle. She had no idea what she was going to say to Elodie, she just knew her heart ached when she thought about not seeing her again. She had to ask Elodie if they could try to find a way to be together. Damn the pedals for not turning fast enough. She pushed harder, puffed harder. The cool air doing little to dampen the heat that consumed her. Turning into the road leading to the vineyard, her heart pounded. Getting closer to the barn, her pulse shifted into her throat.

She recognised the car outside the barn. Her head filled with pressure and caused a ringing sound in her ears that mirrored the thud of her heartbeat. She cycled to where she could see the mezzanine. Mylene was holding Elodie in her arms. Mylene brushed Elodie's hair from her face, cupped her cheek, and looked at her for a long time. Mylene leaned in to kiss Elodie—

Kaye turned, dropped the box outside the door, and pedalled as hard as she could until she reached the narrowboat. Tears still wetted her cheeks as she lay in bed and stared upwards, clasping Winston firmly to her chest. She would go straight home. It really was time to create a new future and forget that Elodie had ever existed.

25.

"FORTY-NINE YEARS WE were together."

A lifetime. Elodie sighed. Whether it was the funeral or just the passing of time, she missed Kaye more than ever with each day. Maybe it was a truism that in times of grief those who came to mind were the people you felt the closest to.

The grave at the cemetery they'd just returned from, untended, overgrown, and unloved was a mark of Elodie's relationship with the mother who had damaged everything that would have made her life complete: her trust, her mind, and her heart. Except that she *had* loved her mother, more than she'd dared to admit. She had been the person Elodie had looked up to, tried to prove herself to, and craved recognition from. Sometimes, even a hug would have made all the difference to Elodie, and whilst she would never understand why her mother couldn't show her that affection, she forgave her. She'd walked slowly past the grave, Yvette at her side, with just a brief glance at the engraving on the weathered stone and consumed by a large dose of guilt for allowing her hurt to get in the way of doing the right thing by her mother. She had vowed to tend to the grave later. Her focus had lingered on the name that still echoed a dull ache in her heart for the love she'd craved as they had lowered Jean's coffin into the ground. A pang of guilt had reminded her she'd never visited the cemetery since her mother's funeral. Another pang said she'd never given it a second thought.

Yvette sighed and put down the photograph of Jean next to the vase of flowers on the table. "Why did he pick the coldest month of the year to die?"

The conversation was banal, a lone voice trying to find humour in the bitterest of moments. It wasn't the coldest month. The winter was only just beginning. January and

February would be much chillier. And yet Elodie too had felt a strange nip in the air, the sort of chill that reinforced a sense of vulnerability.

"It's colder this year." She gave an equally banal response in support of the unarticulated grief of a friend desperately searching for something tangible to hold onto.

Yvette's gloved hand still trembled even though they'd been indoors for a good while already, inside the grand hall of the residence that had been Yvette's home for as many years as she'd been married. Elodie hadn't visited Yvette here often, and she'd never seen the grand hall, but even the other rooms were austere, all straight lines and dull colours, lacking in warmth and comfort. Footsteps in here sounded louder on the stone-tiled floor, and voices echoed in the sparsely furnished chamber. It reminded Elodie of a church, unpleasant and unwelcoming, as if living in a harsh aesthetic and discomfort might give a special dispensation to the wealthy, repentant of their privileges in life as they stood at the gates of heaven. The room didn't have Yvette's imprint on it, at least not the Yvette that Elodie knew. It was as if she'd lived as a shadow in her own home. Maybe that's why she'd been drawn to the club, the spa, and the life she'd created outside her marriage. Elodie put her arm around Yvette's shoulder and tugged her closer. "It was a beautiful ceremony. He would have been proud."

The sun had remained absent of heat, barely peeked over the tops of the houses, and the frost from earlier in the day hadn't lifted in the shadow of the church.

Yvette didn't respond for a long moment. "He never liked ceremony." There was remorse in her tone. She sighed, turned to Elodie as if falling out of a trance, and stared at her through a narrow gaze. "How are you, darling?"

"I'm fine."

"And the harvest is finished?"

"Yes."

Yvette nodded. "That's good. So you have no reason for this." She waved her hand at Elodie.

"For what?"

Yvette shook her head. "I have known you for the best part of your life, and in many respects, I've been like a mother... Anyway, I am probably not the best role model, but I do know that we get one chance at life, and if we never take a risk on love, we may live to regret it."

Elodie plucked two glasses of champagne from the waiter's tray as he passed and handed one to Yvette. "I don't know what you mean." She sipped the drink and had a hard time swallowing. She acknowledged a guest with a smile and a nod simply to avoid Yvette's interrogation.

Yvette downed her champagne, grabbed another glass from the tray, and took a long slug. "You are probably not going to like what I have to say, but at times like this it's important to speak one's truth."

Elodie's throat burned.

"You have distanced yourself from everyone who has loved and cared for you, including me at times, for as long as I can remember. I talked to Mylene."

Elodie rolled her eyes then closed them briefly. "Mylene was a long time ago. I cannot recreate the past. We're different people."

"And you loved her."

"Yes."

"But you never went after her. Never gave her a second thought after she was removed from school."

"That's unfair. She broke my heart, and I thought about her even at university."

"No, *she* didn't break your heart. Her grandparents were responsible for her leaving the school, not her. She had no say in it, and she tried to contact you."

"I didn't know that."

"I know, but this is more than you did for her."

An argument flared at the back of Elodie's mind and died as it reached her mouth. "I didn't know where to start. I thought she'd left me. I was a kid."

"She had not left you though, had she?"

Elodie gritted her teeth. "No."

"And neither did Kaye."

Elodie jolted and shook her head. "This has nothing to do with Kaye."

"Except that you're in love with her, and you're letting her walk away. You are repeating history."

Elodie shook her head. "It's not like that."

Yvette put her hand on her hip. "Then tell me how it is? Tell me you do not love her, that you do not think about her."

Elodie opened her mouth and closed it again. She tried to swallow and the pain in her throat intensified. "I have nothing to offer her."

Yvette sighed. She reached up and swept Elodie's fringe from her eyes, then rested her hand on her shoulder. "Darling, you have the most important gift of all to give to her."

"Which is?"

"Love."

Elodie closed her eyes. The sting became a bite, and tears formed at the edges of her eyes. The trembling bubbled inside her, and she knew she was on the verge of breaking down. She opened her eyes and pulled back, staring up at the tall ceiling to stem the feeling. Yvette's gaze held so much love that her heart squeezed to grab hold of it, and the sadness ached in her chest. "I'm so scared."

Yvette took another deep breath and formed a thin-lipped smile as she released the air though her nose. "Of course. Love is the most frightening of all the feelings when we think we are going to lose it. I spent years convincing myself I did not love him." She pointed at the picture of Jean. "And now my heart tells me how wrong I was. He was my rock, and now that rock has crumbled back into the earth." A tear slipped onto her cheek as she smiled. "Sometimes we do not know what we have until it's gone. But there's only one type of loss that lasts a lifetime. It is this." She picked up the picture of Jean and cradled it to her chest. "*You* still have a chance."

Elodie's hand trembled around the glass. Her heart raced, and her thoughts rambled. "I don't trust myself." The words felt shallow, even though they still had a strong grip in her mind.

"Trust yourself. Pah. Nothing lasts forever, my darling. Nothing. Not you, not me. Nothing. But to let go of someone you love for fear that it may not last has to be the most foolish rationale I have ever heard. You have to give love a chance to blossom and grow. Love comes in many forms, it transforms, and with time it becomes something that you never expected it could be. And then you know you could never feel that same thing about anyone else. Those words you speak, coming from someone with such a beautiful brain, are criminal."

Elodie stared at the glass in her hand while the battle in her mind ensued. What could she have done to convince Kaye to stay? How could they have made a life together when she feared she would push Kaye away eventually. She couldn't do that to her, not after what she'd been through.

"When I got married, it was the most frightening and exhilarating experience of my life. Nothing has come close to it since. And even if Jean had managed his last hoorah, there are no wonders in the world that could compete with a formal declaration of love. That is why weddings are a sacrament, a commitment in front of God."

"I don't believe in God."

"I know. I'm not talking literally, and you need to challenge those damn false beliefs upon which you have carved out an adequate life when you could have an exceptional one."

"That's unfair."

"I said you would not like what I have to say. But it's the truth." Yvette shrugged. "Your mother didn't have to work for anything. She inherited her wealth from her parents, and she didn't have your business acumen. She needed to feel loved, and she was betrayed by the man she gave her heart to. She never turned to anyone else after he left her and now you are repeating her mistakes. It was sad and such a waste of a beautiful life, but she gave up on her future and turned to alcohol and gambling to conceal the heartache. You are not like her, Elodie. You work hard, and you have a strong mind and a loving heart. You have so much to give. I watched you, my darling. The club is fun for people like me, like your mother too, but you deserve so much more than that, and when you get an opportunity, you should grab it with both hands."

Elodie had the faint taste of iron in her mouth from biting the inside of her lip. Her jaw, like steel, refused to concede to words as emotion flooded her. She swallowed back the tears and placed her glass on the table. "I need to go." She turned and took a pace toward the door.

"Elodie."

She turned back to Yvette, who looked blurred. She blinked and wiped the back of her hand across her eyes.

"You need to realise your mother loved you. She was who she was, but you can never doubt her love. I saw her with you when you were a baby. She would have killed to protect you. Yes, she wanted a son, but that was because she thought she needed a man to run the business. She was not strong like you. She did not know that you would grow up to be more than any man. She would be proud of you, if she could see you now."

"She could've worked all that out while I was busting myself in my studies to prove myself to her."

Yvette shook her head. "It was too late for her. After your father left, something inside her died. She changed, in her mind, and the doctors were unable to help her. Your grandmother tried for a while but to no avail. The lifestyle became your mother's life, and she did not know how to change."

Elodie felt her heart squeeze and pain seeped into every cell in her body. She had loved her grandmother deeply as a young child, and her death had been far harder to bear than her mother's. "I need to get out of the club for a while," she said.

Yvette nodded. "I know. I will find someone else to run it."

Elodie nodded. "Thank you." She stepped up to Yvette and hugged her. "I'm sorry," she said and when she let go, a tear slipped onto Yvette's cheek.

"We all make mistakes, Elodie. Some of them are recoverable. When something precious comes to you, you should hold on to it with all your might. One day it will be gone, but don't be the one to push it away before it's ready to leave." She looked to the photo of Jean.

Elodie turned. "I have to go," she said and walked out of the grand hall.

She went to her mother's grave, tended to the frozen plot as best she could, and set a vase of dried lilacs and snowdrops at the foot of the headstone. In the spring, she would bring fresh flowers and wash down the stone. She sat and talked to her mother until well beyond dusk and pondered the questions that she'd never asked. Perhaps the answers had come from the universal consciousness as she stared blankly into the increasing darkness, or perhaps she'd known the truth at some point in her earlier life. Her mother *had* loved her. But she hadn't known how to show it. The icy chill stemmed her tears, and by the time she left the cemetery, she could barely feel her frozen fingers for the gentle warmth that had softened her heart.

She sipped mint tea as she stared through the barn window, the stars clear and bright and with a subtle flickering movement. If she could see the vines now, they would be barren, hibernating, recovering, and repairing to make themselves ready for their next crop. Nature in its stride, without thought or fear, reacted to the present conditions. It didn't question, or second guess, or predetermine a future based on its past.

She'd intended to return to the narrowboat on the night of the baroness's dinner to ask Kaye to stay with her. Instead, she'd stumbled upon the dress in the box outside her front door when Mylene left. She'd changed her mind and locked herself away, thinking Kaye had made her point loud and clear. The following day, seeing the empty mooring where the Papillion had once sat had driven cold through her veins. The Kanab too had gone. She hadn't frequented the spa in the weeks that had passed.

She would be alone again this Christmas. Only this year she'd never felt lonelier. "Do you believe you can create your future?" Kaye had asked. One thing was clear: If Elodie didn't try, if she didn't talk to Kaye, then she'd already determined her future. That meant more of the same, a detached existence, taking what she needed and returning the favour, but without the deep feeling of being at one with another human being. She'd been blessed with a taster of that feeling with Kaye.

Kaye had altered her, like a chemical reaction that couldn't be undone, and Elodie wouldn't be able to settle until she'd given love a chance.

She finished her tea and stepped away from the window. It would be better to have tried and failed than never to have tried at all.

26.

KAYE PAID FOR THE two cups of mulled wine and handed one to Helena.

"Ooh, that smells good." Helena took the steaming cup and sipped.

They crunched their way slowly along the snow-covered cobbled street. The aroma of spiced alcohol mingled with candyfloss from the machine that weaved soft balls of blue and red sugar. And as they ambled, the smell of roasted pig and apple sauce drifted from the hog-roast stand where a queue backed down the street. Around the village square, the speakers belted out *All I Want for Christmas Is You* for the second time, competing with the squeal of excited children and the rumbles and ripples of adult laughter.

"It's like a fairy tale." Kaye sipped her drink. The butcher's shop behind the hog-roast stand threw coloured lights into the street. The vegetable shop next door competed with its gold and silver tinsel wrapped elegantly around wooden trays of parsnips and sprouts. The white flashing lights around the Christmas tree that stood proudly at the edge of the short high-street glistened in the snow, and the carousel close by forced an out-of-tune jingle that was almost more irritating than the song.

"Is it like this every year?"

"Aye. It wouldnae be Christmas without the fair."

She'd never find joyous laughter like this and a dawdling pace on Christmas Eve in London. Yes, London had magnificent light displays that bridged the bustling streets, stalls selling roasted chestnuts and gifts made of plastic or china, and Christmas trees that adorned the main squares inside the city. But here, people knew each other as neighbours even when distance separated their houses, and more importantly they stopped and chatted as if they had all the time in the world.

There were craft stands set up for children to entertain themselves, while adults perused the gift stands close by or challenged their skills with one of the games.

Kaye still hadn't adjusted to the stronger accents but a smile went a long way, and the people she'd met so far had been willing to repeat themselves to help her understand. She'd already become familiar with some of Helena's expressions, such as, "I'm fair puckled" meaning she was short of breath, and "We're a' jock Tamson's bairns" meaning we were all God's children and all equal. Spending time with Helena had been, and would continue to be, an education that brought a smile that stretched Kaye's cheeks until they ached.

"Felicity." Helena hailed a thickset woman almost half her height, who looked as if she was just about to tuck into a hog-roast sandwich and smiled.

"I'll let you blether while I have a wander," Kaye said. She chuckled at her use of the local term for chat and said hello to Felicity as she approached. "I'll see you later."

"Aye, I'll pop in on my way home."

She left Helena chatting to the rosy cheeked woman and strolled down the street until a gift stand caught her eye. Tartan trinkets in a range of pattern and colour combinations were apparent in abundance. Scarfs and neck warmers, ties and bed-socks, teddy bears and hearts, and something that looked like a dead fox which turned out to be a formal dress sporran made from highland cows. They had silver jewellery, antique stag and thistle kilt pins, and antique highland cow brooch. The latter looked odd to Kaye, the lack of eyes and sharp horns gave an eerie feel to the beast.

She moved onto the next stand and picked up a small silver bowl. She ran her finger over the two flat handles on either side of the shallow cup, admiring the fine detail in their design.

"That's a quaich, lassie. You'll only get them in Scotland."

"It's very beautiful."

"That it is. Is it a special gift ye're looking for?"

Kaye shook her head. She didn't know why she was looking for gifts. She'd picked up a sweater for Courtney and a pair of pruning scissors for Helena. She'd already sent a parcel home for her family. She caressed the quaich, which was the size of a small teacup, in her hand. The trinket would go well on the dressing table in her living room.

"I'll take two, please."

The broadset man had a jolly smile as he gift-wrapped the two cups. "Some lucky chap is going tae have a great Christmas," he said. He handed them to Kaye and winked at her, then rubbed his hands together and blew into them. "Tis a proper Christmas night."

"Yes, it's wonderful." A warm feeling spread from Kaye's chest and challenged the cold chill in her cheeks.

"That it is, lassie. Nothing a wee dram won't warm. Make sure yae do the raffle. The proceeds goes tae our local school."

Kaye didn't need alcohol to warm her, though the idea of sharing a drink with Elodie and enjoying this beautiful place together hadn't escaped her. She'd missed seeing her in the weeks since her return to the UK. She missed their conversations and the ambience in Sancerre. But Elodie had given her this opportunity, and that was worth more than anything anyone else had ever gifted her. She loved her place here, and the house was more than she'd ever imagined. In an architecturally rich environment, she found herself settled in an exceptionally pretty part of the world with wonderfully kind and supportive neighbours that she considered her friends.

"I'll head there now," she said and walked toward the stand with the giant cuddly toy panda displayed for all to see.

"Name the panda tae win it," the girl behind the stand said. She had red hair that hung to her waist and rosy cheeks to match. "A pound a go."

"And how much is the raffle?" Kaye asked, eyeing the table with labelled gifts, none of which she particularly wanted to win. It was a donation for a good cause.

"A pound a go," the girl said and her smile revealed the gaps where her top two baby-teeth had once been.

Kaye leaned toward her. "In that case, I'll have to name the panda and have nine raffle tickets."

"That's ten pounds." The girl held out her hand.

Kaye fetched the note and handed it over.

"What name?"

"Gosh, I don't know. What do you think?"

"Cannae say." The girl shook her head, looked as though she was under oath, and grinned.

"Well, let's go with Po."

"Already gone."

"Oh, right. In that case, Yang."

"Gone. So is Ying, and Bamboo, and Liquorice, Noodles, Ebony, Bob—"

"Bob. Ah, okay." Kaye studied the panda's big round eyes and its black shiny fur. It was the height of the girl at its side and carried the faint hint of a smile where the stitching cut in an upwards arch. "I think it's a girl panda. So, I'm going with Millie."

"That's my name!"

Kaye held her palm out. "Well, that's a perfect name then."

The girl giggled and wrote the name on a piece of paper. "What's ye name and number?"

Kaye gave over her details. "Would you like to choose nine raffle tickets for me?"

Millie dived her hand into the small rotating drum filled to the brim with tickets. She pulled a ticket and opened it, then a second.

"Any luck?"

"Nae, needs tae end in a five or a zero." She drew another two tickets and then another two, and as she unfolded them she shook her head.

"Four tae go." Kaye glanced around, noting the chill that came when standing still for a short time.

Millie plucked another two tickets. "Yes. Five hundred and sixty."

A burst of excitement surprised Kaye. She searched the gifts on the stand.

"Here." Millie reached to the back of the table, picked up a bottle of red wine, and handed it to Kaye.

"Thank you." Kaye glanced fleetingly at the bottle and instantly recognised the label. Her heart skipped a beat. *Elodie's wine.*

"That's braw, that is. Lady Babberage gets it directly from France."

Kaye swallowed hard. "Yes, it looks like a very good wine." The taste of the wine lingered on her tongue, together with the memory of her first time with Elodie inside the cave. The sense of Elodie touching her stole her breath for a moment and as she gathered herself, an icy chill slid down her spine.

Millie had pulled another two tickets and shook her head. "That's it."

"Thank you." She wandered past a stall selling Christmas decorations in a daze and picked a small hand-crafted wreath for her front door, a table decoration, and two Christmas-spiced scented candles then ambled back along the street to her cottage. She had the gifts to wrap and mince pies and sausage rolls to cook before Courtney arrived and Helena came over for Christmas Eve supper.

The heat from the coal fire stung her cheeks as she entered the house, the soot seemed to add a slight earthy taste that mingled with the sweet pine from the Christmas tree, and the smell of the gammon she'd roasted earlier was homely. Light and shadow danced across the solid wood floor from the flashing lights on the tree. She closed the curtains to the darkness outside, positioned the wreath on the barn-style kitchen door that led from the living room, and placed the candles on the hearth. She put the table decoration of dried pines and twigs in the middle of the table behind the sprig of holly she'd cut from the bush in the garden. It looked perfect, and yet the dull ache in her heart persisted. She cradled the bottle of wine in her hands and stared at the label, wishing she'd never done the damn raffle. She could have just made a donation, not taken the tickets, and saved herself from the memory. It was definitely a good year, but it was missing a critical ingredient. Elodie.

She studied her phone, tempted to call to wish Elodie a merry Christmas, but what else would she say to her? That she missed her desperately. That she wished things had turned out differently between them. Maybe she'd call her later, after she'd had a drink and when she could sit and relax. She pocketed her phone and went through to the kitchen.

Having put on the kettle, she extracted the ingredients she needed to make the sausage rolls. The kettle boiled, and she decided she didn't want a hot drink. Something stronger would numb the empty feeling, take the edge off the loneliness. She made a snowball, added a maraschino cherry, and took a sip. After the lemonade stopped tingling her nose, the sweet, sticky eggnog brought back memories of Christmas with her family as a teenager. She smiled as she recalled the time her youngest brother had got stuck up the chimney, thus demonstrating that Father Christmas couldn't possibly exist. It hadn't stopped the magic of Christmas Eve from delivering an aura of excited anticipation for the following morning. It was different now, of course. It would just be her, Courtney, and Helena this year, and the illusion of Father Christmas had long since been busted.

Returning from Sancerre and seeing her brothers, mum, and sister again had been like coming home after having lost the battle but won the war, a sweet reunion made bitter by what she'd left behind in France. She wished she'd been able to say goodbye to Françoise, but by the morning after the baroness's event the Kanab had already gone. She picked up the note Françoise had written and read again the words that would always remain with her.

Love is constant and endless. No one can take it from you. It is yours to give, willingly or unwittingly, with or without reciprocity. You will find love in the smallest details, the manner in which something is made, and in the shades that bring colour to your life. If you look closely enough, you will see love in the shadows and in the darkest moments. Love will always overcome fear, and belief becomes stronger when guided by love. Bring love to your endeavours and trust you will find the love you seek. Françoise.

She hoped the words were true. She turned on the radio to the exuberance of a DJ and quickly turned it off again. She selected her favourite Christmas album on her phone and closed her eyes to enjoy Ave Maria, surprised to find they watered within the first few bars of music.

She wiped her eyes and turned her attention to cooking, tipped the sausage meat into a dish, added pepper, thyme, and garlic, and mashed it into a sticky mess. Pastry rolled out, she laid the meat on top, wrapped it to form a long sausage roll, and cut it into smaller chunks, slicing their tops with a sharp blade. Fifteen minutes and they would be beautifully cooked, and puffy...like her eyes were beginning to feel. She swiped a piece of kitchen roll and blew her nose. She'd cried over Elodie more than she'd cried over anyone, but she'd never missed her as much as she did now. She'd kept herself busy, preoccupied with the house purchase in the first instance and then settling in over the past ten days. *All I Want for Christmas Is You* came on and even though it was delivered in silky, smooth tones, she turned it off.

She reached for her glass as the knock on the front door came. She took a deep breath and shouted, "Come in." Her phone pinged. A message from Courtney told her the airports were closed due to snow, and she wasn't going to make it. "Damn it." She'd been looking forward to spending some time with Courtney now that they'd rekindled their friendship. Courtney had agreed not to interfere in Kaye's life unless Kaye asked for her input, and Kaye had shared what she had learned from Francoise. Courtney had been fascinated by the theories and having settled into her new job and become single again, she'd planned to make some changes to her life. Maybe Courtney could make it to Scotland for the New Year celebrations. Courtney would love Hogmanay, which by all accounts was riotous fun, and Kaye had a strong feeling that her new friends would like Courtney too. She sent a text to ask the question. Courtney's affirmation came quickly.

The vague sound of movement through the living room was overshadowed by her attention directed at her phone. She started to text back. "Come on through, Helena. What are you drinking?" She tapped out a response, pocketed her phone, and reached for a tumbler glass from the cupboard to pour Helena her favourite tipple, whiskey. She turned toward the kitchen doorway, gasped, and the glass slipped in her hand. She grasped at it furiously and prevented it from falling to the ground. Her heart thundered behind her ribs. "Elodie?"

Her emerald green eyes sparkled, her teeth chattered a little, and she curved her shoulders a little as if she was bracing against the chill.

Kaye could barely breathe. “What are you doing with that panda?”

27.

ELODIE CHUCKLED. IT WAS a choked sound that emanated from her chest through tension that prevented her lungs from expanding. On the train from Paris to London, her emotions had oscillated between that of a child consumed by the magic of Christmas Eve excitement and the nervous anticipation of an adult consumed by the weight of uncertainty and failure. Never had she doubted herself more. Never had anything meant as much to her. She'd felt every minute of the journey and even as the Eurostar train had pulled slowly into St Pancras, she'd considered the best option might be to forget her foolish quest and get onto the next available train straight back to Paris. Why would Kaye want to be with her now? Maybe Elodie had missed her chance. The risk to her heart that Kaye had moved on from what they'd shared together, and worse still found someone else to love, seemed more life-threatening than the challenge of climbing the east face of Everest without a support team.

She'd stood outside for twenty minutes building up the courage to approach the house. She'd had been on the verge of walking away since the voice in her head persisted in reminding her that she wasn't good enough. It was hard not to give it her attention after all the years of believing it. If Helena hadn't come along, handed her the panda and asked her to make her excuses to Kaye for skipping the evening drink they'd arranged, she might easily be on a train again. Helena's wily smile and the nudge in Elodie's back had given her the impetus she'd needed. She'd never felt more petrified than when she'd knocked on the door and waited for what felt like a lifetime. It had been no more than seconds, and she felt emotionally wrung out as she'd entered the house. And then she'd spotted Kaye in the kitchen with her back to her, and her heart had stopped for a beat. Now, it thundered against her ribs and she felt sick with fear.

"You won it. Helena asked me to pass it to you. She said to say she's heading straight home, and she'll catch up with you for Christmas lunch tomorrow." This was the moment she'd dreaded the most. The first few seconds, when the prospect of Kaye rejecting her was at its highest. If Kaye would just give her a chance to talk and explain, a chance to ask for what she wanted. If she could catch a flicker in Kaye's expression that might give her hope. The worst that would come of her visit would be that they would remain good friends. It was better than nothing, though she wanted much more than that. The warmth from the fire tingled where the cold chill had seeped into her.

Kaye put the glass on the side with an unsteady hand. "What?" She flicked at the flour on her dress.

She looked edible and wonderfully at home, and not like the virtually spotless version of Kaye she'd seen most often in Sancere. Though the dress, in a deep red of a poinsettia beneath the splashes of flour, was well pressed and clung deliciously to Kaye's curves. Elodie held out the large soft toy. "Winston will be jealous, you know?"

Kaye took the panda and held it to her chest.

Elodie evaded Kaye's gaze, which lingered on her unnervingly. Kaye hadn't smiled yet and appeared wary, which was understandable. Elodie had made the biggest mistake of her life letting Kaye go, and now she had to prove herself for Kaye to take her seriously. How the hell could she do that? She smiled. It felt strained, but at least she saw a flicker of a smile in response. It was enough for her to breathe a little more easily. "It's cold here," she said.

Kaye squeezed the panda and pressed her lips to the top of its head, as if seeking comfort. "You came all this way to tell me that?"

Elodie tilted her head and chuckled. She didn't sound quite as strangled and felt the pressure lifting. "And to wish you a merry Christmas, of course."

"You could have sent me a card."

The words stung. She pinched her lips together and rocked from heel to toe in the slightly awkward silence, glancing around the kitchen without seeing. She hadn't even thought about sending a card, though maybe she should have. Maybe she should have picked up the phone and tested the water first, but she hadn't had the courage to do that. Turning up unannounced had been a deliberate plan. She'd taken action to achieve her dream and to carve out a new future, one she hoped Kaye would be agreeable to. "Some things need to be said face to face."

Kaye lowered her head and rested her chin on the panda's head. "I'm sorry, I was a bit harsh."

"You're angry with me."

Kaye cleared her throat and looked toward the oven, still squeezing the panda tightly. "No... I'm angry with myself."

Elodie felt a familiar twinge and fought against it. "You have a lot of snow here. I was lucky to get a train out of London."

"Courtney got stuck there this evening. She'll be here in a couple of days once the snow's cleared in London."

Kaye's face looked pinched, though her tone was soft. Her eyes flicked in unsettled movements between Elodie and the oven. She dumped the panda unceremoniously on the chair next to the small kitchen table and crossed her arms.

"That'll be nice." Elodie's shoulders dropped with relief that Courtney wouldn't be showing up any time soon. This was hard enough and would have been even more uncomfortable had Courtney been here. That was a risk she'd had to take though, to be able to say what she needed to say to Kaye.

"I'm looking forward to seeing her."

Elodie shuffled her feet and heat rose to her cheeks as the voice in her head taunted her that she hadn't been invited to dine with Kaye. "You're baking."

"Sausage rolls. They'll be done in a minute." Kaye uncrossed her arms and ran her fingers through her hair.

She looked troubled by something. "I didn't want to spoil the surprise." It was the best version of the truth she could muster. Why was it so hard to say what she wanted to say?

Kaye started at her, seemingly unconvinced. "Hmm."

It was now or never. She had to be honest and get the words out before Kaye showed her the door. Her chest tightened and her stomach turned. She swallowed hard and took a deep breath. "I didn't want to risk that you might not want to see me."

Kaye smiled faintly and a steady stream of electrically charged particles flowed through Elodie. Reacting to the vibrations, her hands trembled in her pockets. She could even feel a quiver in her lips as she pressed them closed. She ran her tongue across her dry lips. Kaye's smile broadened, and Elodie released a sigh.

"It's a nice surprise. I was just—"

Elodie took a pace toward Kaye. All the words she wanted to say rushed through her mind. She didn't know where to start. What she'd felt in the last two months without Kaye couldn't be explained easily. She'd been like a shell of her former self. Nothing held her attention and even the idea of going to the club hadn't enticed her out of her depressed state. Mylene had travelled back to London soon after Kaye, and whilst it had been cathartic to talk to her, Elodie had had no desire to try and rekindle their love. She had no desire to be with anyone. Her self-appraised perfect life had been unveiled as fake and its deepest flaws spotlighted. She couldn't go back to that life knowing something better was possible, if Kaye would agree to stand at her side...and sleep in her bed. "I couldn't stop thinking about you."

Kaye frowned. "That's what you need to tell me, face to face?"

"No, I had to see you, to—"

"Wish me a merry Christmas. You said that."

Elodie could barely swallow. She noted the dusting of flour on Kaye's left cheek coating her freckles and reached up and brushed the flour away. "I love your freckles," she said, staring into Kaye's eyes. The word love resonated with softness and warmth. Kaye's smile was kind and gentle. Elodie's heart raced and the cold that had numbed her now tingled.

"Let me take your coat."

Elodie removed her coat and handed it to Kaye. When Kaye took hold of it, she held onto it a little longer and smiled. "You look beautiful."

Kaye held Elodie's gaze for a long time, took a deep breath, and then shook her head. "Do you have any idea what you do to me?" Her voice was broken. She took the coat and placed it on the stand in the lobby.

Elodie closed her eyes and inhaled as she got a hit of Kaye's perfume. Relief burned behind her eyes and they quickly watered. She rubbed away the tear before Kaye returned. Yes, she hoped that she did to Kaye what Kaye did to her. "Do you like the cottage?" she asked when Kaye returned to the kitchen.

Kaye removed the sausage rolls from the oven. "Yes, it's more than I could have wished for, and the people here are lovely. Can I get you a drink?"

Elodie took a pace toward Kaye and put her hand in the small of Kaye's back. Kaye trembled and whispered something that Elodie didn't catch, closing her eyes for a brief moment. Elodie glanced at the sausage rolls. "They smell great. I'd love a glass of wine, if you have one?" Her heart thundered as if trying to escape her ribs as she held Kaye's gaze and felt her closeness.

She was so irresistibly close, Elodie wanted to kiss her. But Kaye moved and the heat dissipated too quickly. The thought of kissing her was stronger than ever, and Elodie felt confident that if she did make the first move this time around, Kaye wouldn't object.

Kaye glanced toward the living room briefly. "Red or white?"

Elodie didn't care for any drink particularly. She was already high on the fact that she hadn't been sent back to the bed and breakfast she'd booked for her stay or heading back to France. She spied the remains of the snowball in Kaye's glass. "I'll have the same as you, actually." She watched as Kaye prepared the drink. Kaye still looked a little tense and the voice in Elodie's head was shouting at her to set her cards on the table. "I missed you," she said.

Kaye froze. "What about Mylene?"

If that was all Kaye was perturbed about, she could handle that. She took Kaye's hand and squeezed it tightly. Of course, Kaye would be anxious about Mylene's place in Elodie's life. Elodie had been too self-absorbed to not allay Kaye's concerns before she'd left Sancerre. "Mylene will always be a friend but nothing more than that."

Kaye eased her hand from Elodie's as she looked away. She didn't appear convinced. She made Elodie the drink then began to lift the sausage rolls onto a wire rack. She stopped before finishing the job and took in a deep breath. "I saw you together, the night before I left...when I dropped the dress outside your door. You were...together then."

Elodie's heart thundered as fear gripped her. She shook her head. "I've never lied to you, Kaye. I would never do that. She came by after the event to say goodbye. She was in my past. She's not my future. I promise you."

"And the club? And the other women?" Kaye's trembling hand shook the metal slice. She rested it on the side.

"I'm not a part of the club anymore. Kaye, look at me." Elodie stepped closer and lifted Kaye's chin to force eye contact. "I haven't had sex with anyone since you and I got together. I went to the club once, early on in your visit, but I didn't want to have sex with anyone. When you and I were in the Blue Room together, I was so relieved that you didn't want to be with anyone else too. And I haven't had sex since you left." She smiled and hoped Kaye could feel the love she knew in her own heart. "I fell in love with you, and us being apart isn't going to change that. I drove you away out of fear, and we both lost something precious. I want to be with you, Kaye, and only you. I don't make promises I'm not willing to keep. I've never wanted to be with anyone before. You're the one my heart chose, and I have to listen to it."

Kaye's lips had parted a fraction, but she stood in silence staring at Elodie as if processing the most challenging proposition that had ever been put to her.

Elodie's fingers trembled as she wiped a tear from Kaye's cheek. The burning in her stomach and chest and the anticipated rejection still lingered painfully as she waited for an acknowledgement from Kaye that she wanted the same. "I want to be with you," she said, again, softly, beseechingly. "We can work out the details. I would give up everything if that's what it takes to convince you of how I feel."

Kaye blinked. Her eyes shone with the dampness. "I don't want you to give up everything for me."

Elodie pinched her lips together as she nodded. She swept the loose strands of hair from Kaye's flushed face. "I—"

"I deserted you." Kaye shook her head.

Elodie kissed Kaye's nose. "No, I deserted myself, my love, a long time ago. And I held that against my mother when, in fact, she was struggling with her own life. She did the best she could, and I now accept that. I loved her and yet I resented her for far too long and in doing so I almost destroyed my own life.

Meeting you changed everything for me." She closed her eyes. The heat from Kaye caused fire to flash across Elodie's skin, and the whisper of the kiss that touched her cheek was too brief. "I love you more than life," she whispered, and when she opened her eyes, Kaye's smile claimed her heart all over again.

"I'm in love with you," Kaye said. "And I want to be with you too...more than anything. I'm not going to let you go anywhere tonight, or tomorrow, or the next day, if that's okay with you?" She ran her fingertip along the line of Elodie's jaw.

The hint of a smile crept onto Elodie's face. She tugged Kaye closer and kissed her tenderly. With her arms around Kaye's waist, the flicker she saw pass across Kaye's eyes and the sigh that fell from Kaye's mouth caused her chest to bubble with relief. "I did book a bed and breakfast, just in case you threw me out."

Kaye shook her head. "No chance."

Elodie's smile faded in the increasing intensity that thundered through her heart. Kaye was more beautiful than ever. "I'm glad. I don't want to be anywhere else, ever, unless you are with me." *I will always love you.* The words hovered in her mind, her heart thrumming a steady beat for a long while before she spoke them, knowing without doubt they were the truth.

About Emma Nichols

Emma Nichols lives in Buckinghamshire with her partner and two children. She served for 12 years in the British Army, studied Psychology, and published several non-fiction books under another name, before dipping her toes into the world of lesbian fiction.

You can contact Emma through her website and social media:

www.emmanicholsauthor.com
www.facebook.com/EmmaNicholsAuthor
www.twitter.com/ENichols_Author

And do please leave a review if you enjoyed this book. Reviews really help independent authors to create visibility for their work.
Thank you.

Links to Emma Nichols Books

Visit **getbook.at/TheVincentiSeries** to discover The Vincenti Series: Finding You, Remember Us and The Hangover.

Visit **getbook.at/ForbiddenBook** to start reading **Forbidden**

Visit **getbook.at/Ariana** to delve into the bestselling summer lesbian romance Ariana.

Visit **viewbook.at/Madeleine** to be transported to post-WW2 France and a timeless lesbian romance.

Visit **getbook.at/thisisme** to check out my lesbian literary love story novella.

Visit **getbook.at/SummerFate, viewbook.at/BlindFaith** and **getbook.at/christmasbizarre** to enjoy the Duckton-by-Dale lesbian romcom novels.

Thanks for reading and supporting my work!

Other Great Books By Independent Authors

The Copper Scroll by Robyn Nyx
When ambition and romance collide, can Chase and Rayne's love withstand the fallout?
Available from Amazon (ISBN: 9781838066833)

LesFic Eclectic Volume Two edited by Robyn Nyx
A Little Something More for Everyone
Download free: https://BookHip.com/FAGAST

Call to Me by Helena Harte
Sometimes the call you least expect is the one you need the most.
Available from Amazon (ISBN 9781838066802)

Cosa Nostra II by Emma Nichols
Will Maria choose loyalty to the Cosa Nostra or will she risk it all for love?
Available from Amazon (ISBN 9798690319243)

True Karma by Karen Klyne
Love moves to its own rhythm, if only you stop long enough to hear it.
Available from Amazon (ISBN 97819164443)

Addie Mae by Addison M Conley
An ugly divorce leads Maggie Carlton back to her hometown, where the chance of a new love comes in a surprising form.
Available from Amazon (ISBN 9780998029641)

Nights of Lily Ann: Redemption of Carly by L L Shelton
Lily Ann makes women's desires come true as a lesbian escort, but can she help Carly, who is in search of a normal life after becoming blind?
Available from Amazon (ISBN 9798652694906)

Heatwave by Maggie McIntyre
A quiet weekend in the woods turns into a fight for life.
Available from Amazon (ISBN 9798550424988)

Stealing a Thief's Heart by C L Cattano
Two women, a great escape, and a quest for a soulmate.
Available from Amazon (ASIN B085DW2MZ7)

Printed in Great Britain
by Amazon